THE
SCOTTISH LADIES'
DETECTIVE
AGENCY

BOOKS BY LYDIA TRAVERS

THE SCOTTISH LADIES' DETECTIVE AGENCY SERIES

Murder in the Scottish Hills

THE
SCOTTISH LADIES'
DETECTIVE
AGENCY

LYDIA TRAVERS

bookouture

Published by Bookouture in 2023

An imprint of Storyfire Ltd.
Carmelite House
50 Victoria Embankment
London EC4Y 0DZ

www.bookouture.com

ISBN: 978-1-80314-867-0
eBook ISBN: 978-1-80314-866-3

For my daughters-in-law, Beth and Rosie

ONE

Edinburgh
August 1911

'There.' Maud pinned up the map on the office wall. 'This will serve to remind our clients that we take cases not only in the city but in the whole of Midlothian.'

Daisy looked dubiously at the map headed *Edinburghshire or Midlothian*. 'It's a large area, Maud. Midlothian borders the Forth estuary to the north, Linlithgow to the west.' Her finger followed her speech. 'Lanarkshire and Peeblesshire to the south and Berwickshire and Haddingtonshire to the east.'

'True,' Maud murmured, 'but we can't afford to turn away any cases in the Scottish Borders.' The detective agency opened for business on Monday, and here we are, she thought, two days later with no whiff of interest.

'Aye, we need clients.' Daisy brightened. 'The advertising leaflets should be ready by now. I'll go and collect them from the printers.'

'Excellent idea, Daisy,' Maud said briskly. 'And I'll give the office a dust.'

Although the sun shone through the tall window, there wasn't a mote of dust to be seen in the room. But Maud knew she had to keep busy. She'd put all her money – all that had been left to her by her mother – into her detective agency, and she couldn't allow herself to think it might fail.

Pulling the cleaning cloth from a drawer of her desk, she began to dust. The desk looked impressive with its new Underwood typewriter and a fresh notepad with the fountain pen placed neatly on top, a bottle of ink to the side and the red leather diary beside it. She crossed to the small bookshelf on the wall and took down each reference volume in turn, dusted and replaced it, before fetching the broom from the cupboard and sweeping the floor.

The sash window stood open and, warm from her exertions, Maud wandered over to it in the hope of catching any hint of a breeze. This summer was proving to be the hottest on record, and she longed to loosen the neck of her blouse, or better still to remove her stays. Instead, from her office above the stationery shop, she gazed down into George Street, baking in the morning sun and busy as usual with people, horse-drawn and motor vehicles, and cable trams. Maud sighed as she rested her head against the glass. All were busy apart from her.

It was early days yet and Maud knew she must be patient. And she could always place another advertisement in the *Edinburgh Evening News,* although it would eat into her depleting funds.

She looked down at her clothes, wondering if she looked like a detective. Long plain skirt with a little kick in it: functional but modern. White blouse with a tiered lace frill at the throat: feminine and yet businesslike. She didn't think there was anything wrong with the way she looked and surely someone out there must need the services of a private detective.

'I'm looking for Mr McIntyre.'

At the sound of the voice, Maud spun round. A tall man in his early thirties, unshaven and dressed in rumpled evening clothes and top hat, paused on the threshold of the room. His gaze roamed Maud's small office, painted in sage green, and he grimaced.

'Is he here?' The man removed his topper, revealing dishevelled dark hair.

From the state of his formal attire – the black dress coat and trousers with a white waistcoat – and the wilted carnation in his button-hole, Maud immediately deduced he'd not been home the previous night. Had he failed to reach home because he stayed at his club or for another, more disreputable, reason? A man who appeared in a place of business dressed in last night's clothes had no right to look down his nose at other people's affairs, she thought. Besides, she'd chosen to decorate the room in a practical and yet tasteful style, to demonstrate her modern attitude.

A potential client, however, was one to be nurtured.

Maud stepped forward. 'I am Miss McIntyre.' Her voice was firm, and she gave him a smile that revealed none of her misgivings about him. 'Can I help you?' She indicated the seat opposite hers at the desk.

He ignored Maud's gesture as his eyes flickered to the sign on the office door that read M. McIntyre, Private Detective. Maud ushered him into the room and closed the door. She moved back to her desk and took her seat.

'What can I do for you?'

He crossed the floor in a couple of paces, flicked apart his coat tails and lowered himself onto the chair. 'I saw the advertisement in the *Edinburgh Evening News*.' He placed his gleaming silk topper on the corner of her desk. 'I take it you are Mr McIntyre's daughter. Will he be long?' The man raised an eyebrow.

Maud raised both her eyebrows in reply. '*I* am Mr McIntyre.'

His mouth lifted in a slow smile, and Maud felt her cheeks grow warm. 'What I mean,' she clarified quickly, 'is there is no *Mr* McIntyre. I am Maud McIntyre. Private detective.'

How good it felt to say that!

'You have need of my services, I assume?' Maud continued, picking up her pen, uncapping it and drawing the pad of paper towards her. 'You would like someone found or followed, perhaps?'

'Yes and no.'

Maud's fountain pen hesitated over the page. She looked up and fixed the man with the same hard stare her mother had given her father when she was displeased with him. 'Well, which is it?'

'I would not like someone followed, but something found.' He cleared his throat and drew his brows together. 'The fact is, I find myself in a spot of bother.'

He paused, shifting uncomfortably in the chair. Maud nodded encouragingly.

'I'm sorry,' he said, picking up his silk hat by its slightly curved brim and getting to his feet, his face a little flushed. 'I am in need of a private detective, but it's not something I feel comfortable discussing with a woman.'

Maud rose, too, and hurriedly moved round the desk. She couldn't lose her first client. 'Let me assure you, Mr—?'

Her query hung in the air, so she hurried on. 'Whatever your problem is, let me assure you that I am most discreet and highly professional.' As she said it, Maud hoped that it was true. She'd not had an opportunity yet to put her practice into... well, practice. This gentleman was her first real client. Or he would be if she could just convince him that she was the best person for the job.

He held her gaze. 'I'm sure you are discreet, Miss McIntyre, but as I have said it's not a matter for the ears of a young lady.'

Maud drew herself up to her full five feet seven inches. Although she was tall and willowy for a woman, the man still towered over her. Her height was a useful trait when she wanted to pass herself off as a man – here she paused for a moment to remember when she'd disguised herself as a tramp only a week ago, just to see if she could carry it off successfully, which she had – but it was annoying when it came to finding a suitable dinner date. And she knew she didn't possess the dark eyes and dark hair that marked the fashionable Gibson Girl. Her eyes, though large, were an unremarkable grey and her hair was a pale colour.

'I am at least as competent as any other private detective,' Maud continued with a confidence she didn't feel. 'In fact, more so—'

She was about to tell him of her success in finding the thief of the Radcliffe ruby earlier that summer, but he interrupted.

'I'm sure you are,' he said firmly, 'but there it is. You are undeniably... female.'

'And that is your only objection?' Maud asked quickly. 'That your business is not suitable for a woman's delicate sensibilities?'

With the back of his hand, he brushed a speck of imaginary fluff from his top hat. 'That and you'd be very visible attempting to track down—' This time he interrupted himself. 'Let's just say that a young woman such as yourself would be far too visible to get the job done.'

Maud was beginning to wonder if she actually wanted to work for such an annoying man, but before she could come to any sort of conclusion, he said, 'Good morning, Miss McIntyre,' replaced his topper, turned and let himself out of the office.

Maud stared at the closed door, hope fading and anger mounting. Just as her temper came close to boiling point, the

door opened again and she folded her arms, ready for him. But
it was Daisy who burst in clutching a pile of leaflets, her face
almost as red as her hair. She grinned at Maud.

'Who was that good-looking toff I just passed on the stairs?'

Maud dropped her arms in disappointment. 'If you mean
that wretch, that bounder, that cad...'

'Looks like he made quite an impression,' Daisy said, raising
an eyebrow. She deposited the papers on the desk. 'Will we be
seeing him again?'

'I doubt it. He didn't give his name. Nor did he give us the
case.' Maud went back to the desk and dropped into her chair.
'Whatever his problem is, he wouldn't tell me because he
doesn't deem a *woman* capable of doing the job.'

'Maybe he needs an investigator to go somewhere only a
man can go.' Daisy laughed.

'Perhaps, but I doubt it.' Maud picked up her pen and toyed
with it. 'Oh Daisy, if he's typical of the would-be male clients in
Edinburgh, we'll never get any detective work.'

Daisy slipped off her jacket and hung it on a peg on the
back of the door. 'Dinna worry, miss. I'm sure he's not
typical.'

'Remember not to call me miss,' Maud said, looking up.
'You're my assistant now, Daisy.'

Daisy had been Maud's lady's maid for the last seven years,
ever since Maud turned eighteen and her father deemed she
was old enough to have her own maid. She hadn't been comfortable with the situation as it didn't seem appropriate in this
modern age – it was the 1900s, after all – but Daisy was only a
year younger than her, and she'd soon come to value her friendship. When Maud moved to Edinburgh to start the agency,
Daisy had come as her right-hand woman.

'Sorry, Maud. Old habits die hard.' She smiled at Maud
before nodding at the advertising leaflets on the desk. 'The
printers have made a good job of them. I pushed some through

letter boxes on my way back. I wonder if all our clients will be as good-looking as him.'

Maud picked up one of the leaflets and examined it. Daisy was right; the printers had made a good job of them, and they had charged accordingly.

'I don't care so long as they come over that threshold with easily solved problems and cash in their pockets.'

'You dinna mean that.'

Maud put the leaflet down with a small sigh. 'You're right, I don't, but it would be good to put some money *into* the bank rather than just taking it out.'

'True,' said Daisy. She paused. 'All the same, I wouldna mind following someone for a few days if he looked as braw as that fellow.'

Had he been good-looking? He'd been too objectionable for Maud to notice. It was obvious he thought women should not work, or Maud's class of women at least. No doubt he'd be the first to complain if he couldn't hire a maid to keep his house clean. That was the problem, wasn't it? Women of her station weren't supposed to have a career.

Maud began the following day doing a few warm-up exercises. She had disliked ballet instruction as a child, but her father insisted it was what she should do. Because she was running around after her older brothers and behaving like a boy, he felt it would teach her how to carry herself in a more graceful way. It did. And the physical strength it gave her would surely be useful in her new role.

Later that morning, Maud and Daisy walked as usual to the office, making their way up Broughton Street, past tea rooms and public houses, shops selling watches and jewellery, groceries and confectionery. On the street, flower girls called out to passers-by, attracting them to their baskets of fresh flowers, and costermongers with their handcarts bawled in deep voices to advertise their hot pies, cockles and pease soup. Such a bustle, adding to the noise of the horse and motor traffic.

Ahead, high on the summit of Calton Hill, perched two monuments. The National Monument, to remember those who fell in the Napoleonic Wars, was to have resembled the Parthenon in Athens, but it was never completed due to lack of funds. Despite it being known as Edinburgh's Disgrace, Maud thought it looked like a wonderful ruin. The Nelson Monument was built in the style of the dreadful prison on the side of the hill. What must it be like in Calton Jail, not just in today's stifling weather but any day? Despite the heat, Maud shivered a little.

The women turned right into York Place, left into St Andrew Street, skirted the square with its statue of Henry Dundas towering into the blue sky, and right into George Street. They mounted the stairs to their second-floor office and Maud unlocked the door.

In order that the agency was not left unoccupied, Maud and Daisy took it in turns to post more advertising leaflets through letter boxes. Maud went first as she knew she could trust Daisy to make a good impression should anyone come to the office. She was neat and tidy, efficient and bright.

A couple of hours later, her batch of leaflets delivered, Maud was on her way back to the agency when she decided to do a little detective work of her own and stopped at the newsagents to buy a copy of *The Tatler*.

She sat at her desk and turned the pages of the society magazine, looking for any information on the mystery man who had come to her office yesterday. It still rankled that he'd refused her his business. Before long she found him: Lord Hamish Urquhart. On his arm in the main photograph was an attractive young woman. He and the lady were in evening dress and smiling into the camera. The article mentioned her haughty manner, but praised his 'intelligence, charm and good looks'. As if that wasn't bad enough, the ridiculous caption read *Baron of Hearts*.

So Hamish Urquhart was a peer of the realm. That explained a lot. The feature included pictures of him with six different women – Maud counted them – and described him as 'breaking hearts on the Scottish social scene'. She threw down the magazine in disgust.

Then she noticed at the side of the desk the newspaper Daisy must have been reading. It had been folded to a particular story, and now the screaming headline caught her eye.

ANOTHER COUNTRY HOUSE ROBBERY!

Maud snatched it up and read on.

On Saturday night a second daring jewellery theft took place.

Earlier that evening, Sir Arthur Macall, Bt. and Lady Macall hosted a small house party at Beechwood Hall, their residence near Musselburgh, during which their daughter had worn the large diamond pinned to her dress. Before she went to sleep, Miss Macall's lady's maid replaced the brooch in the jewellery case Miss Macall kept in her bedroom. In the morning, the maid entered the room at the usual hour and discovered the jewellery box lying open and the valuable stone missing. Despite an extensive search of the house by the police, the jewel has not been found.

It would seem that the villain is growing ever more desperate. We remind readers that only a fortnight ago, the Countess of Aichieson had a ruby necklace stolen from Aichieson House outwith Linlithgow. Like Miss Macall, Lady Aichieson had been wearing the item of jewellery during the evening of the same night it was taken from her bedroom.

'Just like in *The Moonstone*,' Maud murmured, tossing the newspaper back on the desk. Wilkie Collins's novel had been one of the many detective stories she'd devoured when growing up. In that case, the thief had been among the dinner party guests to mark the heiress's eighteenth birthday.

Could the two real-life crimes be a case of fiction becoming fact? She leaned back in the chair and considered the various possibilities. As in the book, the guilty person must have seen the lady wearing the jewellery. Which meant that, if the same thief was involved in both cases, there was a strong possibility that he, or she – Maud was always fair in formulating her theories – had been a house guest. With all the corridor-creeping that went on at night during a Saturday-to-Monday, a guest seemed to her the most likely person to be in a position to steal valuable stones. If she could work that out, then surely the police could.

On the other hand, a servant might have taken the brooch and the necklace – but was it likely that two different servants had committed the same type of crime in two different houses? If the same house guest had been present on each occasion and taken their valet or lady's maid with them, then it was possible that a servant was the thief.

On yet another hand...

She looked up as the office door opened. A large and expensively dressed lady of middle years stood on the threshold. Despite the heat of the day, she wore a long wool jacket trimmed with fur at the cuffs and collar. A multitude of lace and tucks peeped out from across her generous bosom. The enormous hat over her dark brown hair was covered in ostrich feathers. Wealth radiated from her, the strong face between feathered hat and fur collar suggesting a person you wouldn't wish to argue with.

Hastily, Maud covered *The Tatler* with the newspaper and got to her feet.

TWO

'Is this McIntyre's detective agency?' the lady boomed.

'Yes, I am Miss McIntyre.'

'I should like to speak to Mr McIntyre. I take it he is the proprietor of this business.' She walked into the office and glanced around as if expecting him magically to appear.

'I am the proprietor of this agency and the detective you are seeking.'

'A woman?' She lifted her lorgnette and looked at Maud with open curiosity.

Maud inclined her head. When she met the lady's eyes, she saw they had a twinkle in them.

'How refreshing.' She lowered the lorgnette. 'Pleased to meet you, my dear.'

'Won't you sit down...?' Not certain how to address her, Maud left the sentence hanging as she stepped forward and drew out the visitor's seat.

'I am the Duchess of Duddingston.' Despite her bulk, she lowered herself gracefully onto the chair.

A Duchess? Things were looking up for the agency, Maud thought.

She resumed her own seat and gave the Duchess her most efficient smile. 'How can I help you, Your Grace?'

The Duchess got straight to the point. 'You have heard about the recent country house thefts?'

'It is my business to know about such things.' Maud indicated the newspaper on her desk. Admittedly, it was Daisy who'd spotted the story, but it *was* her business to know about such things. To be fair to Daisy, she added, 'Both my assistant and I.'

'I will be hosting a modest Saturday-to-Monday house party,' the Duchess went on, 'and it occurs to me that the occasion will be ripe for the plucking. There will be some wealthy guests attending, and I do not wish to have my friends, or myself, plucked.'

Maud immediately admired the old bird. She really was forthright. 'And you would like someone to be there to keep an eye on your guests' and your own jewellery?' Maud wondered if she had sufficient funds for a new gown or two.

'I would like you to do more than keep an eye on it, my girl. I want you to prevent any such theft from taking place at Duddingston. If that is not possible and jewellery is stolen, then I wish you to set your sights immediately on finding the culprit.'

Maud's stomach gave a little flutter of excitement. Her first case, that of the theft of the Radcliffe ruby, had taken place at a country house, so it was a situation she was more than familiar with. She hadn't charged on that occasion, as she had happened to be staying there and was keen to try out her powers of detection. But she liked to think of that as her pro bono work. Now, though, she was running her own agency, and charging clients for her services, so it was a very different matter. She had to succeed; the reputation of the business was at stake.

'Two pairs of eyes are better than one,' the Duchess was saying. 'I think you said you employed an assistant?' She glanced around the office before returning her gaze to Maud.

'Yes, I have—'

At that moment, the door opened and Daisy entered. She stared in amazement at the grand creature seated in the client's chair.

'Perfect timing,' Maud said, giving Daisy a wide smile. 'Your Grace, this is my assistant, Miss Cameron.'

Daisy closed her mouth and curtsied.

'And she is your only assistant?'

'She is.'

'It is a pity about her red hair. It may attract too much attention. But I suppose it cannot be helped.' The Duchess lifted her spectacles again and ran a practised eye over Daisy. 'She will do nicely as your lady's maid.'

Daisy stifled a gasp.

'Close the door, Daisy,' Maud said quickly.

'It is a pity,' went on the Duchess blithely, 'that you do not also employ a male assistant to act as a valet to the Colonel, who does not have his own man.'

Did the Duchess think she ran an employment agency for servants? Before Maud could reply, the Duchess rose, signalling the conversation was at an end.

Maud stood too. 'I'm afraid there are a few details we need to go into, Your Grace.'

She paused. 'Yes?'

'I need to know when the party is to take place.'

'I thought I had told you.' She looked surprised. 'It's a Saturday-to-Monday. This Saturday.'

In two days' time. 'I will need to consult my diary. If you would resume your seat for the moment.'

She did so. Maud sat down, lifted the red leather-covered book and opened it, holding it in such a way that the Duchess wouldn't be able to observe it was empty for the remainder of the week.

'Yes, I think we can manage that.' Maud shut the diary and

replaced it neatly on the desk. She'd write the engagement in later, when her client couldn't see the blank pages. Pulling her notebook towards her, she turned to a fresh page, uncapped her pen and wrote with a flourish along the top: The Duchess of Duddingston. The phrase 'Private investigator to the nobility' was already forming in her mind. If she could put that in her advertising... But she stopped herself in that line of thinking. She prided herself on being discreet.

Maud looked up from her notebook. 'The party is to take place at Duddingston House?'

The Duchess inclined her head.

'A list of the guests would be useful.'

'I will let you have that when you arrive. If that is all?' She moved as if to rise.

'One further matter, Your Grace. Where do your guests keep their jewellery when staying with you? Is there a safe?'

'Certainly not,' said the Duchess tartly. 'Duddingston is a private house, and such a thing is unnecessary.'

As Maud bit back a retort about the logic of that sentence, the Duchess continued. 'Come to Duddingston tomorrow. My butler informs me there is a train from Waverley railway station at five minutes past ten, which will arrive at five and twenty minutes to eleven. I regret the Daimler will be elsewhere at that time, but I will send the pony carriage to collect you from the station. It will be a pleasant journey in such weather for young people such as yourselves. Good day.'

Daisy stepped forward to open the door, and the Duchess made her stately way out of the office. Maud collected her wits in time to set down her pen, rise and bid her good day, shooting Daisy a frown as her assistant pulled a face at the Duchess's retreating back. Daisy closed the door. Without a word, they both moved to the window and peered down into the street. A chauffeur stood holding open the door of a Daimler motor car as the Duchess climbed in.

Maud and Daisy looked at each other. There was silence for a few moments, then they burst out laughing.

'Well,' Daisy said, letting out a breath. 'Wasn't she fierce? Did you see the fur trim on her jacket? I wonder if she killed the mink herself.'

Maud laughed, sure that under that formidable exterior she was a good-hearted person. For one thing, that twinkle in her eye when she had told her that she, and not the mythical *Mr McIntyre*, ran the detective agency. 'She's our first client and that's what matters. We need to earn money, and that means taking each case as it comes and building a reputation.'

'Our first client.' Daisy grinned. 'I like the sound of that. Imagine if the thief strikes when we're there!'

'Then we can't afford to fail.' Maud didn't want to think what might happen if the case turned out to be more than they could handle.

'What a cheek, though,' Daisy went on, 'wanting me to go as a lady's maid.'

'Cheer up,' Maud said with a laugh. 'You were a very good lady's maid, so I know you can carry it off. And it's only for a few nights. The Duchess is correct that it's a good idea to have one of us above-stairs and the other below. You will be able to observe in the background, so you might well learn more than me.'

'Hmm,' Daisy said, somewhat mollified. 'Ach well, at least the woman doesn't want me as a kitchen maid.' She shuddered. 'Up before dawn to start the kitchen fires and put water on to boil, scrub pots and pans and floors, and wait on the other servants.'

Maud looked at Daisy with feigned surprise. 'I thought you were in favour of an egalitarian society.'

She nodded. 'Exactly.'

It was easy to guess what she meant, and Maud half thought about having a conversation on equality, but the slight waft of air through the open window was sultry and the room too stifling to debate the topic. Maud crossed to her desk, picked up a sheet of paper and fanned herself. 'It will be pleasant to spend a few days at Duddingston. I can't wait to get out of the city and away from this oppressive heat.'

Daisy paused in the process of removing her hat with its single feather and she raised an eyebrow.

'Surely,' Maud added, 'even those working below-stairs are allowed to take the air occasionally?'

Pushing aside any prospect of failure, Maud concentrated instead on the opportunity she'd been offered.

This was her chance to prove herself.

THREE

Maud stepped off the train into the heat, Daisy following. Further along the otherwise empty platform, the stationmaster was calling above the hissing of the engine's brakes, 'Duddingston... Duddingston.'

Maud took a tighter grip of her furled parasol and with her other hand smoothed down her long cream linen coat. A uniformed young man, who she took to be from Duddingston House, stepped forward.

He touched his cap. 'Miss McIntyre?'

'Yes.'

He called to the porter to take Maud's trunk from the carriage and turned back to her. 'This way, please.'

Maud set off after him, Daisy close behind wearing a brown poplin skirt and jacket and, bringing up the rear of the little procession, the porter with Maud's luggage on a trolley. The guard blew his whistle; the train jerked forward and moved slowly out of the station. A great burst of steam billowed around them.

'So much for the countryside being clean and fresh,' spluttered Daisy, as they emerged coughing from the clouds of steam.

'It will be soon, as well you know.' When Daisy had been her maid, they had lived at Maud's father's house in the country. But now Daisy liked to pretend she was city born and bred.

On the dusty road stood a varnished open-topped carriage, a coat of arms painted on the side. A large dapple-grey pony stood waiting patiently in the shafts. The driver extended a leather-gloved hand and Maud took it as she stepped up. Daisy was left to clamber up by herself, as the driver and the porter together lifted Maud's trunk onto the back of the carriage and began to secure it with straps.

Maud unfurled her parasol and held it over herself and Daisy. While they waited, she watched a tabby cat slink out of the garden of one of the cottages close by the station. It threaded its way through a profusion of purple geraniums and lupins of assorted colours. The cat paused in their path to give them an insolent stare, before plunging into the rough grass at the side of the road. It had seen through their disguises, Maud thought, as cats are wont to.

'A mile to Duddingston House,' said Daisy, reading the fingerpost. She settled the Gladstone bag on her lap and adjusted the little straw hat perched on top of her low pompadour. 'These things dinna give much protection from the sun.'

She was right. Her usual larger hat had necessarily been replaced by the straw boater, and Maud was grateful for her own wide-brimmed hat trimmed with silk roses.

'There are trees to give some shade.' Maud pointed to a row of beech, heavy with leaves, lining the low drystone wall along the roadside as far as they could see.

'If that dyke is part of the Duddingston estate, they must have thousands of acres.'

Maud's luggage secured, the driver tipped the porter and

mounted the carriage to sit in front of them. He gave the order, and they moved off at a trot.

Daisy drew a sharp breath as the carriage lurched forward and clutched her hat to her head. 'I'm nae used to these carriages any more, and I've never liked them anyway. The wheels hum like a top.'

'When we've solved the case, perhaps we can travel back to the station in the Duchess's motor car,' Maud said, secretly hoping that wouldn't happen at all, as she loved the feel of the breeze on her face.

'If we dinna solve it, it'll be a horse and cart for us, more like,' Daisy muttered.

Maud immediately had a mental image of the jolly days of travelling to Sunday school picnics in sunlit fields. 'I rather like the sound of that.'

The immense landscape stretched around them on every side as they travelled along the road. The sun was warm on Maud's back, and from somewhere in the distance, she could hear the rattle of a reaper-binder. They kept to an easy pace, and she breathed in the delightful smell of warm fields ripe for harvest. Strands of silvery cobwebs stretched along a hedgerow. There wasn't a cloud in the sky, the ditches were deep in grass and poppies, and the barley in the fields bowed in the hazy heat. Apart from the pony carriage making its way along the road, all was motionless around them in the still air.

After a while, Daisy glanced at the driver's back and said in a low voice, 'Do you really think the jewel thief is going to be an upstairs toff?'

They'd spent most of yesterday going through past copies of the society magazines, looking for the names of those present at both of the house parties where jewellery had been stolen.

'I think it's entirely possible. We've identified a handful of names, so let's see if any of them are guests of the Duchess.'

They crossed a stone humpback bridge over a burn and

followed the road round a bend. A lane on their right led to a small kirk standing alone in a field. A red admiral fluttered by and flattened itself against a stone in the sun. A few minutes later, the tall chimneys of Duddingston House came into view.

'Look, Daisy, we're almost there.'

'Thank goodness.' She groaned. 'I'm so hot, I could take off my corset right now.'

'That's best done indoors.'

Before long, there stood the open gates of Duddingston House. The carriage passed between its twin pillars. The drive wound through a deer park and spacious formal gardens.

'Is that a mirage?' said Daisy, raising a hand against the sun to peer ahead.

Maud knew what she meant. As the grand house finally came into view through an avenue of trees, it seemed to shimmer in the late morning heat.

'No, it's the real thing.' Maud gazed at the imposing Georgian mansion standing on rising ground. The sun glinted off its many windows and gave the stone a warm hue.

'Back straight, Daisy,' she instructed, 'ready to play our parts.'

'I keep twenty-two servants in the house: butler, housekeeper, footmen, lady's maids, housemaids, kitchen maids, cooks.' The Duchess indicated Maud and Daisy should each take a seat in the library where they'd been conducted. The room was panelled in reddish-brown cedar wood, with books lining the shelves, paintings of dogs and horses on the walls, papers piled on the desk, low armchairs dotted around and a brown leather sofa in front of the marble fireplace.

'There are a further number of servants who work on the estate.' She waved a hand expansively towards the open French windows where sunlight streamed in. 'Coachmen, grooms, gardeners, forestry men, agricultural workers and the like, but you don't need to be concerned with all of that.'

As Maud perched politely on the edge of her chair, her gaze was caught by the gorgeous red brocade curtains drawn back into thick folds at the long windows.

'Made for me in Paris,' the Duchess said, following her look. 'They are woven with gold and silver thread, and it is that which catches the eye.'

'Very nice,' Maud managed.

'Now your job, Miss McIntyre,' went on the Duchess, 'will involve mixing with the guests and seeing what you can learn about any potential robbery.'

Maud nodded. 'Of course, Your Grace.'

'And you, Miss Cameron, your work will involve assisting Miss McIntyre with her dressing: her hair, dress, jewellery, shoes and any cosmetics she may wear.'

Maud could see Daisy torn between her desire to inform the Duchess she was aware of the duties of a lady's maid, having been one – Maud's, in fact – and the wish to indicate she would never normally consider such a role.

'Cleaning and mending garments if required,' continued the Duchess, 'bringing Miss McIntyre's breakfast tray to her room, seeing to her bath and so forth.'

Belatedly, Maud remembered Daisy's comment about putting on water to boil in the kitchen and wondered if this grand house had plumbing for both hot and cold water.

'Aye, madam.' Daisy smiled.

The Duchess gave her a suspicious stare. 'Yes, well, we must hope that you are able to pass yourself off as required and that the two of you are able to safeguard the various pieces of jewellery over the next three days. The first guest is expected this afternoon – a gentleman whom I consider a *special* friend – and the others throughout the course of tomorrow morning.'

'And who are the guests, Your Grace? It would be helpful to

know a little about them.' Maud had looked up the Duchess in
her *Who's Who* and learned she was a widow. Now she briefly
wondered who the special gentleman might be. Not that it was
any of her business. It was more important that she knew the
names of the Duchess's guests and if any were the same as those
at the other house parties.

The Duchess nodded. 'There will be the Earl of Swinton
and his American wife; Colonel Morrison; Viscount and
Viscountess Drummond; and a promising young advocate-
depute by the name of Douglas Laing. One likes to have a social
mix at gatherings.'

Poor Mr Laing, to be there almost on sufferance.

'And one does like to assist socially any promising young
people,' she added.

Ah, nicely put, Duchess, Maud thought.

'In addition, there will be Miss Esme Taft, the author.'

'Esme Taft?' The name wasn't familiar to Maud, so she
guessed the woman wasn't an author of crime novels. 'What sort
of books does she write?'

'Historical romance, I believe.' If the Duchess had been less
refined, she would have shrugged her disdain. As it was, the
flaring of her nostrils and the downward turn of her mouth said
it all. 'My daughter, Lady Violet, tells me she is quite well-
known in that area of... literature and asked me to invite the
woman. My two daughters, Lady Cynthia and Lady Violet, will
of course also be present, but they will not know the real reason
for your being here. The fewer people who are aware, the
better.'

Maud's brain whirled. All those names were on her mental
list of possible suspects. She supposed it was inevitable that the
same people attended these gatherings, society being so close-
knit. There were a few additional names she'd memorised, but
they had not been mentioned by the Duchess.

'And,' the Duchess concluded, 'my special guest, Lord Urquhart.'

Maud started in her seat. It sounded as though she had said *Lord Urquhart*. 'I'm sorry, what was that name?'

'Lord Urquhart.' It was Maud's turn to receive a stare. 'Do you know him?'

Maud held her gaze. 'I've seen his picture in *The Tatler*.'

That wasn't a lie. And Maud certainly wouldn't tell her that he had rejected her services earlier that week. And now here he was, the Duchess's 'special friend', for goodness' sake.

His name was also on Maud's list of suspects. Her most immediate concern, though, was whether he would give her away to the other guests. It seemed unlikely, not least because he would then have to reveal where he had met her. She couldn't see Lord Urquhart admitting his need for a private detective. That was assuming he even remembered her and Daisy. No doubt he had far more important matters to occupy his mind. Briefly Maud wondered why he had consulted the agency in the first place and decided that his problem must have resolved itself.

'Your Grace, I am sure you have already considered the various possibilities. The jewellery thief may be an outsider, someone keeping a watch on the house; or a person in the house, such as a guest or a servant.'

'Either is possible,' the Duchess agreed, lightly touching the string of pearls around her neck, 'although the evidence points to someone who knows exactly the pieces to steal, having seen them worn earlier in the evening. Unfortunately, this seems to suggest that someone in the house is responsible.'

'Newspapers have reported on the house party thefts and the society pages of magazines comment on forthcoming social events,' Maud pointed out. 'It wouldn't be difficult for a stranger so inclined to identify the next place to rob.'

She fixed Maud with her stern gaze. 'Gaining access to the house would prove less easy.'

Maud nodded in reply. 'We will keep our eyes and ears open for any possible intruders. If you, Your Grace, could alert your servants to do the same, we would appreciate it.'

'Certainly.'

'Miss Cameron and I will also watch for any suspicious activities by your guests or your servants.' Maud glanced at Daisy. 'It's time we began work.'

'I will ring for one of the maids to show you to your rooms.' The Duchess rose, crossed to the fireplace and pulled on the bell rope at the side.

'There will be the usual arrangements,' she went on. 'Miss McIntyre, your bedroom is on the second floor. You, Miss Cameron, as a visiting lady's maid, will share a room in the attic with one of the Duddingston maids. You will have the after-noons off and after eight o'clock in the evenings when we are dining, until Miss McIntyre requires assistance in preparing for bed.'

The door opened and in came a young woman looking neat and tidy in a blue and white gingham dress. She bobbed a curtsy, her brown curls bouncing.

'Show Miss McIntyre to her room, Ada. Her maid will share with you.'

'Yes, Your Grace.' The girl turned to Maud and Daisy. 'Come this way, please.'

They followed her out of the room. As she led them up the magnificent staircase, Maud fell back a little, pretending to admire the polished mahogany banister, to allow Daisy and the maid to speak.

'I'm Daisy,' she heard her say in a chatty voice, 'Daisy Cameron. Have you worked here long?'

'Almost ten years.'

Daisy lowered her voice a little. 'What's she like?'

'I've had worse mistresses than the Duchess.'

'I ken what you mean.'

Goodness, did she mean *me*? Maud thought.

She had to walk a little closer to hear Ada when the girl spoke again to Daisy. 'I've wondered about going to work in one of the factories in the city. You know, tea-packers, biscuit-makers, glue-mixers and the like. But I've heard that the women have to put up with dreadful working conditions and poor pay.'

'Aye, but look at what Mary Macarthur has achieved for the workers in chain factories in England,' said Daisy confidently. 'Things are changing, you'll see.'

The group turned along the broad corridor. Ada looked at Daisy and Maud saw the frown on her face. 'Who's Mary Macarthur?'

'Only the founder of the National Federation of Women Workers and a Scot,' said Daisy, her voice rising a pitch with indignation that the other woman hadn't heard of Mary Macarthur. 'Last year she led the women chain-makers in the Midlands in their battle for fair pay. Thousands of them were on starvation wages. It took a ten-week strike, but then all the employers agreed. And now there's unrest at the food and drink factories in London. It's certain she'll be asked to help the women workers there. Isn't that something?' Daisy's face beamed with pride for Mary Macarthur.

Ada nodded, not looking convinced. They climbed to the second floor in silence. At the top, the corridor ran to the left and right, and they turned right. Maud counted along the number of doors as they passed them. Not only would it not do to forget which was her room, it also would be useful to work out later where she was sleeping in relation to others on the same passage.

Ada stopped outside one of the large mahogany doors lining the corridor. The third from the stairs.

'This is your room, madam.' She put her hand on the brass

doorknob, turned it and opened the door to reveal a sumptuous room: four-poster with lemon hangings, pale-yellow striped wallpaper, Adam-style fireplace with gilt-framed mirror above, paintings and engravings, a thick sand-colour carpet. Maud's trunk stood at the bottom of her bed.

'Thank you, Ada.' Maud turned to Daisy. 'Return as soon as you can, Daisy, to unpack my belongings.'

'Very good, madam.'

Did Maud detect a hint of amusement in Daisy's voice? Her face was that of the perfect servant. Maud stepped into the room and heard the door close softly behind her.

Leaving her parasol propped up against the wall, Maud hastened to the slightly open sash window, tugged it up, put her hands on the windowsill and leaned out. Her room was at the rear of the house, which meant she wouldn't be able to see who was arriving or leaving at the main door, but it would give her a good view of anyone who might be outside enjoying the gardens or, more importantly, outside and up to no good. What she could see at present was a magnificent lawn dotted with oak trees, a yew alley and, in the distance, a shimmering loch.

Maud turned back into the room. It's an interesting thing, but when one is in a strange bedroom, the need to test the mattress as soon as possible is a strong one. She crossed to the four-poster, sat on the edge and bounced up and down. A comfortable bed, but she'd expected no less.

What to do now? She felt at a loss without the shoulder bag containing her notebook and pencil. Daisy had these essentials in the capacious Gladstone bag. All Maud had was this silly little beaded purse, which befitted a lady visiting another house.

Maud rose slowly from the bed, dropped her purse onto the coverlet, beautifully embroidered with climbing roses in brilliant hues, and wandered round the room. Picking up a framed card, she read the times of prayers, meals and postal arrangements, and put it down again. A book had been placed on the low table and she took it up. The lurid cover depicted a hairy fellow in a kilt. *Her Highland Chieftain Lover,* blazed the title, *by Esme Taft.*

Miss Taft, one of the house guests. It didn't seem the sort of novel the Duchess herself might read, but she supposed that, as hostess, she had to show willing. It was hard to imagine this work being left in the bedrooms of the male guests, so what did they have? Bram Stoker's latest book, *The Lair of the White Worm,* perhaps?

She was still holding Miss Taft's novel in her hand when the door opened and in walked Daisy, carrying the small leather case that held Maud's few items of jewellery. She closed the door behind her, came over to Maud and raised an eyebrow at the picture on the book's cover.

'I didn't think that was your type of reading, my lady,' she said with a grin.

'There's no need to "my lady" me when we're alone, Daisy.' It was strange to see her dressed again in the dark-brown silk of a lady's maid.

'Just as well I kept this,' she said, plucking at the skirt with her free hand. Her gaze went round the room. 'Nae offence to your faither's house, but this place is awfa grand.'

Maud couldn't deny it. 'I hope your room is comfortable?'

'Aye, comfortable enough. It's got two narrow beds with a nightstand between them and under the skylight there's a chest of drawers with a wee mirror propped up on top.'

Maud replaced the book on the table. 'Did you learn anything from Ada? Apart from what I overheard on the stairs.'

Daisy shook her head. 'Nae really.' Her stomach growled. 'She told me that luncheon – I mean dinner – is in ten minutes' time, so I'd best get on with your unpacking.' She set the jewellery box on the dressing table and moved to open the trunk.

'I'll give you a hand.' Working together, they took it in turns to lift out Maud's neatly layered costumes, shake them out and hang the garments in the large oak wardrobe. 'We need to remember that we are here as detectives and to be alert at all times. I am beginning to suspect a house guest is responsible for the thefts, but we need to be aware not just of any strange behaviour by one of them but also by any servant.'

Daisy folded into the drawer of the chest a soft woollen cardigan. 'Even though we won't know what is strange and what is normal behaviour by each one.'

'Even though,' Maud agreed. 'I'll finish here, and you get down to the kitchens for your dinner.'

'It will take me a while to get there,' she said, closing the drawer. 'The servants' staircase seems to go on forever.'

'We have the rest of today to get used to the household and its ways. And to present ourselves as convincing when the guests arrive tomorrow.'

FOUR

Disappointingly for Maud's investigation, the talk over luncheon in the dining room was not about the expected guests, but of the proposed National Insurance Act being debated in both Houses of Parliament.

'We don't need such a thing,' said Lady Cynthia firmly, putting down her knife and fork. 'Why should we have to pay thruppence a week for medical treatment and sickness benefit for each of the servants?'

The Gibson Girl might be a fiction created by the American illustrator Charles Gibson, but the woman seated on the opposite side of the table to Maud was real. Maud felt positively dowdy in her smart but plain cream linen dress. Lady Cynthia was tall and slender, yet curvy at the bust and hips. Her dark hair was piled high on her head in the softly swirled pompadour style. Her pale-blue dress fitted tightly to the bodice, with white lace at her long slim throat. If this was what she wore to luncheon with other females, Maud couldn't imagine how she dressed when gentlemen were present.

'Not we, my dear, but I will have to pay,' said the Duchess, referring to the bill being discussed.

'Yes, but I will marry and run my own household one day.' Lady Cynthia indicated to the butler, a plump fellow standing by the sideboard, to top up her glass of claret.

The Duchess eyed Cynthia keenly, and Maud wondered if the mother and daughter had the same gentleman in mind for Lady Cynthia's future husband.

'I suppose it's better that every employer pays the same,' said the other daughter uncertainly.

Maud detected a slight lisp in her voice. Lady Violet was as attractive as her sister but plump, clearly taking after her generously built mother. She looked to be only a couple of years younger than Cynthia, although she wore her fair hair in a long braid as if she were still in the schoolroom.

'It seems an eminently reasonable proposal to me,' said the Duchess.

Hear, hear, Duchess, Maud thought.

'The servants will each have to contribute four pence a week,' the Duchess went on, 'and the government tuppence.'

'You've always looked after the servants, Mama,' went on Cynthia, ignoring her sister, 'as did Papa when he was alive.'

'Perhaps it's a matter of pride, Cynthia.' There was an edge to the Duchess's voice. 'What we do may seem like charity. If the government provides assistance, it can be seen as the servants' right.'

'And,' said Violet, 'you know, Cynth—'

'Don't call me that,' said her sister sharply.

Violet flushed. 'I was just going to say I've heard that in some other large houses if a servant is ill, they are sacked.'

Cynthia sniffed.

'What do you think, Miss McIntyre?' asked Violet, turning to look at her.

Be circumspect, Maud reminded herself quickly. 'I would imagine that anything to help working people must be a good thing.'

'Oh, *must* it?' said Cynthia with a sneer, picking up her cutlery again.

Goodness, she was a nasty piece of work.

'I must apologise for my daughter's manners,' said the Duchess, fixing Cynthia with a stern eye.

The party ate for a while in uncomfortable silence. Maud swallowed the last portion of her grilled sweetbreads in mushroom sauce and dabbed her mouth with the napkin.

'I believe you said another guest will be with us this afternoon – Lord Urquhart?' Maud took a sip of wine and watched to see which of the three ladies reacted in any way to his name. Violet sat up a little straighter. Despite her schoolgirl looks, it seemed Violet was not still a child.

'That is correct,' said the Duchess. 'And tomorrow the rest of the guests arrive.'

Clearly, she was putting a stop to any further conversation. Perhaps she wished to make it clear that she didn't, after all, believe any of *her* guests could possibly be a notorious jewellery thief.

After luncheon, as was normal practice, the party retired for their afternoon rest. Maud had not been long in her room and was sitting in the armchair turning the pages of Miss Taft's novel, when there was a soft knock on the door and Daisy appeared.

'Is there anything I can do for you, madam?' she asked, for the benefit of anyone within earshot. She entered and closed the door behind her.

'What news from the servants' hall?' Maud said in a low voice, putting down the book.

'Talk about the National Insurance Bill,' Daisy replied. Without thinking, she began to smooth the cover on Maud's bed. 'The butler, Mr Thomson, is against it.' She straightened.

'He says making the employer pay would,' she adopted a ponderous tone, '"disrupt the harmony between servant and master".' She pulled a face. 'The first footman, though, said he was happy to pay his bit.'

'Good for him,' Maud said to Daisy. 'You must have approved, surely?'

'I was bursting to speak about it, but I said nothing as I didna want to draw attention to myself.'

'You showed admirable restraint, Daisy.' Maud smiled. She knew it must have cost her friend to remain silent.

'You've warned me that detectives need to stay in the background, listening and observing. As to that first footman...'

'Oh yes? What happened?'

'As soon as the butler's bell rang – do you ken, Maud, that each bell has its own tone?'

Maud knew from expeditions to the kitchen when she lived at home that each bell was labelled with a particular room. Here it seemed servants had to memorise the sound for the area under their responsibility.

'I'm sure I'll never remember mine,' Daisy said.

'I'll try not to summon you too often.'

She grinned. 'Ada said until I get used to it, she'll let me know when my bell rings.'

'You were saying about the first footman?'

'Aye, well, as soon as Mr Thomson had left the room, the fellow winked at me and began to sing "I'm shy, Mary Ellen, I'm shy".'

Maud had to laugh at Daisy's face, which was a picture of indignation. 'What happened then?'

'I told him he was nae Jack Pleasants.'

Maud smiled. He was the music hall performer who played the part of a bashful fool, but whose apparent lack of experience with women had a hidden purpose. This was all very amusing, but it didn't help with their investigation. 'Why did the butler's bell ring?'

Daisy sat on the dressing table stool and faced her. 'It was the early guest.'

'Lord Urquhart?'

She nodded.

'Did any of the servants say anything?'

'Nae about him. But I was told to *wheesht* by Mrs Wood, the housekeeper, for my cheeky reply to the footman.' Daisy huffed with exasperation.

'Tell me about Mrs Wood,' Maud said. 'What is she like?'

Daisy considered. 'She's thin with grey hair in a tight bun. Very proper. She seems all right and said she hoped I'd enjoy my short time here.'

'She's right – our time here is going to be short, and we can't afford to waste any of it. Did you learn anything else?' Maud asked, leaning forward in her chair.

'I asked her if she's worked here long, and she said since she was a wee girl. She came to the house as an under-maid and worked her way up. "So there's hope for me," I murmured. "There is indeed, lass," she said.'

Maud laughed. 'Clearly, there's nothing wrong with Mrs Wood's hearing.'

'And she said, "If you find a mistress as good as Her Grace, you can count yourself fortunate,"' Daisy went on. A wicked glint appeared in her eye. 'So I said, "You wouldna believe how cruel my last employer was, Mrs Wood."'

'It sounds like you are beginning to enjoy yourself here, Daisy.' Maud sighed and glanced out of the window. 'I'm going to take a stroll in the garden while all is quiet and observe the house from the outside.'

'What would you like me to do?'

Maud thought for a moment. 'There's my blue walking skirt. You could undo a small part of the hem and take it to repair in the kitchen. If you're sitting there working quietly, you might see or hear something without raising suspicion.'

'Good idea.' Daisy went to the wardrobe and drew out the skirt. 'I'll see you later.' She let herself out of the room with Maud's skirt draped over her arm.

It was far too hot to pull on the cream linen coat again, so Maud picked up her parasol and set off along the corridor, down the staircase and into the oak-panelled entrance hall. In front of her, the wide main door stood open, and she stepped out onto the broad stone steps that led down into the grounds. A welcome breeze fanned her cheeks as she paused to admire the vast manicured lawn, a large table and chairs set on the grass.

She kept her parasol furled and hurried along the path at the side of the house, following it round to the rear. This was the view she could see from her window: a lawn dotted with the occasional magnificent oak, an alley of yew trees and beyond the sparkling loch. The grass was dry, and she did not need to fear for her elegant boots, so, leaving the path, she set off across the lawn to the yew alley and found herself in a rose garden.

Some of the blooms were already past their best, but the scents of others filled the hot, still air. A bee buzzed past and from somewhere in the distance came the clickety-clack of a mowing machine. The sounds of a country summer. Maud inhaled the roses' soothing, sweet perfume, mingled with the scent of freshly mown grass, and felt all was right with the world.

But it wasn't. It was foolish to think so when she was here on a case. Her *first* paid case too. Someone was stealing valuable jewellery from grand country houses, and it was her and Daisy's job to put a stop to it, to identify the guilty party and retrieve the jewels.

Maud returned to the yew alley. If she angled herself correctly, she could see the whole of the rear of the house, its stone dappled with shafts of sunlight. At first floor level, a broad terrace ran the length of the building. She knew the French windows standing open on the ground floor led into the library, as she had been there earlier. Good: having only one set of these would make it easier for her to observe any comings and goings. It was no use if people could pop in and out, going hither and yon, without the need to use a proper external door.

She watched the terrace for a while, but there was no activity. The house and its occupants seem to slumber in the early afternoon lull. A number of the sash windows stood open to the warmth of the day.

On the second floor, there were – she paused to count them – twelve windows running the length of the house. Assuming her room – large with an equally large window – was typical, that made twelve bedrooms.

As she stood there in the shadow of the yew alley, a female with dark hair leaned out of a window to take the air. Lady Cynthia. The second window in from the other end of the corridor to Maud's. Would it be reasonable to assume that her younger sister Violet occupied the adjacent bedroom, number three, with the Duchess in number one?

The sun's rays were strong. Maud raised her parasol and, like a guest who found it far too pleasant outside to want to return to her room, wandered back to the rose garden. She strolled on a little further and caught the scent from a deep red bloom wafting up to greet her. It was too delightful to ignore. She bent, the better to sample its fragrance...

'If it isn't Miss Maud McIntyre. What a pretty picture.'

Maud froze mid-inhalation. There was no doubting the owner of the voice. He had a nerve to address her so. She straightened slowly and turned to face him. He looked fresh and cool in a white linen suit and a panama hat.

'Lord Urquhart.' Maud's voice was equally cool. Frosty, in fact.

'Ah.' He narrowed his eyes as he looked at her. 'You've discovered my title.'

'Of course. I *am* an investigator.'

Maud found herself studying him. It was good practice to observe others' features. Slim build but muscular about the shoulders, dark hair, clean-shaven today and showing a strong jawline, eyes... what colour were his eyes? She frowned slightly and stared into them.

He drew his head back. 'Is anything the matter?'

She pulled her gaze away quickly. 'Not at all.'

'It's just that you were staring hard at my face as if it displeased you.'

Maud took a sharp breath. His face certainly didn't displease her, not in the slightest. But she was here for business, and he was wasting her time.

'What a pleasant surprise to find you here.' His look became quizzical. 'No, don't tell me. You are on detecting business.'

'Shh.' Maud lowered her voice and glanced around. But they were alone, and no one had overheard. She turned back to him. 'I am working on a covert mission, as you rightly surmise.'

'Then heaven forbid that I should jeopardise it.'

'Good. Now, if you will excuse me, Lord Urquhart, I must return to the house.'

He stood aside to let her pass. As she took a step forward on the path, he said, 'What name are you going by, Miss McIntyre?'

Maud hesitated. What name? Too late she realised she and Daisy had not thought of using pseudonyms. Hopefully, it would not matter as the agency was so new that M. McIntyre, private detective, would not be widely known.

Maud met his eye. 'McIntyre.'

'Then au revoir, Miss McIntyre.'

'Goodbye, Lord Urquhart,' she said firmly as she marched past. Unlike Miss Taft's medieval heroines, the modern woman could not afford to be distracted by the attentions of a man.

A thought suddenly hit her. She stopped and spun round in order to see the expression on his face when he answered. 'Oh, one question?'

He nodded.

'Why are you the Duchess's special guest?'

'I suspect it's because she wants me to marry one of her daughters.'

He looked vastly pleased with himself. And why wouldn't he? Marriage to one of the Duchess's daughters would increase his prestige and fortune. Although what was in it for either of the young women, she could not imagine.

She gave him a curt nod, turned on her heel and walked swiftly towards the house.

Unlike Daisy, Maud had little to do for the remainder of the day. She would spend her time exploring whatever corridors and rooms she could while she had the opportunity. Best to get reasonably acquainted with the place before the rest of the guests arrived.

The first room she entered on the ground floor was the dining room. It had been cleared of the luncheon dishes and not yet set for the evening meal. Briefly, she admired the long mahogany table, the glistening silver candelabra, the bowls of luscious fruit on the sideboard. The next room was the library, where she and Daisy had been taken this morning to meet the Duchess. Passing on, she came to a magnificent ballroom which could surely accommodate some five hundred guests. Maud allowed herself a small smile of relief, grateful that this house party had few guests and correspondingly few suspects.

Up the stairs and onto the corridor of the first floor, she was faced with four panelled doors. The first one stood ajar, so after pausing for a minute or two and hearing no sounds from within, she entered. This was the drawing room. It spoke of good taste and money spanning several generations. Large and elegant with a granite fireplace and armchairs and sofas artfully arranged in small groups around the room. Cut flowers in a silver bowl on the grand piano. An antique rug faded by the sun; old prints and paintings on the walls. Goodness, was that a family portrait by Raeburn? Maud moved closer to get a better look. The Edinburgh-born portrait painter to George IV, no less.

From the next room came the soft click of a billiard ball hitting another on the baize cloth. Maud didn't need to see the room; it was enough that she knew its purpose. Unwilling to open the other two doors, both closed, and thereby risk her snooping being discovered, she decided they probably led to two further reception rooms.

Maud ascended the next flight of stairs and arrived on the second floor with its bedrooms. Curious as she was to see the rooms of the daughters of the house, there was nothing she could think to do to bring this about. Not that she suspected the two young ladies of stealing jewellery from the other houses, even though they had attended both parties. Although it might be amusing if Lord Urquhart's future wife were to end up in prison.

She chided herself at such a thought and turned right for her own room. She entered, closed the door behind her and was wondering what to do next, when she heard the sound of raised voices from the corridor. Slowly easing open her door, she listened.

'Who are *you*?' The female voice was sharp – and recognisable.

'I am Cameron, Miss McIntyre's lady's maid,' said Daisy. 'I was looking for her room.'

'Well, Cameron, you should not be on this part of the corridor.'

'I'm sorry, miss.'

'It's Lady Cynthia.'

The chill in her voice was enough to freeze the cut flowers in the corridor.

'The bedroom allocated to Miss McIntyre is in that direction. Run along.' The door slammed.

Maud stepped back from her door as Daisy hurried in, her face pink and carrying Maud's blue walking skirt over her arm.

'Of all the...' she spluttered, as she closed the door. 'I'd like to slap the woman in the mooth.'

'Lady Cynthia is surely the epitome of the feminine ideal.'

'That'll be right.' Daisy wrenched open the wardrobe door and clattered the hangers together as she hung Maud's skirt on the rail.

'Perhaps only in her looks?' Maud suggested with a smile.

'Aye. Just now she jerked her head towards your room in a most unladylike manner.' Daisy dropped onto the dressing table stool.

'Were you really looking for my room?'

'Of course not. I know exactly where you are. I was just having a wee nosey.'

'And did you find anything?'

She looked crestfallen. 'Not on this floor. But I took your skirt down to the servants' hall and sat at the end of the long table. Only Mrs Wilson, the cook, and the kitchen maids were there, starting on the dinner preparations for upstairs. As I stitched the hem, I nudged the talk onto the country house thefts.

'"I hear that jewellery has been stolen from bedrooms at some house parties lately," I said, really casual.

'"Keep your voice down or you'll catch it from Mr Thomson if he hears you gossiping about guests," said the cook, frowning at me as she looked up from putting pastry into those little tin cases. "But every house gossips about those upstairs," I said. Then a young voice piped up, "I've got my own idea about those robberies."

'It was a wee kitchen maid, and she said, "Stands to reason it's got to be someone who's been a guest at all of the houses." When I asked Mary, that's the wee kitchen maid, why she thought so, she said it can't be a servant because any valet or lady's maid who travels with their master or mistress would have given notice by now and gone off to enjoy their fortune.'

'A sensible argument,' Maud interjected.

'Then the cook told Mary to get on with whisking the egg whites for the raspberry meringue. It was obvious I wasna going to get anything more, so I finished my stitching and came up here.'

'If Mary is wrong and a servant *is* the one stealing the jewels,' Maud murmured, 'and bright enough to be biding his or her time until the thefts are old news, would they know where to sell the pieces for a reasonable price and without being reported to the police?' She paused and then went on, 'And how would they gain entry to the rooms? As you discovered just now with Lady Cynthia, a valet or a lady's maid would find it more difficult than a house guest to move without comment between bedrooms.'

Maud was no further forward in her theorising. She hoped matters would be clearer when all the guests were gathered together for the house party.

FIVE

Afternoon tea was something of a trial. Maud had changed into a tea gown as was expected – a peach creation from Fortuny with lace and tulle bodice and a slight train at the back – and now she sat in the drawing room with the Duchess, her two daughters and Lord Urquhart. Cynthia wore a tight-fitting cerise dress, which perfectly complemented her dark colouring, and a matching silk flower in her high pompadour. For some reason, Violet still favoured the schoolgirl look. She wore a loose-fitting netted tea gown in lemon with a high-neck ruffled collar.

There was some chat, bordering on gossip, between Cynthia and Violet about their friends, which they tried to draw Lord Urquhart into.

'Girls,' admonished the Duchess, 'neither Hamish nor Miss McIntyre has any idea of whom you are talking.'

'Oh, I wouldn't say I have *no* idea.' Lord Urquhart smiled, prompting coy giggles from the girls. The Duchess glared at her daughters.

Maud stifled a yawn. The afternoon was so tedious. She was here to prevent a crime, not to listen to this inept flirting.

The young women were making a play for him, and the man obviously saw himself as some sort of Lothario. As for the Duchess – who knew what she thought? Did she really believe Lord Urquhart would make a good match for one of her daughters? He was a mere baron, after all, the bottom of the aristocracy, whereas the Duchess was at the top. Not quite number one, of course, as she wasn't a *royal* duchess, but she was definitely up there with the toffs, as Daisy would say.

'Miss... McIntyre, is it?' began Lord Urquhart, turning to Maud.

'It is.' As you very well know, Maud thought darkly.

'You are being very quiet.'

'I believe I usually am.' Maud could see he was considering what to say next, and she was wondering if she should engage him in conversation to extract any relevant information, if such a thing were possible, when the door opened to reveal the butler, the tea things and Daisy, in that order.

Daisy? What was she doing here?

The portly fellow held the door open and Daisy, dressed in a maid's afternoon uniform of black dress and white apron, struggled in with a tray laden with the teapot and china, scones, sandwiches and cakes. Good girl that she was, she avoided Maud's eye.

'Ah, tea,' said the Duchess.

Clearly, she hadn't recognised the maid bringing in the tea things, proving yet again, if proof were needed, that servants are invisible to the upper classes. The Duchess's focus was on the delicacies – as if they hadn't only a few hours earlier eaten a very good luncheon. With the image of the Duchess's girth fixed in her mind, Maud realised she would need to do a few extra ballet exercises before dinner.

First, though, she had to suffer the afternoon's activity, a game of croquet on the lawn with the daughters and Lord

Urquhart, before she could find out why Daisy was acting as a housemaid.

As soon as was decently possible, Maud went back to her room and rang for Daisy.

Dressed again in the dark-brown silk, Daisy arrived carrying a brass hot-water can, a clean white face towel draped over her arm.

'Your hot water for washing, madam,' she said loudly, as she placed the can on the side table before returning to close the door.

Maud watched from her seat at the writing desk as Daisy crossed the room to collapse onto the edge of the bed.

'I'm exhausted,' she said in a stage whisper. 'Up and down all those stairs. I didna even get a chance to exchange a word or two with any of the handsome footmen. Can you believe it? The male servants have to use an entirely different staircase.'

'Why have you been acting as a housemaid, Daisy?' Maud asked, pushing back her chair and making her way over to the bed to hear her better.

'I'm helping out Ada.' She yawned. 'The poor lass has got so much to do, what with the afternoon tea things, lighting fires for the evening and carrying water up that steep, narrow servants' staircase. Besides, I wanted to see the family in their natural habitat.' Daisy untied the laces of her shoes and kicked them off. 'My poor feet.' She gave a deep sigh as the first shoe hit the carpet.

'That's very kind, and enterprising, of you.' Maud climbed onto the bed and propped herself up against the pillow. 'So, what did you think of Violet?'

Daisy massaged her stockinged feet. 'To be honest, I barely noticed. I had to concentrate on carrying the heavy tea things in and out of the drawing room, while that bear of a butler held the door open. Him a big strong fellow only having to open a door, whilst delicate little me has to struggle with a tray'—she drew a breath—'laden with two hot teapots, assorted china and three sorts of cake, including chocolate. The chocolate one fairly made my mooth water.'

Maud laughed. 'I hope you didn't drool over them.'

'I might just have licked the top of the cream cake,' she said, her voice casual.

'Daisy!'

She grinned. 'I was only joking.'

'Thank goodness.'

She gave Maud a sideways look. 'I stuck my finger in it and licked that instead.'

Maud decided to ignore her teasing. 'Cakes aside, you're doing a great job, Daisy.'

Daisy stopped massaging her feet and looked up at Maud. 'I did notice the other guest there, though, taking tea in the drawing room.'

'Lord Urquhart.'

She nodded. 'The same.'

'I first saw him earlier this afternoon.' Maud hadn't mentioned it to Daisy before as none of what he said seemed to shed much light on the case. Unless he was in league with one or both of the daughters. That was a possibility she hadn't yet considered. What if they had taken it in turns to steal the jewellery at the first two houses and now it was his turn at this house? It would allay suspicion, but that was too fanciful a theory to give any credence. Surely, they were all too wealthy to risk their reputations...

'Did you speak to him?' said Daisy.

Her question pulled Maud's attention back to the meeting in the rose garden. 'He recognised me, so I had to tell him I'm working on a case to stop him asking questions. What he doesn't know is that I have an assistant here, so your position is still completely secure. After all, we can't be certain he isn't our country house thief. Anyway, it's too soon to expect anything useful yet. The next two or three days will be the important ones.'

With a groan, Daisy pulled her shoes back on and tied the laces. 'I dinna think I'm cut out to be a housemaid. Poor Ada and the other girls have to be up at the crack of dawn every day and canna go to bed until all the guests have gone to theirs. No wonder Ada's thinking about leaving service to work in a factory.'

Maud smiled. 'Does this mean you have changed your opinion of the cruel way you were treated by your last employer?'

Daisy laughed, rose from the bed and stretched. 'Let's get you dressed for dinner. Then I'll be back to help you get ready for bed.'

'There's no need to come back later this evening,' Maud said. 'I know you're tired and I can get myself to bed. If Ada notices or makes any comment about it, tell her I'm having an early night.'

Maud spent the evening after dinner playing whist, she and the Duchess in one team and Cynthia and Violet in the other. Violet kept glancing over at Lord Urquhart and fluttering her cards before her face as though they were a fan. He lounged in the chair by the window and didn't once look up from his book, not even when she let out a little cough. She returned to the game with a deep sigh.

The evening passed slowly, no doubt because Maud was waiting for the rest of the main players in the bigger game to arrive tomorrow.

At ten o'clock, the party wished each other goodnight, and shortly afterwards, Maud was propped up in bed. She reread last September's issue of *The Story-Teller,* which she'd brought with her because it contained the first Father Brown story, *The Blue Cross.* It was one of her favourite tales, introducing the unassuming English priest with superior detective skills. With a satisfied sigh, she finished the story, closed the magazine, extinguished the oil lamp and lay down.

As her eyes began to close, she pictured Father Brown, no physical match for the villain, as the little priest threw soup, knocked over apples and smashed a window to leave a trail for the police to follow. Maud, though, intended to solve the Duddingston case without the aid of any policeman.

SIX

On Saturday morning, Maud was in her bedroom, admiring the arrangement of cream and yellow chrysanthemums in a pretty vase that had been placed there while she was at breakfast, when she heard footsteps in the corridor. It was followed by urgent low chatter. She eased open the door and peeped out. Two footmen were carrying between them a travelling chest.

'Take care!' exclaimed one of the men to the other. 'Don't drop it. And mind the furniture.'

'It's only a Saturday-to-Monday,' grumbled the other man, red in the face from trying to manoeuvre the chest past a little mahogany table standing against the wall. 'Why does he need so much?'

At that moment, Daisy appeared through the green baize door at the end of the corridor. The second man caught sight of her.

'Open the Colonel's door for us, will you, lassie?' he said. 'It's the one there, right by you.'

'Door-opening for footmen is not in my job remit,' she said pertly, 'but I will on this occasion.'

She moved forward, opened the door he'd indicated and

stood back as the men struggled in. There was a soft thump, indicating they'd set the chest onto the carpeted floor.

Maud heard a groan and the second man spoke again. 'I hope they're not all like this one.'

'You're obviously new to this job,' said the other footman. 'You'll learn that most are heavier.'

He must have turned to Daisy next, as Maud heard him say, 'You'd best get yourself to your mistress. You don't want to be found standing about here.'

'And yet it's always a braw sight to see men at work.'

One of the men laughed, presumably the more cheerful one, and Daisy moved away from the Colonel's doorway and came into Maud's room.

Just before Maud closed the door behind her, she caught a glimpse of a tall, slightly stooped man with a long, drooping moustache limping up the staircase.

'It looks like Colonel Morrison is the first to arrive,' said Maud.

'He's always the first, according to Ada.' Daisy moved around the room, automatically straightening things as she had done when she really was Maud's lady's maid. 'She said he's a lovely man, quiet and makes no demands.'

'What do the others say of him?'

'That he's a war hero. That's what Mackenzie, the first footman, said. That fellow's manners dinna improve. In front of the cook, he snatched a handful of raisins from an open jar and popped them in his mooth. When she smacked his hand, he just grinned.'

'Never mind the first footman, Daisy. Tell me more about the Colonel.'

'Apparently, even though he was wounded in the leg, he went to the aid of one of his men who was under terrible fire from the Boers. He took the man up on his horse and back to safety.'

'That was brave of him,' Maud said. 'Come back and let me know when anyone else arrives, Daisy. The Duchess and her daughters are engaged in letter-writing and such like, and I had my fill of Lord Urquhart yesterday.' She sighed. 'I'm feeling useless, but it's expected of me to keep out of the way until all the guests are settled and presentable again after their journey. You get back downstairs and see what you can learn about the other guests as they arrive.'

Maud roamed her room for a short while and found a pack of cards in the drawer of the nightstand. Left behind, perhaps, by an earlier occupant who suffered from insomnia. She would play, appropriately enough, a game of patience. Lacking the concentration for Sir Tommy, she settled instead on Roll Call.

Maud took the pack over to the small writing table and moved to the side the various writing implements set out there by her diligent hostess. After removing from the pack all cards with a value of less than seven, she shuffled those remaining. Taking a card one at a time from the top of the deck, she counted up from seven.

'Seven, eight, nine, ten, jack, queen, king, ace,' Maud murmured as she played.

Each time she turned over a card of the same value as the one she was calling, she removed it from the pack. When she came to the end, she started again. The idea of the game was to continue until she had no cards left, which meant she had won, or no more cards could be removed from the pack, in which case she had lost.

As Maud listened out for Daisy's returning footsteps, she turned each card and murmured its value. The first game she lost. Telling herself it was not a metaphor for the case they were embarked upon, she began a second game. Maud was ridiculously pleased when she won. It might after all be an indication of the outcome of their investigation, she thought.

The noises in the house had been increasing as she'd played, and, at last, the door opened and Daisy burst in carrying a laden tray.

'What news from below-stairs?' Maud asked, immediately dropping the cards onto the table.

'The servants' hall is hooching.' She set her tray on the edge of the dressing table and slid it along, narrowly missing the small pot of cold cream, before plumping down onto the stool.

'There's Mr Thomson, the butler, and the housekeeper, Mrs Wood, bustling about directing matters; the footmen carrying luggage up the servants' stairs; valets, full of importance, talking about outdoor coats that need to be brushed and demanding to ken where their masters' shoes can be cleaned; lady's maids needing to be shown to their rooms. And the maids are hurrying to collect trays of tea and biscuits from the kitchens to take up to each guest as they arrive. That's yours, by the way.' She nodded at the contents of the tray. 'It's mayhem down there, and I'm glad to be out of it,' she added with feeling.

'Who else has arrived?' Maud asked, desperate for information.

'Mr Laing,' said Daisy. 'I've not seen him, or any of the guests, but Ada says he's bonnie and a real gentleman. He apologised for being in the library when she popped in to put a couple more coals on the fire. Very different to the manners of Lord Urquhart, Ada said.' Daisy did a credible imitation of the maid's voice: '"He might be tall, dark and handsome, that Lord Urquhart, but he's a bit on the fresh side. He had the cheek to wink at me when I went to check on the fire in the billiard room."'

'That doesn't surprise me at all,' Maud agreed. 'The man can't help himself.'

'Then the housekeeper said to Ada, "You seem to be taking more care than usual over the fires today, my girl," and Ada laughed and said there was no harm in looking at the young gentlemen.'

Maud laughed, thinking Daisy really was quite a good mimic.

'The Earl of Swinton and his American wife are here,' Daisy went on. 'One of the other housemaids burst into the kitchen with the news. "You should see her," Lizzie said, before sinking into a chair. Then the housekeeper told her to get up, as there was no time to be sitting around. Lizzie got to her feet and said, "The Countess is beautiful, Mrs Wood."

'"From a jar, no doubt," said Mrs Wood with a sniff. "Not as the good Lord intended her to be." These Presbyterians,' added Daisy, raising her eyes, appropriately, to heaven.

'I thought you were Presbyterian, Daisy,' Maud said with some surprise and a glint of a smile.

'I am, but you ken what I mean. Some of them can be like soor plooms.'

Maud nodded; she did know what she meant. Her father's sister, her Aunt Sophy, whom they saw only occasionally, was one of those staunch Presbyterians who can make a person wither with one glance, should they make a comment about something as innocuous as the dull weather. 'If the good Lord chooses to send it,' she'd say, 'we must endure it.'

'And what then?' Maud asked, coming back to the gossip in the kitchen.

'Lizzie said, "The Countess's looks might be natural, Mrs Wood."' Daisy was making the most of relaying these conversations to Maud. '"I saw her lips." Mrs Wood tutted. "They were *scarlet*. You can't tell me that's natural."'

Maud could picture the contrasting emotions that must have flown across the poor housemaid's face. No doubt she longed for a scarlet lipstick of her own, while feeling anxious about the morality of the cosmetic.

'And then,' went on Daisy, 'the housekeeper muttered that the Countess is a Buccaneer.'

Maud knew the expression. And the other phrase used for

such women: 'Cash for titles'. They referred to very rich young Americans who came over in search of a husband with a title. It worked both ways, as the men, struggling with debt and dilapidated castles, crossed the Atlantic to hunt for wives with huge dowries.

'I hear these American heiresses have brought millions of dollars into the British nobility through marriage,' Daisy said. 'I told Mrs Wood that and she sent me a dark look showing she wasna pleased with my interference. Too bad.'

Too bad, indeed. As a woman with some money of her own, Maud knew how important it was to be free of financial dependence on a man, whether father or husband.

'And then,' said Daisy, 'one of the bells sounded.'

'Someone else arriving?'

'Miss Taft. Mrs Wood turned to Ada and said, "Yours".'

'Ada?' Maud was surprised. 'Doesn't Miss Taft have her own lady's maid?'

'Despite Miss Taft being a successful novelist, she claims to be as poor as a church mouse, says Mrs Wood, and that when the Taft woman visits other great houses, apparently, she never comes with a lady's maid of her own. Ada was told she had to take on that job, as well as doing her own work.'

'Poor Ada.'

'That's exactly what I thought,' said Daisy. 'So, I offered to go up to Miss Taft.' She smiled.

Maud frowned. 'Didn't the housekeeper find that a bit strange?'

'Ada and I didn't let on. Mrs Wood was too busy to notice who took up the tray of tea and biscuits.'

Maud smiled back at Daisy's brilliance. 'Excellent. Do go on.'

'Well, I went upstairs and tapped on her bedroom door. She was singing out of tune something terrible.' Daisy paused.

'Yes?' Goodness, she was stringing it out.

'The singing stopped. "Come in," Miss Taft trilled. So I did. And what a sight! A large woman of about forty floating about the room. She has red hair of sorts and was wearing a silk dress in some sort of reddish-pink—'

'Cerise,' Maud said faintly, picturing the incompatibility of the woman's colours. 'It's the French word for cherry.'

'Aye, well, it clashed horribly with her hair colour. Which, by the way,' Daisy added darkly, 'I'm sure isn't natural.'

Maud laughed again. 'Who's being the Presbyterian now?'

Daisy flushed. 'I only meant that it's the strangest red-yellow. I've heard that can happen to women with dark hair who use a mixture of saffron and carbonate of soda, then a rinse of lemon juice or vinegar.'

'How very singular that Miss Taft has changed her hair colour, given that the fashion is for dark hair.'

Daisy shrugged. 'Auburn hair is supposed to show sensitivity and purity of character.'

'Goodness, Daisy, where did you get that from? I don't mean it isn't true,' Maud added, seeing a hurt look cross her face.

'An old book I found. But never mind that,' Daisy hurried on. 'Her dress had three different hem lengths and a wide buckled belt. She stopped floating when she saw me, looked disappointed and asked who I was. I told her I was acting as her lady's maid for the present and that it would usually be Ada or one of the other girls. I'm very glad I won't have to dress her hair,' Daisy added with a shudder, 'as she wears it in those awful side swirls. Then she asked me who else had arrived.'

Maud nodded. 'I wonder if her trilling and floating was for the benefit of another guest – a male, perhaps?'

'I did think she was performing in some way. Anyway, I told her who else was here and then she pointed to a large black trunk and said, "You can start by unpacking." She might be as poor as a church mouse, but she certainly isna as meek as one.

And you should see the clothes that were inside her trunk. There was a fancy yellow housecoat with one huge black button and a black collar.'

Although pastels were still favoured for the daytime, the current fashion was for more jewel-like colours in the evening. Even so, Miss Taft's collection sounded... astonishing.

'Did you notice the label when you hung it in the wardrobe?'

'I made a point of looking. House of Paul Poiret.'

'Good heavens! For a woman supposedly lacking wealth, she has some expensive clothes.'

Daisy nodded. 'She propped herself up on the bed and ate the biscuits and drank her tea, watching me as I unpacked. I think you're right about a man friend, Maud, as she had some awfa bonny silk and lace under-things.'

'Hmm,' Maud murmured.

'I'd just finished putting everything away when Miss Taft climbed off the bed and sat on the stool at the dressing table. "There's an emerald-green cashmere cardigan you've put away," she said, turning her head this way and that to admire herself in the mirror. "It has a stain that needs to be removed." No please or thank you. I drew a deep breath and said, "Certainly, madam."'

'What a cheek to bring with her clothes in need of mending and washing.' Maud bristled on Daisy's behalf. 'Not only that, she could have told you about the cardigan before you put it away. Sorry about my blue skirt, by the way,' she added. 'I should have thought of the sewing earlier.'

Daisy got to her feet, turned to the tray and poured out Maud's tea. She handed Maud the cup.

'Biscuit?' She held out the plate.

'No, thanks.'

'Mind if I have one?'

'Help yourself.'

She took a piece of shortbread and bit into it. 'I wondered if Miss Taft was testing me, when she said about the cardigan. That perhaps she had somehow guessed I wasn't really a lady's maid.'

Maud took a sip of tea and thought about it. 'It doesn't sound as if she'd be that perceptive.'

'You're right. I glanced at her reflection in the mirror, but she was searching on the dressing table. "Where are my pearls?" she said.'

Maud sat up straighter, almost spilling her tea. 'Don't say they have been stolen already?'

'I should hope not! I told her they hadn't been unpacked yet. She glared at me in the mirror and pointed to her leather travelling bag. Inside there was a smaller matching case that held her jewellery.'

'Did you see what she had that might attract the thief's attention?'

Daisy shook her head and brushed shortbread crumbs from her mouth. 'I put the jewellery box on the dressing table and waited, but all she said was, "Come back in ten minutes and help me dress for luncheon. Now take the garment that needs attention and go."' Daisy pulled a face and mimicked waving a hand airily. 'I was dismissed.'

Maud leaned back on the bed, deep in thought. The house party was now almost complete. Only the Viscount and Viscountess Drummond were still to make an appearance.

'Some of the guests at the last two house parties I attended had their jewellery stolen from their bedrooms,' said Miss Taft at luncheon.

Her tightly corseted plump body had been buttoned into a brown and cream floral garment. Maud believed it was called sultana skirts, a very new fashion for those brave enough to wear it. The round neck and sleeves cut to the elbow were a little on the tight side for Miss Taft if one took the time to notice, but the most eye-catching design was the belt, stitched into the fabric at the top of the thighs. A turban of the same material had been secured on her head. Maud had to admit she thought the entire outfit rather stylish, although more suited to a slimmer figure.

'I read of the jewellery thefts in the newspaper,' she said, forking up a piece of chicken in caper cream sauce. It was delicious. She would have to ask Daisy to see if the cook would let her have the recipe.

'Have you not been at any house parties recently yourself?' Miss Taft said sharply, clearly wondering where Maud had been these last few months.

'I'm afraid not. For the last six months, I have been abroad with my father.' Maud glanced down at the asymmetrical hem of her pastel-pink silk two-piece and hoped that her father would forgive her for the lie. 'His doctor prescribed the fresh air of Switzerland for his health and naturally I went with him.'

'And what of your mother?'

The woman was unpardonably rude to ask that question so bluntly. 'She is no longer with us.' Maud didn't have to affect the sad tone in her voice, for even though she could barely remember her, she always felt a little melancholy when she thought of her mother.

Miss Taft nodded, no longer interested, and reverted to the previous subject. 'I confess as an author these crimes set my imagination turning somersaults.' She fixed her eyes on Maud's. 'Who do you think is the culprit? I believe it must be a servant who is responsible.'

'Why do you say that, Miss Taft?' asked the Duchess.

'Because in my experience they are rarely trustworthy,' she said simply.

'Have you read Mr Kingsley's novel *The Water Babies*?' Maud enquired with an innocent expression.

She frowned. 'No. That's a fairy story.'

Mr Laing sent Maud an amused glance. She could see he knew the point she was making.

'I meant perhaps when you were a child,' Maud continued.

'How old do you think I am?' said Miss Taft. 'That book came out almost fifty years ago.'

'Yes, but it's remained fairly popular, I believe.'

Although sadly containing the Victorian era's prejudices, the fable had two very memorable characters. Mrs Do-As-You-Would-Be-Done-By was soft and cuddly. Her sister, Mrs Be-Done-By-As-You-Did was scaly and prickly. The moral was treat people as you would like to be treated and expect to receive the same treatment back.

As they finished the meal, Maud reflected that she would have to be careful not to see Miss Taft as the suspect simply because she didn't like the woman.

SEVEN

After luncheon, Mr Laing drew Maud aside over coffee in the drawing room. 'I'm sorry you were subject to that unpleasant woman's questioning earlier.'

'It was not your fault, but thank you.' Maud looked at him. Although he wasn't to Maud's taste, she could see why Ada thought he was bonnie. His sandy hair grew in waves, he had green eyes and a pleasant face, clean-shaven apart from a natty little moustache above a pair of finely chiselled lips. He was formally dressed in a dark suit and white shirt, like the other men, although it was a shame about the orange spotted bow tie.

'I believe you are an advocate-depute,' she said. 'That must be interesting.'

He smiled and said in a modest voice, 'Everyone thinks so, but really it can become as repetitive as any other line of business.'

'Surely not repetitive? Each of your clients will have a different story to tell.'

'That is true.' He shook his head. 'And some of those stories can be quite heart-wrenching.' He gave a sad smile.

'Tell me,' Maud said. 'Who, in your professional opinion, do you think is responsible for these country house thefts?'

He studied her face and, horror of horrors, Maud found herself blushing.

'I mean in general terms, of course,' she hastened to add, lest he think she was asking him to point the finger at a fellow guest. Although, she thought, that might prove useful.

'In general terms...' He leaned in closer. 'I'd say it was probably one of the servants. A lady's maid, perhaps, who simply found the temptation too much.'

'Even though she would have no legitimate reason for being in another lady's bedroom?'

He straightened. 'I don't know how these things work, not yet being blessed with a wife of my own, but in some circumstances could a lady's maid be sent by her mistress to assist another female house guest?'

'That's quite possible.' Maud prayed the warmth in her face would be seen by him as a result of the day's heat. After all, Daisy, her supposed lady's maid, had been assisting Miss Taft. Clearly, Daisy was entirely innocent of the crimes, but such a situation could arise as Mr Laing suggested. Though would it be likely to happen more than once?

'The question you need to ask yourself is this: is it likely?' He stared deep into her eyes with such a startling familiarity that for a moment she almost forgot why she was at Duddingston House at all.

'I'm afraid we are rather late, but may I introduce myself?'

The soft drawl of an American accent could come only from the Countess of Swinton.

Maud turned to see a beautiful young woman, who was drawing the eye of everyone in the room. The Countess was of a similar height to Maud, which was refreshing. She was perhaps a few years older than Maud, slender and elegant with her fair hair swept up, exposing a delicate swanlike neck. The blue shot-

silk gown she wore was perfect, the kind of creation only a
Parisian designer was able to produce, and it deepened the blue
of her eyes.

The man standing beside her was equally elegant. In his
mid-thirties at a guess, the Earl's dark hair was tousled to advantage. The Countess placed her gloved hand on his arm and
smiled up at him. 'This is my husband, Teddy, and I am
Eleonora.'

Americans were so lacking in formality that it was like a
breath of fresh air, and Maud followed her lead. 'I'm very
pleased to meet you both. I am Maud McIntyre and this is...'

She turned to Mr Laing.

'Douglas Laing,' he provided. 'But of course we have met
before at other house parties.'

'Of course,' the Countess said with a smile.

Before long they all settled down to discuss the proposed
afternoon activities once they had rested. A tour of the garden, a
game of tennis and an expedition in the Daimler to a local site
of interest were all suggested. At the mention of the garden
tour, Lord Urquhart sent a look Maud's way, which she ignored.
He favoured tennis, and Violet, the Countess and the Earl
expressed themselves delighted with the idea of a game of
mixed doubles. The two older members of the party, the
Duchess and the Colonel, declared they would settle down
with their books for a spot of quiet reading. That left Cynthia,
Mr Laing and Maud.

'I'd be very happy to accompany the two ladies on an
outing,' said Mr Laing. 'What do you say to Rosslyn Chapel?'

'I have been there many times already,' said Cynthia, with a
scowl at Mr Laing. 'I'll find something to do here.' With that –
and there can be no other word for it – she flounced off.

· · ·

Mr Laing made an excellent guide. 'Rosslyn Chapel was founded in 1446 by Sir William St Clair,' he said, his voice reverberating off the stone walls. 'It was a Catholic place of worship then, of course. After the Scottish Reformation, the practice was brought to an end. When it was eventually reopened to public worship, it was according to the rites of the Episcopal Church. The beauty of its setting and the mysterious symbolism of its ornate stonework have inspired people ever since.'

He wore a light-coloured jacket and a boater, and Maud was wearing her tailored linen coat. They must have looked like an ordinary couple enjoying an afternoon out, instead of two people each with their own secrets. Maud wondered what Mr Laing might be hiding.

She took her eyes from him and gazed round the candlelit interior. Stone carvings covered almost every inch of its walls, pillars and vaulted ceilings. One ceiling alone was decorated with hundreds, thousands, of roses, lilies and stars. High up, among the carved stars, she could just make out a tiny depiction of Christ with his hand raised in blessing.

'Look there,' said Mr Laing, pointing with his walking cane up to a carving by a stained-glass window. 'An angel holding the heart of Robert the Bruce, which an earlier Sir William St Clair was charged to carry to Jerusalem.'

All around her was the Christian imagery she had expected to see. Angelic musicians playing the harp, drum, pipe, bagpipes and stringed instruments, and scenes from the Bible, such as angels rolling away the stone from Christ's tomb, were carved in arches, pillars and niches dotted all around the chapel.

What she hadn't expected was to see so many representa- tions of a wild-looking face made of leaves. She'd heard some refer to him as the Green Man: a symbol of fertility and rebirth, a bridge between Christianity and the pagan beliefs it replaced.

'There are also plants,' went on Mr Laing, 'such as aloe vera and maize, both unknown in Britain at the time the chapel was built.'

Maud smiled. 'You know this place very well.'

'Indeed, I do,' he said, returning her smile. 'I like to come here whenever I can. Let me show you something else of interest.'

He led Maud over to a frieze on an arch above their heads. 'Here are the seven works of mercy.' He pointed up. 'You can see sheltering the homeless, clothing the naked, visiting the sick, visiting those in prison, and here'– he paused – 'is avarice.'

'Avarice? Surely that isn't a mercy?'

He laughed. 'You are correct, Miss McIntyre. Come round to the other side.'

She followed him and they stared up at the companion frieze.

'There are the seven deadly sins,' he said, gesturing with his stick to each in turn. 'Pride, gluttony, giving drink to the thirsty...'

It was Maud's turn to laugh. 'I can see why that could be easily misplaced.' She thought for a moment or two. 'So in that position should be avarice, the pursuit of material possessions.'

'Yes.'

'I was thinking of the jewellery thefts,' she said. 'Whoever has taken them can't possibly wear the pieces, at least not in public, so the thief must—'

'Let us not think of such matters on this pleasant day.' He smiled and took her arm, tucking it into his elbow, and they moved back to two huge pillars.

'This is the Mason's Pillar, said to be the work of the master mason, and the much more elaborate one there is the Apprentice Pillar. Its beauty is said to have so enraged the master mason that he struck the apprentice on the head with his mallet and killed him on the spot.'

'Is that true?' she asked, looking at the intricate carvings more closely.

'Who knows? It was so long ago. But local lore says the other masons carved the head of the murdered apprentice over there, on the west wall, as a reminder of what envy can do.'

They strolled over to look at it. Above them the face of a man with a gash on his forehead peered down, his sadness displayed for all to see as long as the chapel stood. An unwanted sort of immortality.

Maud turned again to admire the chapel as a whole. 'It seems incredible that during the English Civil War, Cromwell's troops stabled their horses inside this chapel.'

Mr Laing shook his head. 'Such sacrilege.'

How grateful she was to those in the last century who restored the chapel to such glory. Maud pushed aside the image of stabled horses, straw and dung, and instead imagined plain-song rising to the high ceilings as the liturgy was sung.

He sighed. 'It is beautiful here, but we should get back. I have monopolised your time enough for one day.'

Mr Laing was such charming company that Maud was almost reluctant to leave. But she had a crime to prevent, and if that wasn't possible, then a crime to solve.

Maud rang for Daisy as soon as she was back in her room.

'Anything to report?' she asked when her friend joined her.

'Well, I've washed Miss Taft's cashmere.'

That wasn't the type of information Maud had in mind.

'There are nae boxes of ready-made soap flakes here, so I had to grate a few shavings off the block of carbolic soap. What a stink of coal tar.' She wrinkled her nose. 'I washed and rinsed the cardigan and left it spread on a clean towel to dry in the laundry room. After that, I had some time to myself for a wee while, and it was obvious I was getting underfoot in the servants' hall, and that I needed to make myself scarce.'

Maud suddenly realised to her shame how tedious it must have been for Daisy to accompany her when she had gone to all sorts of events as a guest in her own right.

'Dinna look so guilty, Maud,' Daisy laughed. 'I used my time to continue your nosey of the house.'

Maud had earlier told Daisy how far she had got in establishing the arrangement of the rooms above-stairs.

'We already ken on the ground floor there's the dining room, library and ballroom,' Daisy said. 'I stole along the passage on the first floor and the doors were a wee bit open to the two rooms you'd not seen yesterday, so I keeked in. They're the morning room and a small saloon.'

As Maud had guessed from her knowledge of large country houses, but it was good to have this confirmed.

'On the second floor,' Daisy went on, 'I stood and listened for a wee while. The bedroom doors were closed and all was quiet, but I didna dare try any of the door handles. On the third floor, the doors are smaller, so they must have been the bairns' rooms, nursery and schoolroom. I couldna resist a keek and, sure enough, there were cots and wee beds, toys and books.'

For a moment, Maud was reminded of her own childhood with her three brothers, all now married and with children of their own. Perhaps one day she too would have children. She straightened her back. First, though, she had work to do.

'And, of course, the attic floor is where the maids sleep,' Daisy concluded. 'The housekeeper, butler and footmen sleep below-stairs in the basement.'

Maud reflected that, so far, all was as it should be with the house and its inhabitants.

.   .   .

Dinner was served at eight o'clock. Maud went down in her raspberry-coloured embroidered silk with the white gold Krementz brooch pinned to her shoulder, to discover the Viscount and Viscountess had arrived at some point during the late afternoon. They joined the rest of the party in the drawing room before dinner.

Both were thin, elderly and grey-haired; he with wispy side-whiskers, she – Maud tried not to stare at it – with a whiskery mole on her chin. The light from the fire in the hearth gave their skin a sallow hue. Maud observed small burn holes in the Viscount's evening jacket, presumably from ash falling when he smoked; and the Viscountess wore a beautiful but decidedly Victorian boned evening gown in ivory ribbed silk with a princess bustle. From this, she deduced the couple were not as well off as their titles might suggest.

Maud now had an opportunity to make a mental note of the grandest pieces of jewellery on display amongst the gathering. The Duchess wore a relatively modest choker with a single emerald; Lady Cynthia wore a small opal necklace and matching earrings, while a pearl and ruby brooch twinkled on Violet's generous bosom. At the Countess's throat a large pendant of diamonds and sapphires sparkled as much as her blue eyes. A diamond necklace hung about the scrawny neck of the Viscountess. The piece of jewellery she wore, presumably a treasured heirloom, must be worth a few thousand pounds. So, the Countess and the Viscountess were the most likely to be the object of the thief's attention.

Conversation was disappointingly unedifying, and Maud was relieved when the butler announced that dinner was served.

The Duchess was escorted into the dining room by the senior-ranking male guest, the Earl. He had to abandon his beautiful wife in favour of their hostess, while the Countess's partner was the old Viscount. It was quite difficult to think of the Earl as Teddy. Edward, yes; but Teddy, no. For Maud, the name conjured up an image of a teddy bear, and he was much more like Lord Byron.

The remaining guests were also paired according to rank, which meant that Maud was partnered with Mr Laing. Lord Urquhart, as the Duchess's special guest and in lieu of a Duke, accompanied the lady of the highest rank, which was the elder Duddingston daughter, Cynthia.

The table looked particularly beautiful this evening, decorated with vases filled with pink and white roses. The sun hadn't yet set, but it had moved across the sky and candles had been lit in the darkening room. The silver cutlery and crystal glasses sparkled in the candlelight.

'I do so dislike the harshness of the new electric light bulbs,' the Duchess said, as the party took their seats.

When the food was brought in, Maud felt yet another pang of guilt about Daisy at the kitchen table below-stairs. Above-stairs the meal began with soup accompanied by sherry, and they worked their way through fish with white wine, mutton cutlets served with champagne, the remove which consisted of roast beef served with burgundy, then wild duck with claret, followed by cherry tart and cheese.

By this time, Maud was envying Daisy downstairs. The servants' food might be plain, but it was wholesome, and what she was being served was too rich for her liking. Maud took care to eat only a modest amount of each course, as she needed to keep her wits about her. The thief could strike this evening. Her heart quickened at the thought. What better time than when all the guests were full and sleepy?

Finally, the table was cleared, finger bowls brought in and ices served, as well as fruit and nuts. When the port began to circulate, this was the cue for the ladies to retire. The gentlemen could now smoke and discuss important things like politics, while the ladies had coffee in the drawing room.

The ladies' conversation was desultory until the men joined the room again. Cynthia and Violet immediately claimed Lord Urquhart and drew him onto a large sofa by the fire, hemming him in between them. He appeared so uncomfortable that Maud wondered if it was the attention the daughters were paying him or the fire that he wished to get away from.

'Let us play a game of poker,' the Duchess said.

There was a chorus of approval. This didn't surprise Maud, as it was a popular after-dinner game. Lord Urquhart looked as though he wished to join, but his admirers refused to let him leave the sofa. The Colonel, dressed in a baggy suit which complemented his drooping moustache, declined. Maud politely declined too, all the better to observe the guests. The Duchess, clearly realising this, did not press her. That left seven who wished to play. Immediately, the footmen bustled about to set up a card table and chairs. An oil lamp was set on a nearby table and a small pile of white, red and blue chips placed in the middle of the card table.

Seven players at the table, the cosy threesome on the sofa, the Colonel in an armchair, seeming to doze over the unlit pipe in his hand, and Maud – to all appearances – reading Miss Taft's latest novel.

Apart from a muted conversation being held on the sofa and the sound of a log falling in the grate, all was quiet in the room. As the Viscount puffed on his cigar, a memory came back to Maud of the importance of the smell of tobacco in solving the Radcliffe ruby case.

She closed her eyes, leaned back in her chair and saw again the drawn heavy curtains of the Radcliffe's library, its books and curios. Her hostess had given the guests a tour of the house when they'd arrived the previous day and she'd pointed out the beautifully intricate Indian silver bracelet inset with a large ruby, displayed in the glass cabinet which stood against one wall.

That evening Maud had moved on to browsing the book-shelves when she came across a copy of the latest Father Brown novel. She lifted it from the shelf. Music had drifted from the ballroom, but she'd had enough of dancing for one night, so she sank into the nearest chair and began to read. It must have been only minutes later when the door opened quietly and one of the other house guests appeared on the threshold. Maud looked up, book still in her hand, to call hello, but the young woman's manner was so strange that she said nothing and quietly watched her from the depths of her wing-backed chair. The woman hesitated, then stepped quickly into the room. Moving stealthily, she crossed the carpeted floor, reached the cabinet of curios and peered down into the glass. Her hand went out and lifted the lid. She reached in.

At this point Maud felt she had to speak. 'Good evening.'

The young woman dropped the bracelet back into the cabinet and spun round. 'Oh, good evening,' she said, when she saw Maud leaning round from the wing of her chair.

'Is everything all right?' Maud had asked politely.

'Absolutely.' She swallowed. 'I just wanted another look at the bracelet.' She closed the lid and hastened from the room.

The following morning at breakfast their hostess made an announcement. A housemaid had gone into the library to lay the fire, noticed the cabinet lid had not been closed properly and discovered that the bracelet was missing.

An audible gasp went round the table. The bracelet was priceless: a collector's item. The theft was the topic of discussion throughout the meal. Maud thought back to the young woman the previous evening, but somehow felt she'd been telling the truth about simply wanting to look.

'It'll be one of the servants,' Lord Mosley had said, lighting up his pipe. Maud wasn't able – yet – to identify the ashes of one hundred and forty different varieties of tobacco like Sherlock Holmes, but Lord Mosley's blend had a particularly pungent smell.

Now, remembering how easy it had been to catch the thief, she smiled to herself. She'd returned to the library after the discovery of the theft, examined the cabinet and noticed it smelled strongly of Lord Mosley's tobacco. Anyone who smoked his pipe whilst in the act of removing a valuable bracelet from a cabinet deserved to be caught. That success was the reason Maud had at last decided to become a private investigator. If Kate Warne could do it, then so could she. The first female private detective some fifty years ago in America, Mrs Warne had uncovered the plot to assassinate President-elect Abraham Lincoln. A widow by the age of twenty-three, she'd worked for the Pinkerton National Detective Agency, founded in Chicago by a Scot. Mr Pinkerton was from Glasgow, not Edinburgh, but that couldn't be helped.

Bringing her thoughts back to the present case, Maud realised tobacco identification wouldn't be useful here if the jewellery thief was one of the two smokers in the room, as she couldn't detect any distinctive aroma from their tobacco. She opened her eyes and turned her attention to the poker players. The sharp-featured Viscountess was dealing the cards.

Suddenly, Miss Taft spoke.

'Would you mind, Your Grace, if I sent for my lady's maid?'

The Duchess looked surprised, but said, 'Of course not, Miss Taft.' She nodded at a footman who turned and left the room.

Within minutes, Daisy appeared.

Not taking her eyes from the play, Miss Taft held out a plump wrist clasped with an amethyst bracelet and said to Daisy, 'There is a loose thread on this sleeve.'

She had called Daisy in for *that*? The thread hung no more than half an inch from the cuff of her tangerine-coloured blouse. Having a lady's maid had clearly gone to her head.

'Yes, madam.' Daisy removed the tiny scissors from the sewing kit at her waist and snipped off the end of the thread.

'Have you finished?' Miss Taft asked, not looking at her.

'Yes, madam.'

Miss Taft snatched her arm back. 'You can go.'

Maud saw Daisy was holding the scissors like a dagger. For a brief moment, Maud imagined her stabbing the organza-covered arm. How useful to their burgeoning business would the screaming headline be: *Deranged Assistant to Private Detective Attacks Popular Romantic Novelist?* Not very.

As Daisy replaced the scissors in her sewing kit, the Countess sent her a sympathetic glance at being the helpless recipient of Miss Taft's bad manners.

Maud's gaze returned to the Viscountess's shrewd features before dropping to her nimble hands. The woman was quick, but Maud saw her slip some cards from the bottom of the pack to the top. She had taken advantage of the small distraction in the room to perform her trickery.

Maud knew that the Duchess must be told at the first opportunity. If the Viscountess was dishonest in a card game, could she be dishonest in other matters – such as stealing jewellery?

EIGHT

Maud didn't feel the matter could wait, so as soon as there was a lull in the card play and the butler and two footmen appeared with refreshments, she made her way over to the Duchess.

'Your Grace, could I speak to you privately on an urgent matter?' Maud murmured as she accepted a cup of coffee from a footman.

The Duchess gave a slight nod. 'Meet me in the small saloon.'

The older woman drank her coffee and exchanged a few pleasantries with the Countess before leaving the drawing room. Maud waited a few moments so as not to rouse suspicion and also left the room.

She made her way along the corridor, to the small saloon where the door stood ajar.

'Come in, Miss McIntyre,' the Duchess called at the sound of her knock.

Maud entered a comfortable-looking room, not so very small despite the name, with rose silk curtains and carpets, a day bed and a variety of armchairs, sofas and footstools.

The Duchess lowered herself into a chair. 'Close the door and take a seat, my dear. Before you speak,' she added, 'I have an apology to make.'

Maud's eyes widened in surprise. 'You do, Your Grace?'

'Yes, for subjecting your assistant just now to Miss Taft's abominable behaviour.'

'You recognised Miss Cameron?' There went her theory that servants were invisible.

'I could hardly do otherwise, with that red hair.' She smiled and sat forward in her chair. 'Do you wish to see me because you have made progress with your investigation?'

'Not yet,' Maud had to admit, 'but I do have something to report, which I'm afraid you will not like. I'm not sure that it has anything to do with the robberies, but one of your guests is cheating at cards.' She told her of the Viscountess's action at the card table.

The Duchess frowned. 'I see.' She sat back and rearranged the folds of her emerald-green silk skirts. 'Are you quite sure?'

Maud nodded.

'That is a poor way to repay my hospitality. I will watch the Viscountess for the remainder of the evening and, if necessary, deal with the matter in private. It is not what I hoped to discover, but such dishonest behaviour cannot be tolerated. You think she might be the thief?'

'I wouldn't rule out anyone at present, Your Grace.'

'Well, thank you, Miss McIntyre.' She rose.

Maud followed suit. 'I noticed that the Countess is wearing a pendant of diamonds and sapphires, you have an exquisite emerald choker and the Viscountess has on a diamond necklace. Your daughters and Miss Taft are also wearing very attractive jewels.'

'Yes?'

'I'm attempting to establish the most likely person to be targeted by the thief, Your Grace.'

The Duchess wrinkled her brow as she thought. 'Miss Taft has a bracelet of some sort, but I am uncertain if it is a genuine amethyst or not. My daughters, of course, have various trinkets and the gentlemen will have gold cufflinks.'

The so-called trinkets the Duchess had described and the cufflinks were not, Maud was certain, of interest to the thief. He or she would be after a much bigger prize, meaning the pendant or the necklace.

'I must return to my guests or they will be wondering if anything is amiss.' The Duchess moved forward. 'Please let me know as soon as you have anything to report.'

Maud opened the door, and the Duchess went out. The passage was empty, which was a relief. A private conversation between the Duchess and a guest when others were gathered in another room might arouse suspicion.

Rather than go back to the drawing room, Maud decided to return to her bedroom. She would rest for an hour or so while she formulated her plan. The theft, if one were to take place at Duddingston, would be attempted at night once the guests were asleep. Perhaps this very night. As she mounted the grand staircase to the second floor, a frisson of excitement ran through her.

Back in her room, she crossed to the window and glanced out. The moon had begun its nightly climb, clothing the garden in mysterious shadows.

She tensed; someone was creeping out of the dark shelter of the yew alley. Alert, Maud watched as the man's steps brought him closer to the house.

Turning on her heel, she gathered her skirts in her hand and ran back down the staircase, through the green baize door and burst into the servants' hall. The butler and a footman were still seated at the table. They looked up in surprise as she entered.

'Thomson,' she said a little breathlessly, 'there appears to be a stranger, possibly a would-be intruder, at the rear of the house.'

He got to his feet as quickly as his girth would allow it. 'Mackenzie, come with me.' He picked up a lamp, crossed the passageway to a side door and pulled it open. Maud followed. The figure was closer now and was visible in the light Thomson held aloft.

'Hey, you!' the butler shouted.

Mackenzie dashed out, the butler on the footman's heels, their coat tails flapping behind them. Maud waited at the open door. The shouting and scuffling grew louder, until Thomson and the footman reappeared in the doorway, each holding an arm of an elderly, bedraggled man.

'What are we going to do with him, Mr Thomson?' asked Mackenzie.

'That is a matter for Her Grace to decide,' said the butler, his breathing laboured. 'I will not interrupt her evening for the likes of him. Put him in the coal hole for now.'

'That's the best place for him,' said Mackenzie with a scowl. 'He stinks rotten.'

'Let me go.' The man tried to wrench his arms free.

The footman took a tighter hold. 'You would murder us in our beds.'

'He's not here to murder us,' said Thomson, still breathing heavily, 'but to steal whatever he can get his filthy hands on.'

'I'm nae!' protested the man. 'I just want a bed for the night in the stables.'

'Oh aye?' said Mackenzie. 'And what else?'

The man ceased to struggle, and a hopeful look grew on his face. 'Perhaps to cadge a wee bit of breakfast from the kitchens in the morning.'

Maud chose this moment to speak up. 'I wonder if he might be telling the truth.' He certainly looked tired and hungry. His coat was shabby, his trousers muddy and his face and hands in need of a wash. 'We don't need to disturb Her Grace.'

The butler, who had mastered his breathing and his bearing

once again, considered the man's dishevelled appearance. 'I'm inclined to believe Miss McIntyre is correct.'

'I'm sure he's lying.' The footman wasn't persuaded. 'I don't like the look in his eye. The blackguard is wearing a disguise to fool us.'

Was it a disguise? If so, it was a good one, for the man did indeed smell appallingly. In *The Adventure of the Beryl Coronet*, Holmes passed himself off as a common loafer by pulling on a shiny old coat with a turned-up collar and a pair of worn boots. Maud peered again at the man in front of her. She was sure he was genuinely in need.

'Look under his coat,' Maud said, 'just to be sure he's a harmless vagabond and not carrying any housebreaking implements.'

Thomson wrinkled his plump nose. 'Do that, Mackenzie.'

The footman grimaced, but with a finger and thumb opened the coat, which was missing its buttons.

'Now search him,' said the butler.

'Have a heart, Mr Thomson,' groaned Mackenzie.

Thomson's face remained impassive. With a heavy sigh, Mackenzie felt in the coat and then the trouser pockets, and around the old waistcoat hanging loosely on the man's thin chest. 'Nothing there but ribs.'

'This fellow is just some poor wretch,' said the butler. 'He can sleep in the stables tonight and be given something to eat in the morning before he goes on his way.'

'Thank you, sir,' said the man, looking relieved. 'Much obliged. I'll cause no trouble and will be gone at daybreak.'

Later, as Maud rested fully dressed on her bed finalising her plan for the night's watch, Daisy appeared. With a groan she threw herself down next to Maud and stared up at the ceiling.

'Och, my aching back. I lost count of the number of jugs the other maids and I carried from the kitchen up those stairs. And I swear all the guests wanted their hot water at the same time. And I pressed Miss Taft's cashmere cardigan.'

'Only one more day here, Daisy, and then the guests – and you and I – will be leaving.' Maud gave an account of the vagabond in the grounds earlier, and Daisy agreed he seemed an unlikely candidate for the jewel thief. 'With the other two robberies, the thief has struck at night,' she went on. 'Assuming the same pattern applies here, it could be tonight or tomorrow night.'

'Are we going to patrol outside the bedrooms?'

Poor Daisy sounded exhausted, and Maud knew she couldn't ask her to help tonight. 'The likeliest victims are the Viscountess and the Countess. Each of their pieces of jewellery must be worth a few thousand. I can easily keep an eye on those two rooms myself.'

Daisy yawned. 'I can watch one of the rooms. Ada is back to looking after Miss Taft. I'm nae awfa tired.' She stifled another yawn.

'Their rooms are on the same floor as mine, so it's not a problem.'

'If you're sure.' Daisy rolled off the bed. 'Let's hope that the thief doesn't appear.'

She left and Maud read *Her Highland Chieftain Lover* for a while, until she was unable to bear the wait any longer. She crept out of the room, down the stairs and went out of a side door into the refreshing night air. Not only did she need to keep awake, she should also check all was well outside the house. It wouldn't do to have any more strangers lurking about.

She made her way up to the terrace, which gave her a good vantage point over the rear garden as well as inside the drawing room. From the open sash window came the sound of Miss Taft talking. An oil lamp, fashioned as a cut-glass bowl on a long silver stem, glowed in the room and a slight breeze stirred the curtains drawn partially across.

Why only one lamp alight? Maud stole a little closer to the window and peered in. Miss Taft's voice had taken on a low, husky tone.

'*Rory drew in a breath as he pulled the cap from the girl's head and her red tresses tumbled about her face and shoulders.*

'*He rested his hands against the wooden door, one hand either side of her head. Raising his eyebrows, he smiled down at her.*

'*"Let me go," she said, anger flashing in her eyes.*

'*His smile broadened. "Who are you?"*

'*"It's no business of yours. Now let me go!"*

'*He gave her a wolfish grin. "That may not be wise, lassie. You never know who is lurking in the woods."*

'*She flushed. "That certainly is true."*

'*His gaze travelled down her slim and clearly supple body...*'

Miss Taft was reading from her latest novel.

Maud smiled to herself, wondering if Miss Taft had been asked to read or had taken it upon herself to do so, and she moved away from the window. For a little while, she leaned on the balustrade, admiring the night sky, before straightening and returning to her own room.

The thought of remaining fully clothed, including in her corset, was not an appealing one on such a warm night, so she changed into her nightdress and removed the pins in her hair. It would also look more natural, she thought as she folded her hair into a plait, should anything happen to disturb the occupants of Duddingston House that night.

She lay on her bed and, having had enough of Miss Taft's Highland lover, opened Baroness Orczy's *Lady Molly of Scotland Yard*. Lady Molly was a successful detective because she recognised domestic clues which were unfamiliar to her male colleagues. Perhaps one day there would be a real-life counter-part of Molly Robertson-Kirk? Maud gave a little sigh and began to read.

Despite her best intentions, she must have dozed, because the next thing she knew a piercing scream shattered the night.

NINE

Maud scrambled out of bed, pulled on her dressing gown and wrenched open her bedroom door. The lamps were turned low along the corridor, but she could still make out other doors opening and startled faces peering out from the dimly lit rooms behind.

'What's going on?' cried several confused voices.

She turned and saw Mr Laing outside his room, his dressing gown on but not yet fastened.

Further along the corridor, in the opposite direction to Maud and Laing's respective rooms, Lord Urquhart was already tightening the cord on his dressing gown as he stepped fully into the passage.

'Where did the scream come from?' Maud demanded.

'From a room at this end,' called Lord Urquhart, turning to look at the two doors that remained closed.

Maud dashed along the corridor to the first closed door, the rug sliding under her feet on the polished floor and her heart thumping in her chest.

'Wait,' said Mr Laing. 'I'll get the poker.'

'I'll come too,' Maud heard the Colonel call out.

'Oh, be careful, everyone!' twittered Miss Taft from somewhere behind Maud.

Lord Urquhart already had his hand on the door handle of
the Viscountess's room. Pushing past him, Maud burst into the
room.

The Viscountess lay unmoving in her bed, the covers a
tangled mess. A white cotton pillow lay over her face.

'Get the pillow off her,' Maud shouted, running forward
to remove it. Her breath caught in her throat as she was met
with the Viscountess's staring eyes in a deathly white face.
With the wispy grey hair escaping from its night plait, her
white nightdress with its high ruffle collar, the old lady
looked so defenceless. Was she still alive? Maud bent her
head to the Viscountess's open mouth but could feel no
breath.

'A mirror,' Maud called, flinging the pillow across the room.
'Someone bring me a mirror.'

The room became suddenly brighter as the oil lamp was
turned up. Maud glanced round seeking assistance and saw Mr
Laing snatch up a hand mirror from the dressing table.

'Here.'

She took it from him, bent again over the Viscountess and
held the glass in front of the elderly woman's mouth. The
mirror remained unmisted. Maud brought it closer, to no avail.
Turning to the others who had gathered in the room, she shook
her head slowly.

'I'm sorry. She's dead.'

The Countess gasped and her husband gathered her to his
pyjama-clad chest. Miss Taft burst into tears and the night-
shirted Colonel put his arm around her shoulders. Where was
the poor woman's husband? The rest of the gathering stood as if
frozen.

'The police will have to be informed,' Maud said to the
Duchess, who was breathing heavily, her hand to her brocade-

robed bosom. Murder was not in the same category as stolen jewellery, no matter how valuable.

'Yes,' whispered the Duchess, her brows drawn together.

Maud was shaking as she gazed at the silent little party. She had been asked to Duddingston House to detect a jewellery theft, not to deal with murder. That would need a more experienced person than herself and surely one with more powers.

'Everyone should return to their rooms and stay there until the police arrive.'

The Duchess dropped her hand. 'Quite right.' She turned to her guests just as the butler appeared in the doorway, his tailcoat pulled on hastily over his nightshirt. Close behind him was the similarly attired Mackenzie.

The butler gave a started look round the room. 'I heard the scream, Your Grace.'

'It sounded like someone had been murdered,' added the footman helpfully.

'Mackenzie!'

'Sorry, Mr Thomson.'

'Milli?' The Viscount made his way into his wife's bedchamber from the connecting door between their rooms. 'I heard a noise.'

He stared at the gathering, the frown deepening on his brow as he looked from one face to another.

'I'm afraid there's been a...' Maud moved slowly away from the bed.

His face crumpled at the sight of his wife. He hobbled as quickly as he could to her side and all but collapsed on the bed. He let out a wail that tore at Maud's heart.

'The servants should all be awakened if they are not already and told to assemble in the servants' hall for questioning.' Maud murmured to the Duchess.

Quickly, Maud glanced round the room and established that all the above-stairs occupants of the house were present.

The frowning Duchess, and Cynthia and Violet, were huddled together and understandably frightened, while the poor Viscount looked ready to collapse. Lord Urquhart was guiding the elderly man into a chair. All present from this end of the corridor. The Earl and his Countess, Mr Laing, Miss Taft, the drooping Colonel and herself were all accounted for at the other end of the passage. Everyone without exception was in night attire.

'Thomson, telephone for the police,' ordered the Duchess. 'Mackenzie, turn up the lamps in all the passages and rouse the rest of the servants. Get some of the men to check there has been no break-in downstairs. Everyone else, could I please ask you to return to your rooms for the time being? We all need to be ready for questioning when Sergeant McKay arrives.'

Mr Thomson bowed and turned on his heel, gesturing at Mackenzie to follow him out of the room.

'I say—'

The Duchess cut the Colonel off with a wave of her hand. 'I will let you know what is happening as soon as I can,' she said firmly.

The group began to file out of the room, with much muttering about no one being able to sleep after such a dreadful event.

Maud turned back to the Viscountess and stared at her wrinkled face with the tell-tale bloodshot eyes of a person who had been smothered. How long would it have taken for her to suffocate? She was elderly and, if her murderer was strong, then surely it would take only a few minutes, perhaps no more than three, to restrict the flow of oxygen into her lungs and then her brain. She must have woken to see the intruder in her bedroom and...

Her diamond necklace. Was it still here? Maud's gaze lit on the small leather case standing open on a low chest of drawers. It was empty.

The Viscount was sobbing quietly.

'Tell everyone to turn out their pockets,' Maud said softly to the Duchess.

Her face had aged a decade in the short time since dinner. Maud pointed at the necklace case. The Duchess nodded her understanding.

'One moment, please,' she called, stepping out of the room and causing the bustle in the corridor to stop immediately. 'I'm afraid I must ask you all to empty your pockets – those who have them.'

'Surely not us, Mama?' said Cynthia, shock in her voice.

'The Viscountess's necklace has been taken.' The Duchess's tone was remarkably level, considering whoever stole the jewellery must also have killed the Viscountess, and surely she couldn't believe her own daughters had committed murder. 'The police officer will want to know that everyone has been asked to do the same, so yes, my dear, you too.'

Maud followed close on the Duchess's heels and saw the gathering glance from one to another, their displeasure clear. Had it not been for the Duchess's station in life, Maud was sure most of them would have refused to comply.

Miss Taft was red in the face. 'Isn't that a bit much? Surely, we here are all respectable members of society.'

'Her Grace is right, Miss Taft,' said Mr Laing. 'It all happened too fast for the guilty person to have been anyone but one of us. The police will insist on it, I assure you. Better to do it now, whilst we are all together and can provide the necessary corroboration that none of us produce the necklace.'

The Duchess inclined her head towards him. 'Thank you, Mr Laing. And to show that all is equal between us, I shall be the first.' She took a handkerchief from her dressing gown pocket, turned the inner material outwards, and displayed the square of lace fabric on her palm for all to see. Her daughters and Maud followed suit.

With varying degrees of willingness, the guests did as she'd asked. The Duchess called back Mackenzie, who had made it only to the end of the corridor, no doubt listening to the conversation in order to relay it to the servants later, and ordered him to witness the pocket-emptying. Nothing but dainty handkerchiefs were held by the ladies, larger handkerchiefs and boxes of matches by the men.

As Mackenzie approached Miss Taft to inspect the contents of her hand, her colour rose. 'If this is how you treat your guests, I shan't come here again.'

'It is regrettable,' said the Duchess, her meaning perhaps deliberately unclear. They all waited in silence for the footman to finish his inspection.

Mackenzie returned to the Duchess. 'No necklace, Your Grace,' he said, revealing he had indeed been eavesdropping.

The guests continued along the corridor back to their rooms, Miss Taft with a fierce look, the Earl softly consoling his weeping wife.

'You too, girls,' added the Duchess to her daughters, who'd looked set to linger. The tone of their mother's voice told them she would brook no argument.

'All lock your doors behind you, to be on the safe side,' the Duchess called to the retreating backs.

'I'm so sorry I was unable to prevent this happening,' Maud said to the Duchess, keeping her voice low as they returned to the Viscountess's bedroom.

'My dear, no one could have foreseen this.'

A soft knock on the open door indicated the butler had returned. 'I have made a telephonic communication to the police office, Your Grace, and the sergeant will be here shortly.' He made to withdraw.

'Perhaps Thomson could stay for a moment?' Maud said to the Duchess.

He looked at his mistress for confirmation, and she nodded in agreement.

'Are the outer doors locked?' Maud asked him.

'I beg your pardon?' Thomson wore an offended expression.

'Miss McIntyre is a private detective, Thomson,' said the Duchess, meeting his dubious look. 'I'm convinced that being a detective relies more on brains than on brawn.'

Exactly like Miss Gladden, the first British, albeit fictional, female private detective, Maud thought to herself. Miss Gladden solved cases by visiting crime scenes, talking to witnesses and adopting disguises.

'You will give Miss McIntyre every possible assistance in this matter,' went on the Duchess. 'And please keep her identity to yourself.'

'Yes, Your Grace.' Thomson continued to stand there.

'Well, man?'

He turned back to Maud. 'All the outer doors are locked, Miss McIntyre.'

'That includes the French windows into the library?'

'Yes, miss. They were locked at ten o'clock, when the household retired.'

Maud glanced at the small clock on the mantel; almost three o'clock. When she looked up, she met the butler's gaze. He must have guessed what she was thinking. The vagabond earlier this evening. For a moment Maud was afraid she'd misjudged the situation, but the man couldn't have returned to the house because the external doors had been locked some hours ago. She could see the Viscountess's window was tightly closed. Her own window was open to catch the night breeze, but any room on this floor would require an exceptionally long ladder to gain access.

'If that is all, my lady?' the butler asked the Duchess.

'Your Grace, it would seem that the murderer is inside the house. I think it advisable that a couple of your male servants

station themselves on the corridor to ensure everyone stays in
their rooms tonight.'

The Duchess's face was white, but she remained impassive.
'I agree.' She addressed the butler. 'Thomson, please arrange
this.'

'Yes, my lady.'

'And assist the Viscount back to his room, and do what you
can to make him as comfortable as possible. Thank you,
Thomson.'

As soon as the butler had helped the old man into the
adjoining bedroom and closed the door after them, the Duchess
sank onto the chaise at the foot of the bed. 'This is a dreadful
business.'

'I might be wrong, Your Grace, but I'm certain the thief
didn't set out to kill the Viscountess. That is not part of his
modus operandi. She must have woken when he was in her
room to steal the necklace and, naturally, she screamed.'
Maud could picture the scene. 'The intruder panicked,
grabbed the first thing to hand – the pillow – and, well,
silenced her.'

'I'm sure you are correct.' The Duchess ran a hand over her
forehead.

'I need to make a search of this room. It's possible that
whoever did this deed hid the necklace here, intending to come
back for it later.'

Aghast, she stared at Maud, but said, 'Very well.'

Under the Duchess's gaze, Maud looked behind the
curtains, on top of the wardrobe, inside the flower vase, everywhere she could think of. Eventually, she could no longer put
off the awful moment. Carefully, without looking at the
Viscountess's dreadful face, Maud lifted the remaining pillow
under her head and felt underneath it. No necklace.

She took a handkerchief from the top drawer of the tall
chest, shook it out and gently placed it over the Viscountess's

face. An unwelcome thought returned to her, which she knew she should mention to the Duchess.

'Perhaps it wasn't a one-man job, but two. One of your guests may have a partner working outside.'

'I cannot imagine such a thing.'

Nonetheless, Maud continued with her theory. 'One to take the necklace and throw it out onto the terrace...' She crossed the room to examine the window and tried to turn the lock. After a short but determined struggle, she prised it open.

'And the other,' she continued, leaning out to peer at the terrace below, 'waiting outside to pick it up.'

The Duchess drew in a sharp breath.

'But this window hasn't been opened recently.' Maud drew in a lungful of fresh air as she stared along the length of the terrace below. Dawn wouldn't be for another couple of hours, but the stars were already pale, and she could detect a lightening in the sky to the east. On the terrace, there was no sparkle of a diamond necklace, in the garden no outline of a shadowy person. Maud withdrew her head.

'Well?' The Duchess looked hopefully at her.

'Nothing.'

Her shoulders slumped a little. 'I suppose that is to be expected.'

Suddenly, Maud remembered the game of poker in the drawing room earlier that evening.

'I don't believe it is at all related, but I feel I need to ask,' she said to the Duchess. 'Did the Viscountess know she had been spotted cheating?'

The Duchess nodded. 'When I returned to the room after our conversation, I observed her doing just as you described while dealing. I confronted her privately, she admitted her actions and promised to repay the money she had won.'

Maud was impressed with the speed of the Duchess's dealings. And she felt sure there was no connection between the

Viscountess's cheating and her murder. In fact, her death had prevented her from returning her ill-gotten gains.

Maud continued. 'There has been no time to remove the jewellery from the house. How the thief smuggled it out of this room I've not yet worked out, but it might be useful to search the guests' bedrooms.'

'Given that the culprit will imagine that will happen, they are bound to have it carefully hidden.' The Duchess sounded undecided.

At that moment, Maud heard heavy footsteps mounting the stairs and she turned towards the open bedroom door.

'It sounds as if Sergeant McKay has arrived.' The Duchess stood, gave a last glance at the body on the bed and ushered Maud out of the room. 'We had better let him search the other bedrooms.' She closed the door behind them.

'Sergeant McKay,' announced the butler, having reached the top of the carpeted stairs.

The officer was hard on Thomson's heels. He was a beanpole of a man, his nose stuck out more than was usually expected from a face and under the nose grew a thick ginger moustache. 'Good evening, that is to say good morning, Your Grace.' Tucking his helmet under his arm, he bowed.

Her eyes travelled down the length of his uniformed lanky legs to his ankles. The sergeant's gaze followed. 'Begging your pardon, Your Grace.' He bent down and with his free hand whipped off his bicycle clips.

'I believe there's been some sort of a crime committed.' He sounded hopeful. 'I've not had a crime since last year when I caught young Willie Smith with no dog licence.' Catching sight of the Duchess's glare, he went on. 'When I received Mr Thomson's telephone call, I leaped on my bicycle and pedalled here as fast as I could.' He fell silent.

'There's been a murder and a theft,' the Duchess said.

'Dearie me.' The sergeant took a step back, pulled himself

together and placed his helmet on the floor with the bicycle clips inside. Opening the top pocket of his uniform with his knobbly hands, he pulled out a notebook and pencil.

'If it would please Your Grace,' he said, looking up at her, pencil poised over a fresh page in his book, 'I should be obliged if we could start by you giving me a few details.'

'Of course. I was woken by a scream some forty-five minutes ago—'

'Forty-five minutes ago,' said the sergeant, writing it down.

'And when we arrived at Viscountess Drummond's room, we found her dead.' The Duchess indicated the closed door. 'She'd been suffocated in her bed.'

'Suffocated.' He nodded. 'That sounds serious.'

'It is,' Maud snapped. The man was a fool, and she knew she could do better than him. *Sounds serious?* Even the scullery maid with no constabulary training at all would have deduced that.

He turned his gaze on her. 'And who might you be, miss?'

'Miss Maud McIntyre. I am staying here as a guest.' That was true. She felt there was no need to elaborate as it might confuse things for him.

'I'd better have a look at the lady, to be sure she has passed away.'

Once again, the Duchess and Maud went into the room, this time with Sergeant McKay following. He walked over to the bed, bent over the body, listened for a few seconds and straightened.

'Aye, she's passed away, right enough.' He glanced around the room. 'Any sign of a break-in?'

'Not in here. My servants are checking the rest of the house as we speak.'

'And where was everyone at the time in question?'

'In their beds, it would seem,' Maud replied. 'We all came from the direction of our respective bedrooms.'

'There was also a theft, you say, Your Grace?'

The Duchess indicated the open jewellery box on the dressing table.

'Ah,' said the Sergeant. 'I must ask: what is the potential value of the stolen item?'

'It was possibly priceless,' Maud said.

He looked puzzled. 'You mean it was worth nothing?'

Maud stifled a snort. 'No, I do not mean that. A price could not be put on it. A diamond necklace such as that is worth whatever a person is prepared to pay for it.'

His face cleared. 'Ah,' he said again. 'And could I trouble Your Grace for a description of the said necklace?'

The Duchess provided one, while the sergeant made a few more notes.

She directed a steely gaze at the officer. 'My daughters and my guests are waiting for you in their rooms. My servants will do likewise.' She glanced towards the butler, who inclined his head. 'Miss McIntyre and I will now retire to our rooms in order for you to treat us in the same way as everyone else.'

Sergeant McKay flushed. 'I'm sure you and your daughters are beyond reproach, Your Grace.' He pocketed his notebook and pencil. 'It's the middle of the night and I don't like to trouble your guests at this hour. I will return tomorrow afternoon, that is to say this afternoon. That will allow you all to attend kirk in the morning and to rest after luncheon, as I know ladies like to do.' He made a bow to the Duchess, gave a nod of his head to Maud, retrieved his helmet and bicycle clips and clumped out of the room.

His voice drifted back to them. 'Is there any chance of a glass of sherry in the kitchen before I speak to the servants, Mr Thomson?'

The Duchess looked at Maud and sighed. 'Perhaps it is rather late. Very well, then, Miss McIntyre, you may search the rooms and belongings of the guests. It seems inconceivable that the Viscount is to blame, but I will examine his room and those of my daughters. I would prefer the search to be carried out with circumspection. When will you do it?'

'In the morning,' Maud replied, 'when everyone is at church.'

TEN

'Unbelievable,' said Daisy the following morning when Maud related the previous night's events. She'd brought up hot water for Maud's wash and her morning tea tray. 'I was stuck below-stairs and missed it all.' She drew back the curtains with more force than was necessary.

Maud hadn't slept well, tossing and turning as she went over all the possibilities. Daisy looked as bleary-eyed as Maud felt.

'Surely not all,' Maud said, as she climbed out of bed. 'Did the policeman discover anything below-stairs?'

'You've met him – what do you think?' Her tone was crisp. 'That sergeant is a wee sook.'

Maud had to agree. His keenness to please the Duchess could have resulted in lost vital evidence above-stairs.

'He had us all together in the servants' hall,' Daisy said, 'and none of us had seen or heard anything. His search of our rooms found naething either.' She sighed. 'So, are you and me now out of a job?'

'No, we are to investigate the theft as we were engaged to do.'

'Good,' said Daisy.

Maud poured hot water into the bowl and washed, as Daisy laid out her Sunday clothes. Long fitted jacket in midnight blue with velvet collar and cuffs and matching flared skirt.

'I'll pretend to be indisposed shortly,' Maud said. 'That will allow me to stay behind to search the guests' bedrooms while they're at church. Can you give me a hand to do that?'

Daisy shook her head. 'I have to go to the kirk with the other servants. It will look suspicious if we both stay away.'

'There's something you can do at the church.'

'Aye?' She paused in removing Maud's boots from the wardrobe.

'Keep an eye on the guests inside and outside the kirk, to make sure none of them pass a package to anyone who is not a guest at the house.'

'A package that might contain a necklace? Do you think it likely?'

'Perhaps not, but it's important to keep an eye out in case it does happen.'

She nodded, pleased that she had a role to play.

'What did Mackenzie say about the tramp last night?' Maud asked, as she stepped into her skirt and fastened the side button.

'You mean after he wandered into the servants' hall, said, "Morning, ladies. Morning, Daisy," and I swallowed the piece of toast I was chewing, raised an eyebrow and said, "You don't think I'm a lady?" and he replied with a grin, "I'm hoping you're not"?'

'Yes,' Maud said, 'after that.'

'He told me that Mr Thomson had him check the fellow again this morning for any stolen valuables and then give him bread and cheese from the kitchen. After that, the fellow went on his way.'

Maud felt a surge of relief knowing that he definitely wasn't the culprit.

Daisy helped her to dress her hair and she left. Maud drank her fast-cooling tea and went down to the dining room for breakfast.

As was usual at house parties, the sideboard was laden with porridge, devilled kidneys, cold tongue, omelette, kedgeree, scones, honey and fresh fruit for guests to serve themselves. Coffee and tea stood to the side. Maud took a small bowl of creamy porridge and a ripe peach.

'Allow me to help you to a cup of tea or coffee, Miss McIntyre,' said Mr Laing, appearing at her side.

'Thank you. I would prefer coffee. I have a headache and that might help to revive me.'

'I'm sorry to hear you are feeling unwell.' Mr Laing poured her a cup of dark strong liquid from the silver pot, and she inhaled the delicious aroma.

He followed her over to the dining table, set down her cup and saucer, and returned with his own plate laden with omelette, kidneys and kedgeree.

'What a shocking event last night,' he said, taking a seat. 'I can still hardly believe it happened.'

'It is difficult to comprehend,' Maud agreed.

'And yet.' He paused.

'And yet?' she prompted.

'The Viscountess was an old lady...'

'I'm afraid I don't understand you, Mr Laing.'

'I mean only that if any lady here should have lost her jewellery...'

Maud sent him a sharp look. 'And her life.'

'Yes, that too, of course, then at least it happened to one who was advanced in years.'

Before she could respond, Miss Taft, in a surprisingly sober church outfit in grey, placed a cup of tea on the table and dropped heavily into the chair next to Maud.

'Did someone really steal the Viscountess's necklace last night and then suffocate her?' She took a sip of her tea.

'Yes,' Maud said curtly.

'It wasn't a dream?'

'No.'

With a frown, Miss Taft drank more of her tea. Mr Laing and Maud ate in silence.

'This practice of guests being down for breakfast is uncivilised,' Miss Taft grumbled. 'I would much prefer breakfast in bed.'

So would I, Miss Taft, thought Maud. But not this morning, with six guest bedrooms to search: those of Miss Taft herself, Mr Laing, Colonel Morrison, Lord Urquhart and the Earl and Countess of Swinton. The proximity of Lord Urquhart's room to the victim's and the fact that he had been the first on the scene at that end of the corridor, perhaps made him the most likely suspect, but Maud couldn't afford to rule anyone out.

In some country houses, the bedrooms are helpfully labelled. The guests' names are written on cards slotted into brass holders on the doors. The Duchess didn't follow this practice, but by now Maud had worked out the room allocations. She smiled as she remembered her middle brother telling her of a grand country house he'd visited in his single days, where an exuberant young friend of his had leaped onto the bed in a darkened room, believing it to contain his lover, only to find a startled deacon.

Turning the handle of the furthest guest room at her end of the second floor, Maud pushed the door open. She knew this to be the Colonel's room. Sunlight flooded in and for a moment she blinked against its brightness.

A gentleman's bedroom, it was painted in green and contained the usual collection of large bed, chest of drawers, chairs and assorted pictures. A change of clothing had been laid out on the bed, ready for when he returned. Maud stepped into the room and softly closed the door.

There were a dozen places where, if she had a stolen diamond necklace, she would hide it. So where to start? Having no previous experience of searching a room, she decided to draw from the only experts she knew. In *The Eustace Diamonds* by Anthony Trollope, Lizzie Greystock puts the necklace under her pillow. That was too obvious a hiding place. On the other hand, in Edgar Allan Poe's *The Purloined Letter* Monsieur Dupin finds the stolen letter in a card-rack hanging over the mantelpiece. It had cleverly been concealed in exactly the place such an item would be kept. Unfortunately, that method of hiding wouldn't work here. There'd be no hiding the Viscountess's jewellery in the Colonel's personal collection of necklaces. Maud decided she'd start her search in his chest of drawers. She crossed the floor towards it.

A low, grumbling sound came from the corner of the room behind her, and she spun round on her heels.

A small dog with curly white fur rose from its bed. Maud froze. The little animal had soulful eyes, so she gave it a tentative smile. It lifted one side of its mouth. Through its bushy beard and moustache, she could see a set of white teeth. It slunk towards her, blocking off her access to the door. In a flash Maud instinctively jumped onto the dressing table and drew up her legs after her. The dog sat and fixed her with a glare.

If only Daisy were here. She was good with small dogs. What breed was it? Some sort of a terrier. Square body, short legs, sharp teeth...

It let out another low, rumbling growl. The dog was clearly prepared to wait there until its master returned. But Maud couldn't stay to be found. Possibly the animal was all bark, and it wouldn't go for her throat. On the other hand, possibly not...

Time passed. Maud considered taking off her smart Sunday

skirt and throwing it over the creature's head to allow her to escape, but at best the fabric would end up covered in dog hairs and at worst ripped to shreds by those evil-looking teeth. And running into the corridor in her chemise, corset and drawers probably wasn't a good idea. Could she toss the garment over the dog's head, spring off the dressing table, wrap the animal tightly, deposit it in the wardrobe, whip back her clothing and shut the door before it knew what was happening? No. Its black eyes alert under the bushy white eyebrows, the dog continued to stare at her. Maud could swear there was saliva trickling from the corner of its mouth.

Now she noticed the items scattered around her on the dressing table. No doubt they had been neatly laid out, but in her scramble to evade the dog's jaws she had spoiled the arrangement. She picked up a hairbrush. Weighing it in her hand, she considered throwing it, trying to judge the fine line between sending the animal to hide under the bed and inflicting actual bodily harm. The former was desirable, the latter not. Maud met the animal's silent stare. Who would blink first?

The door opened and the Colonel entered. He looked at the dog. 'Hello, Roger.'

His gaze followed the dog's glare up to the dressing table. Now two pairs of eyes stared at Maud. One pair dark, the other very light blue in their weather-beaten face. The Colonel gave her a sharp look.

She set down the hairbrush. 'Good morning, Colonel. I thought you were at church.'

'I set out to walk there but changed my mind. What are you doing in here?'

Maud had her excuse ready. 'I mistook my room.' It sounded rather feeble now.

He bent to pick up Roger, tucked the dog under his arm and said casually, 'I suppose you came in to look for that missing necklace?'

Maud knew her face gave her away.

'And what did your search find?' he went on, tickling Roger behind an ear.

'I was barely in the room before Roger made his presence known.'

The Colonel tickled him behind his other ear. 'What a good little guard dog you are.'

There was a pause while he set Roger back down on his feet. Maud had missed her chance to slide from the dressing table.

'If you could just take hold of Roger again, Colonel, I will get down and leave you to your room.'

At the mention of his name, Roger responded by returning to the dressing table, fixing her with his penetrating gaze and barking.

'You had no right to search my room,' the Colonel said, raising his voice above the noise, his cheeks a dull red. 'Just who exactly are you, Miss McIntyre?'

Maud certainly wasn't going to answer that question truthfully. Nor did she want him to demand the police be called, as that would be too embarrassing for her. On the other hand, it would be embarrassing for the Duchess if it were known she had authorised the search of her guests' rooms. Respect for the laws of hospitality and so on.

She decided to stick to her story. 'I'm afraid I entered the wrong room.'

Whether he believed her or not, she didn't know, but after a pause he scooped up the dog again and glared at her. Maud thanked him, climbed down, straightened her skirt and left the room with what she hoped was a quiet dignity.

ELEVEN

In the corridor, Maud bumped into Lord Urquhart.

'Good heavens!' she said. 'Has no one gone to church this morning?' Thank goodness she wasn't, after all, in her petticoat and drawers.

He frowned. 'I was just about to catch up with the others, when I heard barking from the Colonel's room and thought I should investigate.' He smiled. 'Were you in there to search for the missing necklace?'

Maud sighed. 'Yes, I was.'

He raised an eyebrow. 'Any joy?'

'If you mean did I find the item, the answer is no. As to experiencing any joy, the answer is again in the negative.'

'I gather you met Roger, the miniature schnauzer.'

'Oh, is that what he is?'

'Small but spunky, wouldn't you say?'

'He certainly has quite a marked personality.'

'Look, why not let me help you unmask the villain? I could carry out the dangerous side of the operation.'

Maud drew herself up to her full height. 'Lord Urquhart, I cannot allow you to assist me in any way.'

'Why not?'

'Because *you* could be the villain.'

'I could be – but I assure you I'm not.'

She fixed him with a businesslike stare. 'How was it you were so quickly on the landing last night when the Viscountess screamed?'

'I could ask the same of you.'

'I am a light sleeper.'

'As am I.'

There was that slow smile of his, but she wasn't about to let him deflect her from her purpose. 'Did you hear any footsteps along the corridor shortly before the intruder entered her room or immediately afterwards?'

'No.'

'You went to bed at the end of the evening and stayed there until you heard the scream?'

'That's correct.'

'I only have your word for that.'

'It's the word of a gentleman.'

'Aren't all the men here gentlemen and the ladies, ladies? Yet one of them must be guilty, given the very short time between scream and discovery.'

'True.'

While he was considering this, Maud slipped past him and returned to her room. When Lord Urquhart had left to purge his soul in the kirk, she would return to her search of the rooms. Apart from Colonel Morrison's... for the present.

The Colonel remained in his room after their earlier meeting, no doubt in order to ensure Maud didn't slip back in. Instead, she quickly and quietly searched all the other guest bedrooms and found nothing. It was frustrating. She was coming round to the idea that she would just have to ask the Duchess to come with her to the Colonel's room to search it.

Shortly after eleven o'clock, the group returned from church. Within minutes, the footmen entered the drawing room with coffee and tiny fancy cakes. The party consumed the refreshments and chatted, the atmosphere subdued, before going to their rooms to change.

'Anything?' Maud asked Daisy hopefully, as soon as she appeared in her bedroom.

She shook her head. 'I didna see any package.'

They were getting nowhere in their investigation. 'Something will turn up soon,' Maud said, with more conviction than she felt.

Maud changed into a pale-blue cotton pinstriped day dress with lace at the collar and cuffs and a small train at the back, and returned to the drawing room.

The activities laid on for the remainder of the morning included playing tennis and riding. Miss Taft, who had changed into a dress of lime-green with purple feathers, opted for the piecing together of a jigsaw puzzle. It was less physically strenuous than the other pastimes on offer, but not unlike trying to solve a crime, Maud thought. Was Miss Taft the criminal mastermind?

Determined to stay close to the house should the guilty person, whoever they were, attempt to smuggle out the necklace, Maud expressed a wish to see more of the gardens. Later, she would make her request to the Duchess to search the Colonel's room. As she laid out her plans, Maud was uncomfortably aware that time was slipping away.

As soon as luncheon was over and the upstairs occupants had retired for the afternoon siesta, Maud hastened along the corridor and tapped on the door of the Duchess's bedroom.

'Enter.'

She turned the handle and went in. To her relief, the Duchess's lady's maid had finished her work for the present and wasn't in the room. The Duchess sat propped up on the bed, her lorgnette raised and reading *The Phantom of the Opera*. She lowered her spectacles and put down the book.

'You have something to report, Miss McIntyre?'

Maud related how she'd searched all the bedrooms bar the Colonel's, and the reason why. 'I'm afraid I must ask you to come with me and insist he allow the search. If he refuses, the only other option will be to inform the police.' Not that the local constabulary would be much use. Last night's performance confirmed Maud's admittedly limited experience that the more rustic the officer, the more doltish his behaviour. Such men were honest, but hopeless at detecting crime.

'Certainly, I will speak to the Colonel, my dear, but it must wait until we've all rested.'

'I think it would be best if the search were done as soon as possible, Your Grace.'

'I'm sorry, but after all the excitement last night I can hardly keep my eyes open. And Sergeant McKay will be returning this afternoon.' She closed her book and set it down with the lorgnette on the nightstand. She shut her eyes. 'Please close the door on your way out.'

There was nothing for it but to do as she said. Resisting the temptation to slam the door with frustration, Maud left the room.

It was clear that she needed to examine the situation carefully and methodically, so she returned to her chamber, took the pad and pencil from the Gladstone bag and went back into the corridor. Listening outside the Colonel's door, she heard him moving around. At this end of the passage was a tall plant in a large pot on a pedestal. The bright green leaves of the Boston fern cascaded down over the pot and the stand. This would do

Maud very well. She slipped behind it, sat on the floor and leaned against the wall, making herself as comfortable as possible. All was quiet.

In the case of the Radcliffe ruby, the mystery almost seemed to solve itself. This time something more organised was required. She would try the method of writing down the questions that remained unanswered and next to each put a possible means of approach. Maud opened the pad, turned to a fresh page, divided it into two neat columns and headed one *Questions* and the other *Answers*.

The first question, in chronological order, concerned the order the bedroom doors were opened last night, so she wrote:

1. Can Lord Urquhart be trusted and is he interested in one of the Duddingston girls?

That was not what she had meant to write. Maud crossed out the words and began again.

1. Who was first onto the corridor?

In the answer column she wrote: *The most likely was Lord Urquhart, whose room is next to the Viscountess's, and the second most likely candidate Mr Laing.* She'd noticed Mr Laing first, but that was because he spoke to her and his room was closer to hers. Also, Lord Urquhart was already tying the belt on his dressing gown, whereas Mr Laing's was not yet fastened. *Lord Urquhart*, she wrote firmly. She moved onto the next question.

2. Who was close enough to have time to smother the Viscountess when she screamed, snatch the necklace and leave the room without being caught red-handed?

This, of course, was the crux of the matter. Lord Urquhart. Although it was possible another guest might have sped out of the room, returned to their own and closed the door before any of the rest of them appeared. In Baroness Orczy's story, *The Woman in the Big Hat,* Lady Molly discovers the murderer is the victim's wife. Maud frowned. It was too big a stretch to imagine the distraught old Viscount stealing jewels at country houses, attempting to do the same from his wife and, when caught in the act, smothering her. Maud paused as a fresh problematic thought came to her. The scream.

3. *Who screamed?*

If it was the Viscountess and it took several minutes to kill her, then during this time the murderer would have been discovered. Maud stared at the words she'd written, looking for an answer. She would have to revise her opinion of the length of time required to suffocate a frail old lady. The scream the Viscountess had uttered must have taken most of her breath. Two minutes might well be sufficient. Further, when the rest of the party were woken from sleep, and no doubt they were all, apart from the killer, in a deep slumber given the amount of food and drink consumed at dinner, it would have taken a few minutes for each of them to gather their wits. Yes, Maud concluded, the Viscountess's scream, her suffocation and the murderer's escape from the room could fit into the time span.

4. *How did the thief smuggle the necklace out of the bedroom?*

Maud had entered within a few minutes of the theft. An immediate search of pockets and then of the room had yielded no necklace. Had one person smothered the Viscountess and another grabbed the jewellery and thrown it out of the window?

Yet why would two intruders enter the bedroom to steal one necklace? She sighed and wrote down the next question.

5. Was the presumed tramp involved in the crime?

The outer doors were locked at ten o'clock, which was the usual practice. The theft took place after that, and the doors remained locked until the sergeant arrived. The logical answer to this question had to be no.

6. Did the thief pass the necklace to an accomplice?

Daisy had reported no sight of an item being passed from a guest to any other person inside or outside the kirk. What if the diamonds had been passed only minutes after being stolen? Who was in the immediate vicinity shortly after the discovery of the body and the theft, but hadn't been searched? Apart from herself and the Duchess, there'd been Thomson and Mackenzie. Neither the butler nor the footman could have been involved in the thefts that had taken place at the other two houses, as they would have been working at Duddingston.

7. Assuming that the scoundrel had somehow got the necklace out of the room, where was it now?

The only room still to be examined was the Colonel's. Maud couldn't see him being able to move fast enough in the short space of time – unless the limp was a faked injury. That was the sort of disguise a master criminal would adopt. But if he was the thief, and the necklace now hidden in his room, how had he managed to secrete it out of the Viscountess's bedroom?

This brought Maud back to question number four. There were more questions than answers. The weight of the evidence, such as it was, seemed to point to Lord Urquhart, the Colonel and Mr Laing.

This gave Maud another thought, and she added a further question.

8. Which of these three was in greatest need of money?

It might not be a question of need, but done for the thrill of the act. Did the elderly Colonel fit this last objective? Not only did he have an injured leg, assuming it was genuine, but also he appeared content to shuffle about and to doze off frequently. By the same token, his needs appeared to be modest. Mr Laing was a successful advocate and should be earning a reasonable salary. Maud had no reason to think Lord Urquhart was short of funds – but she could imagine him doing something purely for the thrill of it.

Miss Taft suddenly came into her mind. She pled poverty but had expensive gowns. As to the thrill of committing a jewellery theft, if she wrote crime novels Maud might be able to believe she sought ideas for her books, but she was a writer of romance. This led on to the next question and from a practical standpoint perhaps the most important.

9. Who has the necessary contacts to dispose of the item?

Given that the thief couldn't be seen wearing jewellery known to be stolen, they would need to sell the pieces to someone they trusted to ask no questions. It was easy to see Lord Urquhart as a Raffles character: a person who mixes in society and has at least some questionable friends.

Maud wrote the name *Lord Hamish Urquhart* at the bottom of the column, then closed the notebook. Could she knock on his door now and speak to him privately? As the saying went, there was no time like the present. It was still the guests' after-luncheon rest period, but she couldn't picture Lord Urquhart reclining on his bed. Her face and chest suddenly flushed hot. That is, she *shouldn't* picture Lord Urquhart reclining on his bed.

The unmistakable sound of a door opening reached her ears. Was it the Colonel's? Would he take his dog with him, which meant she would be able to slip into his room? Should she search the room or follow him in case he was sneaking out to hide the necklace somewhere else? Perhaps he wouldn't go far and would secrete it on the landing. Maud tried to remember what was here. Paintings on the walls, a few vases of flowers on tables, a rather nice Turkish rug on the floor. No obvious hiding place, but the noise mustn't be ignored. Whoever it was, those footsteps were soft and too stealthy for her liking.

Sliding her notebook and pencil into her pocket, she got to her knees to peer through the lush green foliage and was just in time to observe the Earl of Swinton ease open the door to Miss Taft's bedroom. Maud heard her murmur one word, 'Darling!', before a pair of naked arms appeared and pulled him into the room. Motes of dust disturbed by the Earl's progress danced in a ray of sunlight.

Good Lord – who would have thought it? So was that how the woman could afford such expensive clothes? Maud shrugged. Her concern at that moment was gaining access to the Colonel's room. His door remained stubbornly closed.

Maud resumed her hiding place on the floor behind the fern and watched Lord Urquhart's door, wondering if his would be the next one to open. Which room would he creep into? she wondered. One of the Duchess's daughters? The Countess of Swinton?

The door remained closed, but she decided against speaking to him privately for the time being. The afternoon seemed to be busy enough, and she had no wish to give him the wrong idea.

Feeling disinclined to return to her room, she went down

the stairs and out into the rose garden. As she expected, no one else was there; all the guests were dozing or otherwise engaged in their bedrooms. The sound of bees going from flower to flower seemed to deepen in the stillness of the hot August afternoon.

The scent of rose after perfect rose filled her senses. Yet Maud's hearing remained acute, and someone was behind her; she could hear their ragged breathing.

Maud spun round. A dark shape, with a stone clutched in its raised hand.

She screamed.

TWELVE

A stab of pain shot through Maud's head. The world keeled over as she fell forward, landing on the grass on her hands and knees, her heart pounding. For a moment, there was utter silence.

Then a shout in the distance. She was vaguely aware of the thud of running feet. Strong hands seized her, and she tried to cry out, but there was a roaring in her ears and the roses swam in her vision. She closed her eyes as nausea swept over her, and she was lifted and cradled by a pair of muscled arms.

'Put me down,' she managed to gasp.

The arms lowered her softly to the ground. She lay on her back on the grass, letting the spinning in her head come to a stop. Careful hands moved over her body, patting, searching for injury.

'It's my head that's hurt,' she whispered.

The hands were taken away. When she opened her eyes, Maud let the world re-focus before she made any kind of move. When she dared to look for her rescuer, he had hoisted himself up onto the garden wall and was staring at the woods beyond.

Gingerly she felt her head, and when she took her hand

away, she saw a smear of blood on her fingertips. She pushed herself up into a seated position. The man jumped down off the wall, strode over and squatted in front of her. His dark eyes anxiously searched her face.

'Here.' Lord Urquhart drew a folded white handkerchief from his jacket pocket and dabbed gently at her head. 'Hold the fabric there.'

'I hope it's clean,' she mumbled.

He pulled back, the expression on his face quizzical. Why did she have to say that? He was only being kind. Maud started to get to her feet; she needed to go after her attacker.

'Stay still. You may be more hurt than you realise.' He put a hand in front of her face. 'How many fingers?'

'Three.'

'No concussion.' He gave a pleased nod.

'What are you doing here?' Her brain was still not quite clear, but she could work out that once again he was on the spot after a disturbing event at Duddingston House.

'I'd just come into the garden when I heard your cry and I came running. You have a bit of a bump on your head and there's a small cut that needs attention, but thankfully nothing serious.' He put his arm round her shoulders and scanned her face. 'Are you feeling a bit better now? Can you move?'

'I will be able to if you let go of me.' With his help, she climbed to her feet. The garden swirled, then settled. 'Thank you. I think I'll be all right now.'

'You're as pale as a ghost.'

Maud pushed strands of hair back from her forehead. Her pompadour had come loose from its pins and her legs were shaking. He gently led her along the gravel path towards the house.

She removed his handkerchief from her head, saw the white cotton smeared with bright red blood and kept the fabric in her hand.

'Did you see who attacked me?' she asked.

'I'm afraid not.' His voice was grim.

'But you could make out if they were male or female?'

He shook his head. 'I can't say either way. Whoever it was, they were wearing a long cloak with the hood up.'

Maud couldn't remember seeing an opera cloak in any of the rooms she'd searched, but she hadn't been looking for a garment, and it was possible the owner had hidden it amongst other clothing.

She lowered her voice. 'A cloak?'

He lowered his voice too. 'Yes, a cloak. Why are we whispering?'

Good question, she thought. They were walking along the garden path and still alone. Maud spoke normally again. 'Why would someone have brought such a garment for a stay in the country in August?'

'Because the weather might change?'

'It's been hot for weeks. What about their height?'

'It's hard to say. You were already down when I saw the person standing over you.' He drew his brows together. 'But if you were to push me on the point, I'd be inclined to say that the person was tallish.'

Tallish? That word could describe almost any of the guests, Maud realised. The Earl was tall. The Colonel was another possibility, but he was an elderly man with a limp and her attacker had moved quickly. Miss Taft and Mr Laing were a little over medium height but of a stocky build; could that make them appear 'tallish'? The Duchess's two daughters were each a little taller than average for a female; the Countess about Maud's height, five foot seven. And of course Lord Urquhart was tall. Yet, if guilty, why would he describe a feature of her attacker – the height – that he himself had?

Maud had a fleeting physical memory of being held in his arms and now she came to think of it she was surprised by the strength in his muscles. He could easily have smothered the Viscountess in a minute or two.

Maud frowned, but it hurt her head, so she stopped. 'Why didn't you go after my assailant?'

'When I shouted at them, they took off over the wall and into the woods beyond.'

Who would be fit enough to scale a wall, jump down the other side and run away? The Earl? The daughters perhaps, Maud wondered.

'Besides,' he continued, 'my priority was to make sure you were not badly hurt.'

Maud passed a hand across her forehead and gave a shaky laugh. 'I must be getting closer to finding the jewels and the culprit.'

'You think the attack on you is connected?'

'Of course. Don't you? Why else would someone wish to assault a lady in a rose garden on a quiet Sunday afternoon?'

They'd reached a rustic bench, and he made her sit down. 'Are you sure you're all right?'

'Yes, perfectly,' she said, looking up at him. 'I'll rest here for a minute, then I need to return to the house and see if anyone's room is empty.'

'Whoever attacked you will be back indoors and resting on their bed by now.'

'There must be some sign.' Maud got to her feet. 'I must ask you a favour, Lord Urquhart.'

'Ask away.'

'Please don't reveal to the Duchess what happened.'

'Surely she ought to know about the attack.'

'If she finds out, it will be clear for certain that another knows why I am here. Lord Urquhart, I—'

'Hamish.'

'Lord Urquhart,' Maud continued, 'I want to succeed in this work. It is possible that my future depends on the outcome of this case. So, you must promise me that you will keep what happened here a secret.'

Her look must have shown how earnest she was, for he nodded. 'Of course.' He held out his arm.

Maud let out a breath. 'Thank you.'

She accepted his arm, and they slowly returned to the house.

'What the dickens has happened?'

Daisy stood in the doorway of Maud's room and stared at her seated on the dressing table stool with the bloody handkerchief in her hand. She closed the door and hastened in.

'Someone attacked me with a stone when I was in the garden,' Maud said. 'It must have been the thief, as I can't see why anyone else would want to do such a thing.'

With careful fingers, Daisy examined Maud's wound. 'I suppose it's a good sign, as it means you must be getting close to finding the villain, but you've taken a fair dunt. You might have been killed and then what would I say to your faither?'

'I have a bit of a headache,' Maud admitted, 'but that's all.'

'Next time you might not be so lucky.'

'I hope there isn't a next time...'

'So do I,' Daisy said, straightening. 'The cut looks clean and isna deep, thank the Lord, but I will fetch water and wash it.'

She was gone only a few minutes, returning with a bowl of warm water and clean towels.

'Whose handkerchief is this?' she asked, taking it from Maud.

'Lord Urquhart's. He came along shortly after the attack.'

Daisy was silent as she rolled up her sleeves and cleaned the wound. Maud tried hard not to flinch.

'Do you think we can trust him?' Daisy said, dabbing the cut dry.

'I don't know. Did you notice if any of the servants were missing for a while this afternoon?'

Daisy dried her hands and rolled down her sleeves. 'Not that I'm aware of.'

'I must solve this, Daisy. The reputation of the agency depends on it.'

Daisy sat on the edge of the stool next to Maud and took her hand. 'Never mind the agency's reputation. You need to be safe, Maud. Weren't you feart?'

'No,' Maud lied.

'I would have been.' She stared at Maud before speaking again. 'Did you see who attacked you?'

'No, but Lord Urquhart did. He heard my scream and came running.'

'Maud, are you sure he wasn't the one who attacked you? I mean, it would be so easy for him to claim that he rescued you, when in fact it was him who almost knocked you out cold.'

'Whoever it was ran away when he shouted to them.'

Daisy released Maud's hand. 'Then the Colonel can be ruled out. I doubt he could move fast with that limp. What else did Lord Urquhart say about the assailant?'

'He said they were wearing a dark cloak with the hood up and they were tallish.'

She snorted. 'That's not much help. It could be any of the guests, apart from perhaps Miss Taft and Mr Laing. Although,' she added, 'I suppose even they could be described as tallish.'

Tallish... what kind of a word was that? Lord Urquhart would never make a detective with that kind of observation. 'Whoever it was, they might have some blood on their clothing. I know it's a long shot, Daisy, but it's all we have at present. Can you keep an eye open for any maid or a valet cleaning the blood off a cuff or sleeve of someone's clothing?'

'Of course I will. First, though, you had best get yourself to the Duchess's room and tell her what's happened.'

Maud shook her head. Her brain followed a split second behind, hitting the sides of her skull, and she winced.

'No,' she said, feeling nausea rising again. 'It's best she doesn't know that my reason for being here has been exposed.'

Maud rested for a while and, by the time the afternoon siesta was over, was feeling much better. She changed into a fresh gown. The bump on her head was small, and Daisy had concealed it by pinning her hair in a simple but high arrangement. Maud joined the others for afternoon tea – all were present save Lady Violet – and found herself surreptitiously examining their garments, but as expected finding nothing to indicate blood.

As soon as she was able, Maud drew the Duchess aside to ask her why Sergeant McKay hadn't yet appeared.

'It seems he fell off his bicycle on his way here,' the Duchess said, 'and has returned home to rest for a short while. He assured Thomson on the telephone he will be with us before dinner.'

Just as well this part of Scotland didn't have to rely solely on Sergeant McKay, Maud mused. Not that she was making much progress with the case herself.

The Countess wanted to chat to the Duchess, so Maud moved to take a seat on the sofa. Putting aside for the time being the matter of the assault on her, she had to find out if anyone had noticed exactly when Lord Urquhart had stepped into the corridor last night, but whom could she ask? It was possible a nervous guest had opened their door and peeped out, waiting for another to be the first to set foot on the landing. The question had to come naturally in conversation, so as not to arouse suspicion about her role here. The difficulty was resolved when Miss Taft took a seat next to her.

'What a beautiful gown,' Maud said to her as she accepted a

cup of tea from the footman. She really did admire the dress: lemon silk with a long waistcoat of dark-lemon lace.

'Thank you.' She glanced at Maud's ivory tea gown with an embroidered panel down the front, but said nothing and took the tea offered to her.

'I see Lady Violet isn't here,' Maud continued. 'I do hope she's not unwell.'

'I've heard she's hurt her arm and is resting in her room. Apparently, it happened when she was playing tennis a short while ago.'

Maud's heart jumped. Was she getting somewhere?

'How unfortunate. Who was her partner?' Maud knew she needed to check Violet's story.

Miss Taft shrugged. 'I have no idea.'

Maud let out a slow breath. 'How are you, Miss Taft? Have you recovered from the shock last night?'

'I feel that I have, although it was quite horrid at the time. To think that the evil man is one of us is enough to make you shudder.' She shot an uneasy glance at the men – Lord Urquhart, Mr Laing, the Earl and the Colonel – who were standing talking together. The Viscount had understandably chosen to remain in his room.

'Do you really think it was another guest?'

'Who else could it be?' she asked sharply.

'It was fortunate that Lord Urquhart was able to respond so quickly,' Maud went on conversationally, refusing the slice of Victoria sponge the footman was offering. 'It seems he was the first person to come out of his room.'

Miss Taft directed a pair of suspicious eyes on her. 'Have you been spying on who goes in and out of bedrooms?' Maud understood that she meant bedrooms that were not the occupant's own.

'Of course not.'

'It's astonishing how some people can be mistaken in what they see.' She accepted a plate with a slice of cake.

'Then Lord Urquhart wasn't the first out of his room?' Maud kept her voice deliberately light, while butterflies danced in her stomach. What had Miss Taft observed?

'Oh, he was,' said Miss Taft, a small smile warming her face. She took a bite of the sponge, chewed and swallowed it. 'Earlier in the evening I caught him gazing at me in that intense way a young man does when he finds something that piques his interest. Hamish is such a gentleman. Naturally, when the Viscountess screamed, he was the first to respond.'

Lord Urquhart had designs on Miss Taft? Stranger things have happened, Maud mused.

Later that afternoon and once again in her room, Maud rang for Daisy.

'Sorry about bringing you up and down all the stairs,' she said, 'but there is something I wanted to discuss with you.'

'Violet and her sore arm? Her lady's maid mentioned it, and I was on my way up to tell you anyway.'

'Did she say who was partnering Violet?'

'She didn't know.' Daisy sighed. 'Which means we can't be sure Violet is telling the truth.'

'I can't believe that young woman is capable of a violent assault on me,' Maud said. 'She and her sister had been at the other house parties, but surely neither of them would steal from a guest at their mother's party? Violet can't be the culprit.'

'I dinna see why not. She could have been in and out of the Viscountess's room as fast as anyone else. And all the tennis playing she does will have given her strong arm muscles to hold down the pillow.'

There was something in that. 'But where did she hide the necklace, to get it out of the room?'

'Where did any of the guests hide it, for that matter?'

Maud frowned. 'One of them must have.'

'Exactly. And why shouldn't it be Violet?'

'Why would she steal the necklace? Surely she isn't short of funds?'

'The gossip below-stairs is the girls are given only pin money from their mither and that Violet likes to gamble.'

Gambling: the curse of the bored moneyed class. Maud hadn't searched either of the girls' rooms, but the Duchess said she would. Had she? Could Violet's lady's maid, acting on behalf of her mistress, be the villain they sought? Maud would have to tread carefully when finding out the answers to those questions.

That evening as the guests were beginning to gather in the drawing room for drinks before dinner, Maud left her room, slipped down the stairs and out onto the darkening terrace for some air before the next large meal.

The sun was sinking and there were shadows all about. She stood at the balustrade and took a breath of the sweet-smelling, warm night air. The trim lawn with oaks stretched away down to the water, golden in the last rays of sunset. A slight breeze stirred the trees and wafted up to her the scent of roses.

She closed her eyes and found herself imagining a tall, dark, handsome man coming to stand behind her, his hands on her shoulders. *"Isn't it beautiful?" he said softly.*

"I suspect it's something better viewed in company," she *replied.*

He slipped his arms around her and held her close. "Especially if the company is agreeable."

She turned to face him. The shadows highlighted the masculine contours of his face. His eyes were dark, unfathomable pools...

At least, that's how Miss Taft would have written it.

Maud smiled at the girlish notions and turned to lean her back against the balustrade. Above her, lighted windows pricked the gloaming, but where she stood was in shadow. It was a pleasant, peaceful scene and she breathed in deeply.

As she did so, something flashed in the light from an upstairs window, passed inches from her face and fell with a soft clunk on the gravel at her feet.

THIRTEEN

The diamond necklace gripped firmly in her hand, Maud looked up. Where had it come from? A number of windows were open to the sultry evening. The one on the second floor above where she stood seemed the likeliest source. It was the Colonel's room.

Maud ran back into the house, reached the drawing room door and threw it open. One by one the face of everyone in the room turned towards her as she paused in the doorway, holding aloft in her hand the stolen necklace.

For a moment, no one spoke. Quickly, she surveyed the room. The Duchess, Cynthia and Violet, Miss Taft, the Countess. With a choking cry and a rustle of skirts, the Countess rose from her seat and her hands went to her cheeks. 'You have caught the murderer!'

Maud shook her head.

The Duchess's response was suitably measured. She lifted her lorgnette. 'Where did you find the necklace, Miss McIntyre?'

'On the terrace, Your Grace.'

'The terrace?' She frowned, lowering her spectacles. 'How very strange.'

Maud knew a more detailed explanation was required. 'I was taking the air on the terrace when something came flying from above. I picked it up and saw it was the diamond necklace.'

'Thomson will be able to tell us who is in the room directly above.' She turned to the butler who stood stiffly beneath the Raeburn portrait, his eyes huge as they followed the events in the room.

'It is the Colonel,' Maud said, unable to wait any longer to voice her theory.

'Then we must see what the Colonel has to say about this,' said the Duchess, getting to her feet. 'Come with me, Miss McIntyre.'

She sailed from the room, and Maud followed in her wake. Behind them came the sound of multiple footsteps and assorted exclamations from her guests.

'Your Grace...'

She stopped walking and turned to look at Maud, who indicated their retinue.

She fixed the gathering with a steely glare. 'There is nothing to see,' she said, telling a blatant untruth. 'Please go back to the drawing room.'

The door to the Colonel's room was open. Thankfully, there was no sign of Roger, just the Colonel and, to Maud's surprise, Daisy. They stood facing each other across the room. Daisy held the poker in her hand.

'Colonel,' said the Duchess, 'Miss McIntyre informs me the stolen necklace has been dropped from the window of this room.'

He turned towards them. 'The woman is mistaken. I have only just entered my room. If a necklace has been thrown, it must have come from one of the other windows. It is easy to get confused when the sun is low and in one's eyes.'

Maud held the Colonel's cool, light-blue gaze. 'I was standing directly under it, and I do not think I am mistaken.'

She turned to Daisy. 'Did you see anything?'

'Aye, I came into the room to turn down the bed to help out Ada and found the Colonel standing by the open window, looking at something in his hand. As soon as I entered, he turned, and when I asked him what he was looking at, he told me I was impolite and that he would be having words with my mistress. He must have dropped it out of the window then because I saw something glint in his hand and now it's gone. It must have been the necklace.'

'Well done, Daisy,' Maud said, moving further into the room.

He sent Maud a startled glance. 'Are you two women in league?'

Maud drew herself up. 'We are private detectives, engaged by the Duchess after the recent spate of jewel thefts from country houses.'

'Now look here...' He started towards her.

'Your limp,' Maud said, stopping him in his tracks.

'What about it?' His voice was curt.

'It's less marked.' Maud realised she also hadn't noticed him limp into his room when she'd been cornered by Roger. Things were starting to fall into place.

'It's the warm weather, good for the joints.'

'Oh, really?' There was an edge to her tone. 'I put it to you—'

He took another step towards her, and she stepped back. Daisy took a tighter grip of the poker.

'That is,' Maud continued, 'I believe you have no war wound at all. It was a feigned injury to persuade others you had an infirmity and so dismiss you from any suspicion of the thefts.'

His eyes were watchful. 'I'm a war hero.'

'You mean there's nothing like pretending to be a war hero to put people off the scent,' said Daisy.

'We believe you stole the Viscountess's necklace and those other pieces of jewellery, and that you murdered her.' Maud stared at him. Detectives knew that silence was the best way to get information, including a confession, so she waited.

'You are completely mistaken, young woman. I was looking at my pocket watch when the girl came in and it was that she saw glinting.'

'And where is your watch now?'

'Where do you think, you stupid creature? Back in my pocket. She' – he indicated Daisy – 'was too busy lifting the poker from the hearth to notice.'

Could this be true? Maud kept her face expressionless. 'Please show us your watch.'

Scowling, he pulled the watch from his waistcoat pocket and held it out on his open palm. 'Satisfied, my dear?'

She gritted her teeth at his patronising attitude. 'You're not a war hero, but a fake.'

'And what about you? A woman pretending to be a detective.'

'I *am* a detective. And my disguised identity at this house was for an honourable purpose.' Maud could hear the pride in her voice, but trading insults would not get them any further forward and there was something she wanted to know.

'Why did you make up that story about your heroism in the Boer War?'

He curled his lip. Maud didn't know such a thing was actually possible. 'There are some things a lady never asks a gentleman.'

'You, sir, are no gentleman.'

'And you, madam, are no lady.'

Maud's face felt hot. The nerve of the fellow. 'I may be a detective, but I also consider myself a lady.'

He gave a nasty laugh to indicate she couldn't be both. 'If you must know,' he said, 'being a war hero provides sympathy and invitations to country houses. My income is too small to allow me to live as I wish.' He shrugged. 'As to my leg, I broke it some years ago and it failed to heal properly. I'd had a little too much to drink, climbed onto a table to sing a hunting song and fell off the damn thing.'

'You sing?' Maud failed to hide her surprise.

He inclined his head. 'That's not quite the response I was expecting, but yes, I do have a rather pleasant baritone.'

'Then sing your way out of this mess,' said Daisy, raising the poker. Maud was beginning to worry that she was enjoying herself a little too much.

'Colonel,' said the Duchess, 'I hate to interrupt this informative chit-chat, but I must insist you stay in your room until Sergeant McKay arrives. I will lock your door and take charge of the key.'

The Colonel started. 'You can't invite a man to your house and then lock him up.'

'I'm afraid I can, and I most certainly will.' Her tone left no room for discussion.

As Daisy lowered the poker, Maud was struck with sudden doubt. Did the Colonel have an alibi for his whereabouts immediately before the necklace was thrown?

'So the thief is caught at last?'

She turned at the voice behind her and saw Mr Laing.

'Perhaps,' Maud said slowly. 'But it's up to the police to gather sufficient evidence to charge him.'

FOURTEEN

'So, you'll be going back to Edinburgh in the morning?' Mr Laing asked as they sat side by side on a sofa in the drawing room. The curtains were drawn, the lamps lit and the other occupants of the room chatted amongst themselves.

Daisy had changed back into the brown poplin skirt and jacket she'd worn on arrival, the only costume she had with her apart from her lady's maid brown silk dress, but Maud and she were once again Miss McIntyre and Miss Cameron, detectives at the M. McIntyre Agency. The guests had attempted to ply them with questions, which the Duchess fended off. Daisy was now in animated conversation with Violet.

The necklace had been returned to the Viscount, but Maud wished she could be sure they had the right man. She and Daisy had gained experience from their first real case, but was it a success? The Earl had corroborated Colonel Morrison's story, that they had been in the Earl's room chatting about the Colonel's supposed war adventures. But there were still too many unanswered questions. Exactly what time did the Colonel leave the other man's room? Neither could be sure, but the Earl's chamber was at the same end of the corridor as the

Colonel's, and it would have taken almost no time at all for the
Colonel to return to his room and throw the necklace out of his
window. Were the Colonel and the Earl in league? The latter
had two women to support, after all, which must be a drain on
his finances. If someone else had thrown the jewellery from the
window, who was it? The alibis of Lord Urquhart and Mr Laing
were thin, to say the least; the former claimed to have been in
the library, the latter in the billiard room, each solely in his own
company. It seemed strange that whoever the thief was, he was
now prepared to dispose of the necklace in such a manner,
when he might well have got away with keeping it.

The Duchess had sent her motor car to collect Sergeant
McKay and bring him to Duddingston House. The policeman
looked proud as Punch as he took Colonel Morrison into
custody and escorted him into the back of the Daimler to return
to the police office.

Maud became aware that Mr Laing was smiling down at
her and waiting patiently for an answer.

'Yes,' she said. 'We're going back to Edinburgh in the morning. There's a train leaving a little after ten o'clock.' The butler
had consulted his Bradshaw's Guide for the train times.

'I also leave in the morning. I wonder if instead of catching
the train, you would accept a lift in my motor?'

'I'm awfully sorry, but no. We have tickets for the train, and
I feel we must travel that way.'

'Then at least allow me to take you both to the station. It
would save my manly pride, since it was Daisy wielding the
poker and not me.'

Maud laughed, drawing attention from the other end of the
room. His offer was tempting and surely could do no harm. He
was simply being a gentleman. 'Thank you.'

'Your presence will make that part of the journey more
enjoyable.'

Maud doubted she would see him – or any of the

Duddingston folk – once they were back in Edinburgh, but meanwhile there was no harm in enjoying his company.

'Both Mr Laing and Lord Urquhart admire you,' said Daisy, as they climbed the staircase to bed.

Daisy had said it was simpler for her to return to the attic to sleep, than to accept the Duchess's offer of having a fresh room made up, and that anyway she was tired enough to sleep standing up.

'Sorry, what did you say?' Maud said, her face growing warm.

'I said,' repeated Daisy, 'both Mr Laing and Lord Urquhart admire you.'

'I think you'll find they admire the detection business.'

'I don't think so, not if the way they look at you is anything to go by.'

'You mean with both eyes instead of just the one?'

Daisy threw up both her hands in surrender. 'I'm just pointing out that it's possible...'

Maud wondered why two men might suddenly be interested in her, but she was too tired to think clearly. They reached her room, and she pushed open the door. On her bed lay an envelope.

She had asked the General Post Office to forward any post for the agency to Duddingston House, as they were to be away for a good three days. Maud hastened over to the bed, Daisy following, snatched up the envelope and tore it open.

'Another case?' asked Daisy hopefully, as Maud scanned the closely written single sheet of paper.

'Yes. Listen to this.' Maud read the letter aloud. '*Dear Sir.*' She paused to tsk. '*I saw your advertisement in the newspaper and wish to engage your services. The fact of the matter is that my daughter, who is to marry in a fortnight's time, has disap-*

peared.' Maud glanced at Daisy. 'A missing person. I wonder if her parents have informed the police.' She continued reading. *'Naturally, I am very concerned as to her whereabouts, but do not want a scandal and so have no wish to involve the police.'* No mention of a wife, Maud noted. *'I will attend your office at ten o'clock on Tuesday forenoon, which I hope will have allowed sufficient time for you to consider accepting this case. Yours faithfully, A. Miller.'*

'Do you know the name Miller?' Daisy asked.

Maud shook her head. 'It doesn't ring any bells.'

'I wonder why he talked about a possible scandal. Perhaps he's a high heid yin.'

A bigwig... Maud knew the term originated in the eighteenth century, when it was fashionable for men to shave their heads and wear a wig – the bigger the wig, the greater the authority of the fellow. And then she remembered... all those cases she had followed in the newspapers.

'I think it must be the Honourable Lord Miller. He's a judge in the High Court of Justiciary.'

Daisy raised her eyebrows. 'Scotland's highest criminal court. No wonder he doesna want publicity.'

'I wonder if his daughter's disappearance is anything to do with one of his cases.'

Daisy made a scoffing sound. 'More like the lassie came to her senses about marriage just in time.'

'Whatever the reason, we have a fortnight to find her.' Maud glanced at the top of the letter. It was dated Friday. 'Just under two weeks, in fact.' She returned the letter to its envelope. 'We'll get a good night's sleep and travel back tomorrow, ready to deal with whatever the Honourable Lord Miller brings us on Tuesday.'

.   .   .

The following morning, they were up and ready for Mr Laing to take them to the railway station. Maud had even found time to perform a few additional *pliés*, arabesques and chassés to make up for her lack of ballet exercises over the past couple of days.

The Duchess had thanked them warmly for their work, and Mackenzie had taken their bags out to the car the minute it pulled up in front of the main door. As Maud and Daisy trod down the front steps of the house, Maud still felt misgivings about the outcome of the case.

The morning sun glinted on the Vulcan's yellow bonnet. 'Your carriage awaits, ladies.' Mr Laing jumped out of the driver's seat, swept off his tweed driving cap and gave them a courtly bow. 'As you see, it's a two-seater I'm afraid, but it does have a dickie.' He gestured to the wide seat already folded out from the back of the car and held his hand towards Daisy to help her in.

She giggled. 'Thank you, kind sir.'

Maud shot her a look, surprised at her sudden coyness, and Daisy grinned at her before clambering into the dickie seat. Mr Laing moved to the front passenger door. He opened it and smiled at Maud.

She inclined her head. 'Why, thank you.'

She smiled and climbed into the rear seat beside Daisy. He gave a laugh before shutting the passenger door. The pair settled into the thickly padded leather upholstery and, with a toot on the car hooter, Mr Laing drove off as the three of them waved farewell to the Duchess standing on the top step of the house. Behind the Duchess, Mackenzie blew a kiss at Daisy and smiled.

'Cheeky loon,' muttered Daisy, her cheeks pink.

Mr Laing was inclined to chat about the evidence against the Colonel, but Maud's distance from the driver's seat and her monosyllabic answers soon discouraged him. The journey was too pleasant to talk, she thought, as the soft breeze fanned her face. Flocks of sheep grazed in fields where the grass had faded in the fierce sunlight. In a field of barley, a reaper-binder, its sails white in the sun, tossed out sheaves, as men, women and children formed stooks. Whatever else happens in the world, the hairst must be brought in.

All too soon Maud felt the car slowing down and saw the railway station coming into view.

'Here we are.' Mr Laing spoke over his shoulder. He brought the car to a halt and came round to their seats in the back.

'Thank you for the lift.' Maud took his proffered hand and climbed out. 'It was kind of you.'

A porter with a trolley appeared to collect her trunk, and Daisy picked up the Gladstone bag.

'Goodbye, Mr Laing,' Maud said, and they set off towards the station.

'Miss McIntyre, one moment,' he called.

She turned back as he approached her and was aware of Daisy walking tactfully on.

'Something for you to remember the rose garden by.' He lifted his hand, which she saw now held a red rose, and pushed the flower into the band of her straw hat. 'There.'

She met his gaze, but before she could decide how to reply, the whistle of the approaching train cut into her thoughts, and she glanced round to see its steam billowing in the air.

'I must go,' she said and hastened towards the station.

The following morning, Maud and Daisy were sitting in their office, discussing the Duddingston case as they waited for the Honourable Lord Miller to arrive, when the telephone sprang into life. They both jumped and stared at it.

'Daisy, answer it, quickly!'

She lifted the black receiver. 'Who is it?' she said in a suspicious voice.

'Use our name,' Maud hissed.

Daisy straightened and spoke slowly into the handset. 'Hello. M. McIntyre Agency.'

Maud watched her face as the operator connected the call. Her eyes grew wide at whatever the caller was saying. 'I will ask her, sir.'

She held the receiver away from her mouth, covered it with her hand and whispered to Maud. 'It's Lord Urquhart. He wants to meet you this morning, somewhere other than here, to discuss business.'

'Really?' Was he so impressed by her detective skills? 'Tell him...' Maud glanced at her wristwatch. He could pay for lunch by way of apology for his behaviour when he visited the agency. 'Tell him I will see him at half past twelve in Café Vegetaria.'

Daisy nodded and repeated her message down the telephone wire. Maud heard the man laugh, and he said some further words before ending the conversation.

'Well?' she asked, as soon as Daisy had replaced the receiver on its cradle. 'What did he say?'

'It will be the first time he's been in a tea shop favoured by the local branch of the Women's Freedom League.'

'But he agreed?'

Daisy grinned. 'Aye.'

It was Maud's turn to laugh, although she had to admit she was a little annoyed. She'd been hoping to make him feel uncomfortable in her choice of meeting place. Never mind, lunch would do nicely.

Feeling they could get no further forward with the Duddingston mystery, Maud and Daisy turned their attention to familiarising themselves with the street map of Edinburgh. Maud knew the main thoroughfares in the New Town, of course – Princes Street, Queen Street and so on – but she didn't know her way about the Old Town with its numerous narrow closes. It was no longer the disease- and crime-ridden area it had been up to the last century, but it still wasn't a place that ladies visited. Maud McIntyre, private detective, was a different matter, though. She would do what was necessary to solve any case that came her way. True, the only case she had definitely solved so far had been that of the Radcliffe ruby, but...

On the stroke of ten, a short, almost painfully thin man entered the office. He wore a black cut-away jacket and pinstriped trousers, and carried a top hat and cane. Even if Maud hadn't known who he was, his formal, slightly dated clothes spoke of a professional gentleman.

'Lord Miller,' he said, 'to see Mr McIntyre.'

There was the usual confusion over the sex of M. McIntyre. Lord Miller accepted Maud's explanation with a nod of his head, but under his hairy eyebrows there remained a suspicious look in his eyes. Inevitable in his line of work, she supposed. Daisy rose from the visitor's chair.

'Please,' Maud said to Lord Miller and indicated he should take the seat.

She introduced Daisy to Lord Miller and, pad and pencil in hand, Daisy took the chair at the side of the desk.

Maud gave him her most professional smile. 'You wish me to find your daughter, who is missing?'

'That is correct.'

'You have come to the right place. To begin, could you furnish me with your daughter's name and address, Lord Miller?'

'Diana Miller. She resides with me in Rose Street.'

Maud nodded. 'Forgive me for asking, but is there a Lady Miller?'

'Sadly, no. My wife died some years ago.'

'I'm sorry to hear that.' After a brief, polite pause, she

continued. 'Tell me about your daughter, sir. When precisely did you last see her and what were the circumstances?'

Maud glanced at Daisy, to make sure she was writing this down.

'It was on Saturday morning. She told me she was going for the last fitting for her wedding gown.'

'And where was the fitting to take place?'

'At Madame Escoffier's in Shandwick Place.'

'Did Miss Miller go alone?'

'She was to have called at her friend's house on the way to the eleven o'clock appointment. The two girls had arranged to go to the dressmaker's together.'

'The friend's name and address, please,' said Daisy.

'Angela Grant. She stays in Hope Street.'

'You say your daughter was to have called at Miss Grant's house?' Maud asked.

'That's correct. But she never did.'

'You have checked that at the Hope Street residence?'

'I have. Both Angela and her mother are adamant Diana never arrived that morning.'

The first question Maud asked herself was, if Diana had been abducted, had it been planned or was it a random act, a matter of the young woman being in the wrong place at the wrong time? If planned, the abductor knew exactly where she would be at that time. But in either case, if she'd been snatched as she walked the short distance between her father's house in Rose Street and her friend's home in Hope Street, in the middle of a Saturday morning, surely her struggle would have attracted attention. This prosperous area at the west end of Princes Street was busy with shops, churches, people.

'And Madame Escoffier – you have spoken to her?' Maud went on.

'Yes. She confirmed that my daughter failed to keep her appointment.'

'What time did Miss Miller leave your house?' asked Daisy, glancing up from her note-taking.

'At a little after half past ten. This would have allowed her sufficient time to call for Angela Grant and for the two of them to walk to the Frenchwoman's premises.'

Maud nodded. 'Were you at home when your daughter left?'

'I was.'

'How did Miss Miller seem to you on Saturday morning before she went out?'

'Diana was her usual self. She gave me no cause for concern.'

The judge spoke as precisely as Maud imagined he did in court. She continued in a similar manner. 'Could you have been distracted by a case you were to hear?'

'Certainly not. My mind is alert to all matters at all times.'

Is that possible? She shot him a doubtful look, but he didn't as much as blink before he continued.

'I noticed nothing different about my daughter.' He paused for a moment to consider. 'If anything, she appeared more eager than usual to leave the house, excited about her wedding dress.'

'When did you realise that she hadn't returned home?'

'She didn't appear at luncheon, which concerned me as Diana always tells me if she will not be present. When she wasn't home at the hour for tea, then I became most anxious. I wrote to you that evening.'

Maud nodded. 'Her fiancé – what can you tell me about him?'

'His name is Douglas Laing, an advocate-depute – I'm sorry, did you say something?'

In her astonishment, Maud had almost choked. It had to be the same Mr Laing, the man she had spent time with at Duddingston House. Where to her knowledge no mention of his being betrothed, to Miss Miller or anyone else, was uttered.

'Would you like me to get you some water?' asked Daisy, half up from her chair, probably to hide her own surprise.

Hastily, Maud swallowed and waved a dismissive hand. 'No, thank you, Miss Cameron. Please go on, Lord Miller.'

'As I was saying, Mr Laing is a young advocate-depute who shows a great deal of promise. I have made it my business to follow his progress in the High Court and have found him to be a man of high moral standards.'

From the corner of her eye, Maud saw Daisy's pencil falter on the page.

'How do you feel about his and Miss Miller's marriage?' Maud asked.

'I have not pressured my daughter into this wedding, if that is what you are implying,' Lord Miller said stiffly, 'although I am delighted that Diana is to marry Mr Laing.'

She gave him her best smile. 'I take it that you agree to my interviewing Mr Laing, Miss Grant and Madame Escoffier?'

'Of course. I realise that is an essential part of your investigation. All have agreed to speak to you – I took the liberty of informing them you were to work for me – but I made it clear they were not to talk of the matter to anyone else. I wish them and both you young ladies' –he indicated Daisy with a brief nod of his head – 'to be most discreet, you understand.'

Did he imagine any of her clients wished her to be indiscreet? 'Do you have a portrait of your daughter, sir?'

He opened his jacket, revealing a black waistcoat, and removed a card from an inside pocket. 'This too I have already thought of.' He placed the photograph on the table and pushed it towards her. 'She had this likeness taken for me a month ago, so it is a faithful image.'

Maud and Daisy peered at it. Not a modern *carte de visite*, Maud noted as she took the stiff piece of card. This was more formal: cabinet card with a cream mount and bevelled edges finished in gold.

'Was there any particular reason for the photograph being taken?' It seemed a strange thing to do a few weeks before her wedding, given that another with her new husband would be taken at the nuptials.

'She told me it was to mark the end of her being an unmarried woman.'

Maud frowned at the oddness of his statement and looked at the picture more closely. The image showed the head and shoulders of a handsome young woman, with her dark hair piled fashionably on top of her head. She wore a pretty, high-necked lace blouse. There was a slight smile on her lips, but her dark eyes, as they looked out of the picture, not quite meeting the viewer's gaze, were large and sad.

'Miss Miller is a very attractive young woman,' Maud said.

She didn't need to ask him the age of his daughter, as the young woman was clearly over twelve years and so could marry, but Maud asked anyway.

'Diana is twenty-two,' Lord Miller replied to her question.

She had her father's blessing for the marriage to Mr Laing, but could there be another man she secretly wished to marry? Maud wondered. Although Scots law had no requirement for parental consent, it could be hard to marry against a father's wishes.

Maud turned her gaze to the card itself. The photographer's name and address – Ovinius Davis, 16 Princes Street, Edinburgh – was printed in copperplate script at the bottom.

'May I keep this while I investigate?' She looked up in time to see the worry on Lord Miller's face before he resumed his businesslike mask.

He nodded, tight-lipped.

Maud obtained Mr Laing's address in Lawnmarket, and Daisy advised Lord Miller of their usual terms. Maud assured him of their best attention, and he bid them good day.

'Well, that's a turn-up,' said Daisy. 'Mr Laing having a fiancée.'

'My father always said the quiet ones are the worst.' Maud wasn't sure she believed that, but it had stuck in her mind.

Daisy smiled, a twinkle back in her eyes. 'I canna say that has been my experience, but if it's true, then Lord Urquhart is a paragon of virtue.'

'Never mind him, Daisy. What is far more important is Mr Laing. Is there a connection between the crime at Duddingston House and the case of the missing Miss Miller?'

'Too much of a coincidence, you mean?'

'Exactly that. I can't think what it might mean just yet. What I do know is Mr Laing was charming at Duddingston... perhaps too charming, now I come to think of it.'

'Why would Miss Miller run away, if she has run away, from such a charming fellow, unless his behaviour was an act?'

'He can't have abducted her, although I cannot think why he might want to abduct his own betrothed, because he has an alibi – everyone at Duddingston. There would not have been sufficient time to seize her, take her elsewhere and arrive at the house party in time for luncheon.'

'On that subject,' Daisy glanced at her wristwatch, 'it's quarter past twelve.'

'Thank you, Daisy.' Maud stood and patted her hair to ensure the clips still held the pompadour secure on the crown of her head. Daisy handed her the wide-brimmed straw hat and Maud pinned it into position. 'I expect to be back about two o'clock.'

She slid paper and pen into her leather satchel, slipped the strap over her shoulder and sailed out into yet another hot August day in Edinburgh.

Despite her frustration at the outcome of the Duddingston case, Sherlock Holmes couldn't have been keener than Maud to solve the new cases presented to her. What her fellow Edinburgher Sir Conan Doyle had done in fiction, Maud remained determined to do in fact. The notion prompted her to give a wry smile. A man passing by on the pavement caught her eye and, mistaking her meaning, returned the smile. Averting her gaze, Maud strode on.

Had Holmes ever had to put up with unwanted attention from the opposite sex? Not as far as Maud could recall. No matter, she was engaged in the occupation she'd dreamed of since she was a young girl.

Maud strode out with more purpose.

FIFTEEN

Arriving at Café Vegetaria, Maud pushed open the door and walked in.

Lord Urquhart was already there, seated at a table tucked into a corner of the mainly female establishment, although for someone who apparently wished to be unobtrusive, his choice of blazer was rather garish. The bell above the door drew his attention her way, and he got to his feet.

'Miss McIntyre.' He pulled out a chair for her.

'Thank you.'

He took his seat opposite, and they looked at each other.

'You have decided to use my agency's services, after all, My Lord?'

'Nice hat,' he said.

'Thank you,' she said again and waited for him to reply. The rumble of carriage wheels and the neigh of an agitated horse in the street outside floated in through the open window, adding to the hum of women's voices.

Just as he opened his mouth again to speak, a young waitress, smart in her black dress, white apron and frilly cap, appeared.

'Sir; madam. What would you like to order?'

Maud picked up the menu.

'What do you recommend?' Lord Urquhart asked the waitress.

'Well,' she said, smiling shyly at him, 'there's cheese and vegetable hotpot, and roast cod with parsley sauce.' She lowered her voice. 'The cod is the best dish.'

'Then the cod it is for me. And a glass of water.' He turned his gaze on Maud and lifted an enquiring eyebrow.

She glanced back down at the menu and made a play of consulting it. She'd already decided she would choose the cod, but it wouldn't do to agree with him too quickly.

Handing her menu to the waitress, she said, 'The cod. And water for me, as well. Thank you.'

'So,' Maud said, pushing on, 'how can I help you?'

'It's interesting that you have chosen this tea shop for our meeting.'

Maud pretended she did not know what he meant. 'Interesting in what way?'

'Because many suffragettes gathered here on the night of the second of April to evade the census enumerator. If I were a suspicious man, I might think you were trying to tell me something.'

That women did not have the right to vote was a disgrace. On her census form, Maud had been very tempted to write, 'No persons here – only women', but it wasn't a good idea for a private detective to have a criminal record. That same night, to boycott the census, Emily Davidson had hidden in a broom cupboard in the House of Commons and other suffragettes had a midnight picnic on Wimbledon Common. How brave they all were.

Maud looked at him. 'I didn't know you followed the movements of the Women's Freedom League.'

'I don't *follow the movements*, as you put it, of the WFL. It's simply that it's impossible not to be aware of what they did. "No vote – no census!" is quite a memorable slogan.'

She couldn't tell if he supported the aims of the League or not, so she nodded and brought the focus back to the business in hand. 'What made you change your mind about using my agency?'

'Your performance at Duddingston House.'

Performance sounded about right. She'd behaved like a detective, but she remained uncertain she and Daisy had named the right man.

'Well, My Lord, are you going to tell me what your case is all about or do you intend to make me wait until after the waitress serves the fish?'

He rearranged his cutlery on the table in front of him. Finally, he said, 'I need some stolen letters found.'

Maud raised an eyebrow. 'Have you informed the police about the theft?'

He raised both eyebrows. 'No.'

She had no intention of engaging in competitive eyebrow-raising, so she composed her features and said simply, 'Why?'

He lowered his brows into a frown. 'Why do you think, Miss McIntyre? They are letters of a romantic nature.'

How could Maud have expected it to be anything else? The man exuded confident charm of the type silly young ladies fell for.

'I see. I assume you've been having an affair, been foolish enough to write to the lady in question and now she won't return your imprudent billets-doux?'

He shook his head. 'Quite the opposite.'

'I beg your pardon?'

'You are right in that the lady and I had been involved in a liaison, but it was she who wrote the letters to me. Then she ended our relationship and married another. I was upset, of course—'

'Of course,' she murmured.

He sent her a quick glance before continuing. 'But I respected her decision and thought that was the end of it. Recently, she wrote to me again, saying she had made a terrible mistake in marrying the man and that she wanted to resume our... acquaintance. Foolishly, I'd kept her letters, including those which expressed her dissatisfaction with her new husband. I did not leave them lying about, but neither did I store them in a safe place as it turns out, as now they have been stolen.'

Maud didn't know what to say; so many questions jostled to be first. Eventually, she asked, 'Did you write any letters to her?'

'No.' He looked torn between shame and relief that he hadn't reciprocated. 'I've always found it best not to put anything of that nature in writing.'

Before Maud could make a caustic response, their meals arrived. 'The food smells wonderful,' she said politely.

The pair made small talk as they ate. The cod really was excellent.

'It is rather pleasant here. I may come again.' He smiled.

Maud made a mental note not to return to the restaurant.

When they had finished eating and their plates had been removed, Maud drew him back to the matter of the missing letters.

'Where were the letters kept, Lord Urquhart?'

'In the bureau in my study.'

'And when did you notice they were no longer there?'

'On Wednesday morning, after I'd returned from... ah... a night out.'

When he had come to her office.

'I keep only a small number of servants in Edinburgh – a manservant, a cook and two housemaids. I questioned them about the missing letters, without saying what they were. All denied knowing the whereabouts of any correspondence.'

'Was anything else taken?'

He shook his head. 'Only the letters.'

'Interesting.' She pulled the pen and notebook from her bag and began writing down the details. 'Do you keep the bureau locked?' she asked as she wrote.

'No.'

She tsked. 'Was there any sign the room had been broken into?'

'None. There would have been no need if entry was made during daylight hours, as it is my practice to leave the window in my study slightly open on warm days.'

Maud shot him a look suggesting that was another mistake.

'I like fresh air,' he continued, 'and you may have noticed the heat this summer.'

'Nonetheless, one could be forgiven for thinking that leaving a window open in one's study, where one's personal papers are stored, is not a very bright thing to do.'

He leaned back and folded his arms. 'Do you have governess blood in you?'

There had been no call for that comment. Maud took a deep breath and continued her line of questioning. 'Therefore, it could equally have been someone who entered from outside. What about inside? Who has access to your study?'

'Apart from my servants, only a handful of friends. They have not been left alone in my study, and I cannot believe any of my servants would open my bureau and steal the letters.'

'Then do you have any idea who might have taken them?'

'No, but I do have a suspicion as to motive.'

'Yes?'

'It could be political.'

'In what way?'

'The lady's correspondence, if it fell into unscrupulous hands, could be used to discredit her husband.'

This was proving to be more interesting than Maud had originally expected. 'To whom is the lady married?'

He paused, then replied, 'Sebastian Ferguson.'

'The Tory MP!' Despite her astonishment, she managed to keep her exclamation low.

Lord Urquhart gave a brief nod of his head. 'The same.'

'Goodness.' Sebastian Ferguson was known for his extreme right-wing views and an advocate of the birch for even the most minor of offences. 'If he knew about your correspondence with his wife, the consequences for you could be... uncomfortable.'

'I doubt it would harm me in the long run, but for Stella it would be catastrophic.'

Maud had to ask: 'Do you still love her?'

'That is none of your business,' he said.

Maud bit her lip. He was right. She was curious, nothing more, and it was not a question she should have put to him.

'Perhaps that was unfair of me,' he added. 'Since you ask, the answer is no, I do not. I did love her, but she chose another. My concern now is to protect the honour and the person of the lady.'

'Quite right,' Maud said.

He raised a hand and called for the bill before telling her, 'Come to my address at 72 Frederick Street tomorrow afternoon at three o'clock. I will let you have an advance on your fee and will show you how I believe the thief may have entered my premises.'

'Tomorrow at three,' she said, rising.

He got to his feet. 'One other thing, Miss McIntyre.'

Maud turned back. 'Yes?'

'Mr Ferguson is away on business at present, but he returns to their house in Charlotte Square next week. That gives you seven days to find the missing items.'

SIXTEEN

Seven days to find the stolen letters, Maud thought as she strode back to her office. When she'd pointed out how foolish he'd been in not engaging her services earlier, Lord Urquhart had the grace to admit he had been wrong. Surely she could indeed rise to this new challenge; it was simply a matter of applying herself. Back in the office, Maud found Daisy in her seat and looking pleased with herself.

'We have another client,' Daisy said with a grin.

'Another one? That's wonderful news. The agency is doing well.' Maud felt vindicated in setting up the business. 'What is the case?'

'A missing dog.' She went to rise from the chair.

'Keep your seat, Daisy.' Maud unpinned her hat and hung it on a peg behind the door. 'Missing pets are the bread and butter of detective agencies. That reminds me. Have you eaten luncheon?'

'Yes, thanks. I nipped out and bought a pie from a coster-monger. I was gone only a couple of minutes and I kept my eye on the street door.'

Maud slid into the client's seat on the other side of the desk. 'Tell me about the missing dog.'

Daisy picked up the pad in front of her and began to read from her notes. 'Lady Argyll, resident at 70 Frederick Street—'

Maud's mouth fell open. 'Frederick Street?'

'Aye.'

'Number 70?'

Daisy frowned. 'Aye.'

'That's the house next door to our other new client, Lord Urquhart.'

'We've got his case then?'

Maud nodded. 'He's had intimate letters stolen and wants them back.' She gestured to the notebook in Daisy's hand. 'What else did Lady Argyll tell you?'

'The dog, a Pekingese, went missing from her back garden on Wednesday morning.' She saw the look on Maud's face. 'What is it?'

'Wednesday morning was when Lord Urquhart noticed the letters were missing.' Curiouser and curiouser. 'Why did she wait so long before coming to us?' A thought struck Maud. 'Don't tell me, she didn't want a female detective?'

Daisy shook her head. 'The first agency she went to got nowhere with the case. But it was run by a man, so what do you expect?' She grinned.

Maud relaxed. 'Go on.'

'Well, apparently, the dog often barked when it was in the garden, so Lady A. didn't take much notice at first. But when the yapping became more lively, she went outside to find out what was upsetting wee Maximilian.'

'The suggestion being that he'd been grabbed by a stranger and was voicing his objection to the enterprise?'

'Exactly,' said Daisy, settling back in the chair. 'By the time Lady A. was outside, the barking had stopped and she couldn't see him, so she had the servants search the garden and there was nae sign of the wee fellow.'

'Does he have any distinguishing features?'

'He was involved in a rammle with another dog a couple of years ago and lost the end of his tail. Instead of it being carried jauntily over his back, poor Max's tail now sticks up like a wee flagpole.'

That must be embarrassing for him amongst his Peke chums, but it was good news for them.

'The rest of him,' added Daisy, 'is much as you'd expect. A biscuit-coloured body with a black face. The colours you most often see.'

'Could you deal with this case?'

'Nae problem. It shouldn't be too hard to find a Pekingese with that tail. Or to spot the dognapper, if he's had a bite taken out of his nose.'

'Can you get some posters made and display them in the window of any shop that will take them? Offer a small reward; see if that encourages anyone to come forward with information. I'll start the interviews with those on my list regarding Miss Miller. We'll also need to begin work soon on the missing letters case. We have only seven days to find them.'

'Why only seven days?'

'The lady's husband, an MP, is due to return from a business trip next Tuesday. If he arrives home before the letters are recovered, our client will not be recommending our fledgling business to anyone. Quite the opposite, I imagine.'

'So Lord Urquhart lives next door to Max's owner?'

'He does.'

'Is it possible—?'

'That the two events are connected?' Maud smiled. 'I wouldn't rule it out.'

. . .

When Daisy left the office to go to the printers, Maud gave further thought to the missing letters.

Anyone wishing to discover where Lord Urquhart stayed would simply be able to consult *Who's Who* in the public library. They could then make their way to his house, open the window and help themselves to his correspondence. But how would the thief know about the existence, content and where-abouts of the letters? And where, if at all, did the missing Pekingese fit into all this?

First, though, she must interview Diana Miller's friend, Miss Angela Grant. Although time was of the essence in the letters case, it also had to be with a missing young woman.

It was only a ten-minute walk from George Street to Hope Street. She found the Grant residence and pulled the bell set in the wall by the side of the door. No response, just the sound of birds tweeting in the trees in nearby Charlotte Square. As she lifted her hand to try the bell again, a maid opened the door.

'Yes, madam?'

'Is Miss Grant at home?'

'Whom shall I say is calling?'

'Miss Maud McIntyre. I believe she is expecting me.'

'Please come in.'

The maid opened the door wider and stepped back for Maud to enter. Indicating a chair in the hall, she disappeared along the corridor. Maud took a seat and waited. The house was so quiet that she could have heard a pin drop if she'd taken the one from her hat. Eventually, a door opened and a petite young woman in a dark-green blouse and skirt and with a solemn face came towards her.

'Miss McIntyre.' She held out a hand. 'I'm so glad you could come.'

She made it sound like Maud was a welcome guest to the house, presumably for any servants who might be eaves-dropping.

'Let us go into the garden,' she continued. 'It's too lovely a day to be indoors and we can talk as well there as in a stuffy drawing room.'

'Thank you. I should like that.' Maud followed her along the passageway. At the end Miss Grant paused to remove from a hook on the back of the door an old straw hat with a wide brim. She set it on her head, and they passed through and out into a delightful flower garden. A lawn with a bird bath took centre place, the water sparkling in the sun. In this heat, the stone bath must have to be filled often. The borders burst with white daisies, red geraniums, orange lilies, yellow chrysanthemums and purple hydrangeas.

'What vibrant shades. Who is the gardener in the family?'

'I am. My mother is happy to look, but I like to plan which plants go where. I spend as much time out here as I can.' She gave a quick smile. The array of colours and the sweetness in her brief smile made Maud think she was by disposition a cheerful young woman. The loss of her friend, or perhaps something she knew about her friend's disappearance, was clearly having an effect on Miss Grant's spirits.

They moved to a shady bench at the side of the lawn and Miss Grant sat down, gesturing for Maud to do the same. Maud watched her face to see if it revealed more than her words might say. That the young woman did not meet her eye aroused Maud's suspicion.

Staring ahead at the bird bath, Miss Grant said, 'You've come about Diana.'

It was a statement, rather than a question.

'Yes.'

'It's looking bad for her, isn't it?'

Maud nodded.

Miss Grant turned her head to look at Maud. 'I want to do what is best for Diana, to help her.'

What a strange thing to say, Maud thought. 'The best thing

for your friend is for you to tell me whatever you know about her disappearance.'

Beads of sweat had formed above Angela Grant's top lip. Admittedly, it was hot out here, but was there more to her perspiration than this?

'Miss Miller made an arrangement for you to go with her to Madame Escoffier's for her dress fitting,' Maud continued, 'but I believe she never arrived here?'

Angela Grant didn't miss a beat. 'Diana was to have called for me about twenty minutes to eleven and we were to walk together to Shandwick Place for her eleven o'clock appointment, but she didn't appear.' She spoke as if she'd learned her reply by rote.

'Why do you think Diana didn't come?' Maud asked.

Miss Grant looked uncomfortable. 'I cannot say.'

Maud softened her voice. 'You cannot say or will not say?'

The other woman's cheeks flushed, but she shook her head.

Further questioning produced no variation on her response, so Maud thanked her for her time and got to her feet. She left Hope Street dissatisfied and hoping for a more useful interview with the next person on her list, Madame Escoffier.

Maud hastened down Shandwick Place, keeping an eye on the horse-drawn cabs, trams and motor cars. It was a notoriously busy street but, despite the hustle and bustle, she easily spotted Madame Escoffier's premises on the other side of the road. Maud crossed the street, weaving through the traffic and taking care to step over the tram rails.

An awning protected the dressmaker's shopfront from the glare of the sun. She stood under this for a moment and admired the attractive window display. A mannequin, draped in a bolt of pastel-blue silk which fell in pools on the floor, dominated the space and drew the eye. On closer inspection through the window, the prospective customer would notice the wall which artfully displayed an array of gloves and belts, hats and scarves, all presumably commercially made.

The bell jangled above the door as she pushed it open. The shop was empty of customers, but a number of ladies' dresses made up in miniature sizes lined the walls, giving a rather eerie effect. Books of Butterick Patterns arranged on a central table next caught her gaze, but before she could examine them, a thin, elderly woman dressed in black emerged from the back of the shop.

'*Bonjour, madame.*' Her businesslike gaze took in Maud's white blouse with striped black and white waistcoat and skirt.

Forcing aside the desire to ask for a dress made in the blue silk in the window, Maud introduced herself. 'I wonder if I might have a word with you about Miss Diana Miller?'

'Miss Miller?' She pursed her lips. 'Please, come this way.'

Maud followed her into the back of the shop and into what was clearly the fitting room. It wasn't large, but two long mirrors standing against opposite walls and the chandelier suspended from the ceiling gave the room a brightness. In the centre on a small platform was displayed a life-size mannequin, clothed in a wedding gown of white silk and lace. Little bunches of pale-pink silk rosebuds clung diagonally across the fitted bodice. To the side of the dress, a tall stand displayed a long veil with matching rosebuds stitched onto the headband.

Maud let out a breath. 'How beautiful. Is that Miss Miller's gown?'

'*Oui.* I 'ope it will not go to waste.'

She turned to Madame Escoffier. 'Why do you say that?'

'Miss Miller knows if I cannot be satisfied very soon that the dress fits perfectly, there will not be sufficient time for any alterations before her wedding day.' She frowned. 'I cannot allow any robe less than *parfaite* to be worn by my customers.'

'Miss Miller's father has told me that she did not appear for her fitting on Saturday morning.'

'That is correct.'

'And she sent no note to explain her non-appearance?'

'That, too, is correct.'

Maud had to ask the same question she'd put to Angela Grant. 'Why do you think Miss Miller did not come?'

Madame Escoffier shot her a look. ''ow can I answer such a question? But I will tell you what I do know. I know I will need to be recompensed for the fabrics and for my valuable time, whether the young lady marries or not.'

'You sound as though you don't expect the wedding to take place.'

She gave a Gallic shrug. 'I 'ave seen a lot of brides in my time. Usually, they become more excited about the marriage as the day draws near. They fantasise as to the look on their fiancé's face when he sees 'er walking down the aisle and *naturellement* they are obsessed with 'ow beautiful they will look in one of my creations. What they do not do, mademoiselle, is become less talkative and less keen.'

Maud's pulse quickened. 'Is that what happened? Diana Miller appeared to have gone off the idea?'

'You put the changing of the 'eart in an odd way. But *oui*, I think she very well may 'ave "gone off the idea".'

'But she never referred to another young man?'

Madame didn't answer for a while, just looked at Maud. Had she pushed her too far? A dressmaker, like a coiffeuse, must hear a lot of secrets. Was she considering whether or not to reveal some infidelity of Diana Miller's? Eventually, she spoke.

'I am like a priest, you understand? Women confess the feelings of their 'eart as I measure them for a gown.'

Maud held her breath and watched the other woman's face.

'Miss Miller did not confess to me anything of that nature.'

She let out her breath and her shoulders sagged.

'But,' she continued, 'I do believe she was not looking forward to her wedding day. We Frenchwomen notice these things. All the little details that do not add up. Miss Miller's eyes lost their sparkle, she spoke less frequently of 'er betrothed and, worse, she did not exclaim over the beauty of the gown. To summarise, Miss Miller had lost 'er *joie de vivre.*'

Madame Escoffier ran a finger lightly over an embroidered sleeve of the wedding dress and shook her head. 'I spare no effort when making my works of art, so it is painful to me to see such a *médiocre* response from a client.'

Maud left Shandwick Place and made her way back to her apartment through streets busy with hot and tired shop-, office- and factory workers who'd finished for the day. So, she thought, Miss Miller's friend knows something but isn't letting on and her dressmaker can provide no actual evidence but has her suspicions. Did this get her any further?

SEVENTEEN

'Any news on the missing Max?' Maud asked Daisy over dinner at their apartment, as she forked up a portion of *macaronis au fromage*. All this investigative work was giving her an appetite.

'Naething helpful so far,' Daisy admitted. 'I thought I'd found the wee blighter this afternoon when I was on my way back here, but it turned out to be a red herring. Or, rather, an angry Pekingese and its crabbit owner.' She shuddered.

Maud's fork paused in midair. 'What happened?'

'The dog was trotting along on a leash and our eyes met. I was sure I read in them a plea for help. So I snatched the animal. The leash slipped from the hand of the man who'd been holding it and I turned to run.' She frowned. 'The man cried out and the dog bit my hand.'

Remembering the incident with Roger at Duddingston House, Maud set down her fork on her plate and looked at her friend. 'You can't trust what you read in the eyes of a dog, you know.'

Daisy shot her a vexed look.

'What happened next?' Maud asked.

'I yelped, came to a sudden halt and felt the man's hand on

my shoulder. I tried to shrug him off, but he held fast. I shouted the dog's name, and the man said his name was not Maximilian.'

'The dog's name was not Maximilian?'

'No, he said *his* name was not Maximilian.'

'How did he get the idea that you thought it was?'

'I canna imagine. Anyway, I turned towards him and told him that I'd thought this was my dear employer's dog that has gone missing and that the man had found Max on the street and taken him.'

'What did he say to that?'

'His face went red, and he said, "Are you accusing me of dog theft?"

'"No, sir," I said. "I took you for a kind gentleman who had found little Maximilian."

'His colour faded a little. "Humph. Well..."

'I could see a police constable approaching, so I handed the dog back to the man, bobbed a curtsy and left smartish.' She took a gulp of tea. 'The mutt still had his tail. Pity I didn't see that before I grabbed him.'

'And your hand – is it all right?' Maud glanced down to where Daisy's palms were wrapped around her cup.

She nodded. 'I washed the bite thoroughly and put on some turmeric.'

'Keep an eye on it, to be on the safe side.' Maud lifted her fork again, chewed as she thought and swallowed. 'Now we have to decide on our next step in the Miller case. Mr Laing is still to be interviewed, but he's in court during the day and it's too late to call on him this evening. The question is, is there another gentleman in Diana Miller's life?'

Daisy set her cup in its saucer. 'A sweetheart, you mean?'

'Assuming Miss Miller hasn't been kidnapped and her body disposed of, someone is providing a safe hiding place for her. A visit tomorrow morning to Mr Davis, the photographer, might provide an answer.'

Daisy looked at her hopefully. Maud took the hint. 'Would you like to come?'

Daisy smiled her answer. Maud didn't like to leave the office unattended for too long, but as she looked at Daisy an idea came to her. Lord Miller had told Miss Grant, Madame Escoffier and Mr Laing presumably people he felt he could trust – to expect a visit from Maud. He didn't want anyone else, including the photographer, to know his daughter was missing. While Mr Davis was engaged in photographing the sweetly smiling Daisy, Maud would extract information from him.

'Here we are,' Maud announced to Daisy, as they came to a halt on Princes Street. Daisy was dressed in a fetching tailored nautical jacket and skirt with a light-coloured blouse. Maud, as her plain best friend, wore a neat lace blouse and brown skirt.

'Number sixteen.' On the shop window it stated OVINIUS DAVIS PHOTOGRAPHY STUDIO. 'Remember, Daisy, you wish to have your photograph taken for your sweetheart.'

'Aye, right.' She rolled her eyes.

'Daisy!'

She grinned. 'Dinna worry, I can play the part well enough. Here we go.' She pushed open the door and a little bell rang. Maud followed her in.

They took seats and as they waited in the otherwise empty shop, Maud read the notice on one of the walls. **PHOTOG-RAPHY FOR SPECIALTIES IN ARTISTIC PORTRAITURE.** EDINBURGH, GLASGOW AND LONDON. PORTRAITS. MINIATURES. PHOTOG-RAPHY OF EVERY DESCRIPTION. FIRST CLASS CARTES DE VISITE FROM 5S. PER DOZEN. CABINET PRINTS FROM 6S. 6D. ROYAL PATRON-AGE. WORLDWIDE REPUTATION.

Very impressive. And expensive. Perhaps this wasn't a good idea, after all.

Before Maud had a chance to comment on this to Daisy, the inner door opened. A man of medium height with dark hair and moustache stepped out. Maud was pretty sure his plain black suit wasn't off the peg.

'Ladies. What can I do for you?'

She opened her mouth to speak and then remembered that she was here as Daisy's friend.

Daisy smiled at him. 'I'd like my portrait taken, please.'

He came towards them, his arms open wide. 'What luck! My last appointment has not long left, and I am free at present. This way, please.'

He led them through the door and into the studio. It was a large and airy room, with a Turkish rug covering most of the floor and a camera on a tripod to one side. At the other side of the room, natural light poured in through the long windows. There were various props, but Maud's eye was immediately taken by the huge canvas at the back of the studio.

Painted with an idealised rural landscape, it stretched from floor to ceiling. Trees filled the left-hand side of the picture and a crumbling ivy-covered pillar stood to the right. In the centre, a path faded away into a misty scene of yet more trees.

'Where would you like to be photographed, miss?' Mr Davis asked.

'The country estate is bonnie,' began Daisy.

He smiled encouragingly. 'It is very popular.'

And no doubt the most expensive background, Maud thought.

Daisy turned to the left wall of the studio. 'On the other hand, I quite like the hearth.' A padded chair with a matching footstool had been placed by the side of a carved wooden fireplace.

He nodded. 'Many ladies choose the domestic arrangement.'

'I'm not sure...' Her gaze moved to the other side of the room. 'Perhaps I'd photograph better by the side of the aspidistra.' The leafy plant stood in a pot on a tall, ornate table.

'You cannot go wrong with a traditional setting,' he said.

Daisy turned to Maud with a gleam in her eye. 'What do you think, Mildred?'

The cheeky besom had chosen for Maud a name she knew Maud disliked. Maud would get her own back. 'The domestic arrangement, without a doubt, my dear. It is exactly how Ernest would wish to see you.'

Daisy frowned. 'You are mistaken, Mildred. He would rather picture me in a rural idyll.'

'I distinctly remember hearing him say how much he favours women by the hearth and home.' Maud turned to smile at Mr Davis. 'We wouldn't want to disappoint him, would we?'

'Indeed not. Make yourself comfortable here, miss.' He gestured to the velvet padded chair and lifted the camera on its tripod into position.

Daisy turned to scowl at Maud. She made her way to the chair and sat down, arranged her skirts and struck a smiling pose.

'You are a natural subject in front of the camera,' Mr Davis exclaimed. He ducked his head under the cloth.

'I am now looking at the image formed on the focusing screen,' he said, his voice muffled. 'And moving the lens forward and back to focus the picture. There. Perfect. If you could keep that pose.' He removed his head from under the cover and took hold of a photographic plate.

'What exactly is it that you are doing, Mr Davis?' Maud wanted to establish a rapport with him, but she was also genuinely interested.

'I am about to put in this plate, which has a coating

containing light-sensitive silver salts. I find this method gives the sharpest image.'

'You must get a lot of young ladies asking for photographs as keepsakes for their loved ones.' She kept her voice casual.

'Indeed, yes. And of course young men who are desirous of pictures to give to their young ladies.'

Maud wasn't interested in this topic. With only a very short time available to them in the studio, she needed to go straight to the matter. 'You were recommended by a friend of ours, a Miss Miller.'

She watched his face as he clearly went through names and faces in his head.

'Ah, Miss Miller. A charming young lady. She also wanted her photograph taken for her... for her...' He flushed.

Maud let the sentence hang.

'Her young man,' he concluded.

Did he mean her fiancé? Maud tried not to let her disappointment show. Foolishly, she'd been hoping the photographer would mention another name. But she supposed, if Diana Miller had run away with another man, she'd hardly admit his name to Mr Davis.

'A very pleasant young fellow,' went on Mr Davis, his hand still on the plate. 'And he cut quite a figure.

'You met him?' Maud was interested in spite of herself. She wasn't sure she would describe him as cutting a figure. Stocky and sandy-haired, yes. She could understand the description if he were tall, dark and...

'The gentleman accompanied Miss Miller to the studio and stayed while her image was being taken.'

Maud nodded slowly. 'You mentioned that he caught your attention?'

'An exceptionally tall man and very dashing in his kilt – Buchanan hunting green, if I'm not mistaken.'

Daisy made a squeaking sound.

'I must ask you to remain very still until I say otherwise, miss.' Mr Davis eyed her severely and slid the plate into the camera.

Her fixed smile was turning into a grimace. And no wonder. Miss Miller's lover did not sound at *all* like Douglas Laing.

'The photograph must be taken before the gelatine coating dries out. No more than ten seconds is all that is required.'

They waited in silence.

'And relax,' said Mr Davis.

Daisy's shoulders sagged.

'Excuse me,' he said. 'I must now take the plate to the dark-room as it needs processing.'

'We'll return tomorrow for the photograph. A *carte de visite* – just the one,' Maud said hastily. 'Come, Doris.'

They all but burst from the shop onto Princes Street. Daisy worked her mouth to get some life back into it.

'Doris,' she finally spluttered. 'What made you give me that name?'

'Don't you like it? And for that matter, why did you call me Mildred?'

'It was the first name I thought of. I read somewhere that when we have to choose another name for ourselves, we opt for something beginning with the same letter of the alphabet. Hence Mildred.'

'There you are. That must be why I called you Doris.' Maud was a little breathless from the speed at which they were moving along the street. 'But never mind that. You heard what Mr Davis said about Miss Miller's gentleman friend?'

'Why do you think I squeaked? The description certainly didn't fit our friend Mr Laing.'

'No wonder the photographer coloured. He couldn't bring himself to use the word lover. So why do you think she might have had her portrait taken for her father? A farewell gift for him; something to remember her by?'

Daisy stopped and put a hand to her side. 'Do you think we could walk at a normal speed? There's no one chasing us and now I've got a stitch.'

Maud came to a halt. 'I'm famished. Let's eat. After luncheon I must attend Lord Urquhart's house to examine the scene of the crime and then I will interview Mr Laing. He should have returned from court by then.'

'Would you mind if I had the afternoon off?' Daisy straightened. 'I've heard from an old friend in service who can't get away at present. Her mother is feeling poorly, and I promised to visit as soon as I could. She stays not too far away.'

'Of course you must go, Daisy.'

'Thanks, Maud. I'll stop off at the office and leave a note on the door with the telephone number, just in case a new client comes looking for us.'

Maud smiled. 'I don't think we can cope with any more cases at present.'

Maud was pleased to arrive back at her apartment in Broughton Street. The day was still uncomfortably warm, and she longed to strip off her clothes and bathe, although that would have to wait until the evening.

As she entered the small hall, she heard the sound of movement in her sitting room. There was someone in her apartment. Had Daisy not gone out, after all? Taking no chances, she quietly drew her parasol from the stand. It wasn't much protection, but it did have a useful point at the end.

Holding her breath and the parasol aloft, Maud turned the handle and carefully opened the door to the sitting room.

'Father!' She dropped her hand holding the weapon. 'What a lovely surprise!'

He eyed the parasol as he rose from the chair to greet her. 'I'm sorry if I gave you a start, my dear.'

She propped it against the wall and turned to him. 'It was just that I heard a noise.'

He kissed her on the cheek. 'I thought I'd drop by as I was in the area.'

'Did Martha let you in? She comes to clean and tidy in the mornings on weekdays and to prepare a simple meal for Daisy and me to heat up in the evenings.'

'She did. A pleasant young woman. You are fortunate to have found her.'

Taking off her jacket and hat, Maud dropped them on an armchair. Her father resumed his seat and placed on the side table the book he'd been reading. She sank onto the sofa facing him.

'You're looking well, father.'

Maud's father was tall and a little too thin for her liking. His hair, though silvery as expected in a man of his years, was thick. It gave him the appearance of a comfortably off, land-owning gentleman, which in fact he was. Maud gazed at him, her only surviving parent, who was the dearer to her for it. Her mother had died of consumption when she was only ten years old and so, unlike her three older brothers, Maud had few strong memories of her mother. She and her father had grown closer to each other as one by one the brothers departed to live their own lives. So, she was grateful to him for encouraging her when she announced she wanted to be a private detective. Not many fathers would do the same. Maud was sure he would secretly like her to be married and giving him grandchildren, but he already had six of those from her brothers.

'And you look well too, my dear,' he said. 'Your new occupation clearly suits you.'

She smiled. 'I already have a small number of cases.'

He returned her smile. 'What are they?'

'Father, you can hardly expect me to tell you! It would be most unprofessional.'

'Of course.' He cleared his throat.

'Would you like a cup of tea?' she asked.

'No, thank you, my dear.' He paused and she could see he wanted to say something further, so she waited.

'Your brother Archie is working in Egypt for a month or two and he and I wondered if you would like the use of his motor car while he's away. He's thinking about taking the vehicle with him when he next goes abroad, but he thought you could try it out first on the roads in Scotland. You'd be doing him a favour.'

Maud loved her Foreign Office brother dearly, but she knew he never would have thought of this on his own. It was her father's doing.

'You are a darling.' She leaped up and gave him a kiss on the cheek.

'Me?' he said, but he beamed. 'Archie will deliver it to you tomorrow morning. Now, all this calls for a celebration. Will you allow me to take you out for luncheon?'

'That would be delightful.'

He got to his feet, and she plucked her hat and jacket from the armchair.

'Carstairs will drive us,' he said. 'Where would you like to go?'

'Anywhere, apart from Café Vegetaria.'

EIGHTEEN

Maud thanked her father for luncheon at Mr Boni's, the charming little Italian café on Gilmore Place, and bid him farewell, promising to visit soon. Refusing her father's offer of a lift, Maud made her way to Lord Urquhart's house in Frederick Street. She liked to walk not just because it kept her fit, but also for the variety of people to be seen on the streets. They never failed to give her ideas for disguises.

As she walked along George Street, a charwoman, tired by the work she must have done earlier that morning, shuffled towards her. Maud smiled at the realisation that impersonating a charwoman would enable her to enter almost any public building without comment. The woman caught Maud's eye and smiled shyly back.

They nodded to one another as they passed, and Maud knew she would add the woman's look to her growing number of disguises. All she would need would be some padding to make her shape more matronly, a dusty black dress with an apron tied round her waist and on her head a battered straw hat. That and some soot to darken the hollows of her eyes, to make her seem older and less healthy than she was.

A man sauntered past. Men were an easy disguise to adopt. Loose shirt, trousers, tie, hat, a swagger. Two other impersonations she had already practised on the streets of Edinburgh were a clergyman and a tramp. Costume, tone of voice and gait were important. Get those right and people saw what they expected to see.

A gypsy girl, a grocer's boy, a nurse... Maud was eager to try them all. A wardrobe in her house contained a variety of costumes, whiskers and cosmetics bought from Mutrie, the theatrical outfitters. Such a cornucopia of delights!

Smiling at the thought of donning whiskers, Maud strolled on towards the statue of a cloaked William Pitt the Younger. He stood in the middle of the road where George Street met Frederick Street. Although she didn't approve of Tory politics, Pitt deserved his statue. To think that he became Britain's youngest ever Prime Minister at the age of twenty-four. Maud was twenty-five... and the way their current Prime Minister Mr Asquith, ironically a Liberal, was dragging his heels over female suffrage, women would never be able to vote, much less become Prime Minister.

'If there's one thing Edinburgh isn't short of,' Maud said to Pitt as she passed him, 'it's grand statues.'

The thoroughly unpleasant politician Henry Dundas, posturing on his one-hundred-and-fifty-foot pedestal in the middle of St Andrew Square, immediately came to her mind.

Maud turned into Frederick Street. Her blood boiled as she marched down the hill, the heat from the cobblestones under her feet propelling her on. The people of the city like to boast of statues of important Edinburghers such as philosopher David Hume, physicist James Clerk Maxwell and many more. All *men*. Even Greyfriars Bobby, the Skye terrier who famously spent years guarding the grave of his owner, had his own wee statue on a three-foot-high polished granite column.

Where were the statues of women? There were none of

women who had achieved something in their time and yet there was no shortage of candidates. Take the Seven Against Edinburgh, she thought, as she strode on down the brae; women who had to campaign to be allowed to become doctors. Surely these women were worthy of a statue.

In her preoccupation, Maud tripped on a cobblestone and slackened her pace. She was almost at the bottom of the hill and now she looked at the house nearest her to make sure she hadn't missed number 72. At the end of the road, Queen Street Gardens looked green and peaceful in the sun. Maud took a breath and tried to think calming thoughts.

She had reached number 70 and she glanced at the smart town house as she strolled past. This was where Lady Argyll lived and so had her Peke until some days ago. Close by, a narrow lane off the street presumably led to the rear of this group of houses and the garden from where Maximilian had been snatched.

Moving on, Maud came to number 72. It was a mirror image of the house next door. Impressive, stone-built, three storeys plus a basement and attic. Wrought-iron railings in front of the basement area and on either side of wide stone steps. At the top of the stairs, a grand portico and the door painted in what she believed was called Brunswick green.

Maud mounted the steps and lifted the heavy brass knocker.

After a few moments a manservant opened the door, and she quickly stored the image of him in her memory bank of disguises. His portly shape Maud knew she could manage with a lot of padding, but how would she achieve such rounded facial features? She would need to place something – a piece of apple peel, perhaps, or better still a fig – in each cheek to fatten her face. A few wisps of hair decorated the sides of his otherwise bald pate. With some whiskery tufts poking out from under a hat, Maud thought she could carry off a man of some minor importance.

'Madam?'

'Miss Maud McIntyre,' she said, reverting to herself once more. 'His lordship is expecting me.' She held out her business card.

The manservant took the card and asked her to enter and wait in the hall. Gazing round at the fine paintings hanging on the walls, her eye was caught by a ceiling light fitted with the new electric bulbs. The man returned and, her boots tapping on the parquet floor, she followed him through the hall and along a corridor, past a number of closed doors. He stopped at the end one, tapped lightly on the panelling and turned the handle.

'Miss Maud McIntyre,' he announced.

Lord Urquhart looked up from his desk. 'Thank you, Beech.'

He got to his feet and came forward, looking fresh and cool in a white shirt and cream waistcoat and trousers. Maud drew her gaze from him and sent it around the room. So this was the famous – or should that be infamous? – study.

'So this is the study?' she said, voicing her thoughts. It was a good size, with a marble mantelpiece, a full bookcase and a couple of charming watercolours. Her eyes lighted on a piece of mahogany furniture against a wall near the window. 'And that is the bureau in question?'

'You are on form today, Miss McIntyre.' He smiled.

She took a breath. If she was going to be a successful private detective, she would have to grow a thicker skin to put up with the attitude of clients.

'I'm glad you approve, Lord Urquhart.'

'This, as you rightly say, is the study and that is the bureau.' He crossed the room and lowered the flap of the bureau to reveal a green leather-topped table for writing. Behind sat a row of small drawers and narrow slots filled with paper and envelopes.

'Where exactly were the letters kept?' she asked, coming to stand next to him.

'In here.' He pulled open one of the drawers. It was empty, save for a piece of red-coloured thread. 'Seven letters, tied in a bundle with ribbon.'

'Seven?'

'One for each of the six weeks of our... relationship and one written after the lady's wedding.'

Maud looked at him. It had been a short but presumably intense affair. And the bundle lovingly tied with a ribbon? He was something of a romantic, it would seem.

'What colour is the ribbon?' she asked, feeling she already knew the answer.

'Does it matter?'

'If it were unusual, that might help to ensure I find the correct letters quickly.'

'You don't expect to read them, to see if you have found the correct ones?'

He was right. She might have to. What a distasteful thought.

'Assuming the thief has kept them bound in the same ribbon and the envelopes are addressed to you, I hope that will be sufficient to identify them.'

'I see. The ribbon is red.'

Red ribbon. Clearly, he lacked imagination, Maud thought.

'The lady sent it to me in the first letter and bid me use it around other letters she would send me.'

Perhaps she had judged him too quickly. It was the *lady* who lacked imagination.

'That is a little careless of you both. The ribbon itself would indicate the nature of the letters to anyone who was browsing in the bureau.'

'No one should have been going through my private papers in the first place.'

Maud walked to the sash window. The room faced the back of the house and had a view of the shrubbery and lawn in his garden and in that of the neighbour next door, Lady Argyll.

She pointed to the window, already ajar. 'Does this open easily?'

'Yes. Do you wish me to demonstrate?'

She nodded for him to proceed. He went to lift it, but she stopped him. 'On second thoughts, I should try it for myself. That way, we can learn what degree of strength is required.'

He stepped aside and Maud placed her fingers in the brass rings on the lip, lifted and the window glided upwards smoothly on its sash. 'So, a woman could be the thief as easily as a man.'

'I doubt that—'

'Let us stick to the facts for now.' She turned back to face him. 'As the study is on the ground floor, it would not take an intruder long to climb in through the window—'

'I doubt that a lady would find that an easy thing to do, being hampered by her clothing.' He looked a little smug, as if he'd scored a point.

'Some female cyclists, those who support the Rational Dress Movement, have worn divided skirts for the last few years,' she pointed out.

'That is true. I must confess when I pictured a woman scrambling in through my study window, I was thinking of the new fashion for the hobble skirt.'

'I think we can assume our thief was not wearing one of those ridiculous garments.' Maud's voice was cold. 'May I continue?'

'Please do.'

'Thank you,' she said. 'Having gained access to the room, the intruder needed only to walk quickly and quietly to the bureau, open it and remove the letters. He, or *she*' – Maud sent him a sharp look – 'would return the way they came and the whole episode would be over in a matter of minutes.'

Maud turned back to the open window and leaned out, careful not to dislodge the cheerful blue feather in her hat. 'Have you noticed anyone loitering around outside your house in the last few weeks?'

'No,' he replied firmly.

'The thief must have been watching the place, and you have made it rather easy for him, leaving such a convenient bench below this window.' She drew her head back in. 'No matter,' Maud said, catching sight of his dark expression. 'It is done now. And I am here to help you.' It was her turn to look smug. 'I need to examine the bench,' she went on. 'If I with my height can't reach the window, then you're probably right, it wasn't a woman.'

She followed him out into the corridor. Instead of turning left for the hall, he turned in the other direction and led her to a plain door.

'This takes us into the garden,' he said, sliding a bolt and opening it.

In front of her was a lawn with a stone sundial in the centre. Around the four sides of the garden ran a path. The boundary was marked by stone walls on either side and a higher wall at the bottom. Only a faint sound of traffic from Frederick Street could be heard. Maud walked along the path taking her in the direction of Lady Argyll's garden next door.

Maud was peering over this wall, when Lord Urquhart came to stand beside her.

'You are interested in my neighbour?'

'Does she come into her garden often?'

'Hardly at all. She's an elderly lady and spends most of her time indoors with the curtains drawn to keep out the sun. She lets her dog into the garden and when he barks, she calls him back in.' He paused. 'Now I come to think of it, I haven't heard the animal for some days.'

When Maud made no comment, he said, 'Do you think the intruder climbed over the neighbour's wall to get into my garden?'

'It's possible.'

'But unnecessary. Come with me.'

He strode across the lawn to the back wall of the garden, and she followed. He lifted a cascade of sweet-scented honeysuckle to reveal a low wooden door. 'It leads into a close that runs the length of this section of houses, although this entrance is no longer used.' He dropped the tangled vine to hang back over the door.

The hinges were on the side where they stood, which meant the door opened into the garden. Maud examined the honeysuckle but could see no damage. It looked unlikely that the door had been opened and in the process torn the plant. She looked down. There had been no rain for a while and so the path was dry with no obvious footprints.

Turning the handle, she pulled. The door creaked open. Stepping into the alley, Maud saw only a path of rough grass running to the left and right between the walls of the gardens in this street and those behind. No lighting. At night, it would be very dark here.

She stepped back into Lord Urquhart's garden and considered the rear of his house. There was his study on the ground floor, with its window open as she had left it. Despite the lack of damage to the honeysuckle, the intruder had to have entered through the garden. What if the thief were slim enough to slip through a slightly open door, thereby causing no disturbance to the vine? From the corner of her eye Maud caught Lord Urquhart watching her, but she continued with her train of thought.

There was the matter of the barking dog. Had one thief

snatched Maximilian and another, entirely unrelated, taken the letters? That was surely too much of a coincidence. Or was one person responsible, removing the little creature because he was loudly announcing the presence of the correspondence thief?

Once again Maud wondered how the thief knew the letters existed and where they were kept. Anyone standing here, watching the study window before the packet was taken, would have been able to see very little of any activity taking place in the room. The bureau stood close to the window, but not that close. There were too many factors against a random thief. He – or *she* – had at least to have known of the existence of the letters.

Yet if the dog had disturbed the intruder, why had they taken the animal, as that had surely increased the ferocity of its barking?

'Now I wish to see how tall an intruder would have to be to lever themselves up off the bench and into your study.' Maud set off briskly across the lawn.

The wooden bench was immediately below the window. 'Could you help me up, please?'

She held out one hand, with the other lifted the hem of her skirt an inch or two, and began to raise her foot to step up. Before she could do so, Lord Urquhart's hands were round her waist and he lifted her onto the bench.

'For goodness' sake,' Maud spluttered.

'It was clear you weren't going to be able to climb up unaided.' He glanced at her skirt. 'Not in that outfit.'

She was sure she would have managed, but this was not the moment to discuss the rights and wrongs of men's behaviour. She didn't want his hands around her again, so she looked over her shoulder and said in a firm voice, 'I will not be climbing in through the window, simply trying to ascertain how tall or muscled the intruder had to be. Kindly take a step or two back.'

'Certainly.' He moved a little away.

She could now concentrate on the window. If she climbed onto the back of the bench, it would surely be an easy matter to sit on the sill, swivel round and slide down into the room. Easing up her skirt a tiny bit further, she put one foot on the seat's back and raised herself on to the deep windowsill.

'As you can see, Lord Urquhart,' she said, a note of triumph in her voice, 'it would not be so difficult to enter your study through the window.'

Before he could step forward to help her from the bench, Maud slid off the sill, onto the seat and jumped nimbly to the path. She brushed her hands clean, straightened her clothes and checked her hat was still securely on her head. 'Shall we go indoors?'

He led her back into his study, where she reminded him of her daily fee and added that she had every reason to believe she should have the crime solved within the week he had given her. He didn't blanch at the amount, even though it was the equivalent of an office clerk's salary for an entire year. But Maud knew this was what male private detectives charged and she was sure she would prove to be worth the same as any of them.

Lord Urquhart went to the bureau, opened a second drawer and removed a bulky envelope. 'Half the payment now.' He handed it to Maud.

'You are still keeping valuables in there?' She wasn't able to keep the surprise out of her voice. She took the money without being so vulgar as to count it in front of him, dropped the envelope into her satchel and secured the fastening.

'I now keep the bureau locked,' he said, 'and the key with me. I opened it just before you arrived.'

Maud nodded her approval. 'Let us consider motive. You said yesterday that you believed it was political.'

'I did.'

'And do you still think that?'

He indicated the two leather chairs placed near the hearth.

A finely woven fire screen hid the empty grate behind. Maud took a seat, and he sat down opposite her.

'A political explanation seems the most logical one,' he said. 'Sebastian Ferguson is a young and ambitious man. A Tory Member of Parliament with his eye on the top job, if I'm not mistaken. Imagine if it got out that his new wife pined for her former love and had written the gentleman a letter saying so. It would embarrass the husband and doubtless hamper, if not outright ruin, his career and destroy all hope of his rise in government.'

Maud's foot tapped on the plush carpet as she took a moment to think. Certainly, the newspapers and society magazines were trumpeting Sebastian Ferguson as a possible next leader of the party.

'Who do you think is the likeliest candidate to wish Mr Ferguson political harm?'

Lord Urquhart gave a short laugh. 'It could be almost anyone in his parliamentary party or indeed in the Commons.'

Maud frowned. 'It would be an impossible task to investigate all of them, not least because we have less than six days to retrieve the correspondence. Do you have any thoughts on who else might want the letters – someone with no political design?'

He shrugged. 'If the thief simply wished to blackmail me, I imagine I would have heard from them by now.'

'That does seem likely.' She thought for a moment. 'And you had no callers at the time the letters vanished?'

'It must have happened last Tuesday night or Wednesday morning. Shortly before I went out in the evening, for some unfathomable reason I removed the letters from the drawer, intending to dispose of them. I wish to God I had now! Something stopped me: a misplaced sense of loyalty to the love we'd had, I suppose. I put them back in the drawer.' He shook his head.

'What made you notice they had gone?'

'When I arrived home in the morning, I could see that the bureau had been opened. Whoever had done it must have closed the flap too quickly and the edge of a sheet of writing paper was caught in the hinge.' He frowned. 'It didn't take me long to discover the letters had been taken.'

He bent his head and rubbed a hand across his forehead. For the moment, his confident manner had forsaken him. The clock on the mantelpiece chimed the half-hour, and he raised his head, revealing just how pale he had become.

'My apologies, I am forgetting my duty as a host. Can I offer you some tea, Miss McIntyre?'

'No, thank you,' Maud said. 'I must interview your servants.'

NINETEEN

It was late in the afternoon by the time Maud had spoken to Lord Urquhart's servants and made her way to Mr Laing's lodgings. He opened the door to his rooms and removed the cigar from his mouth. 'Miss McIntyre. Pleased to meet you again.' He extended his free hand to her, and she shook it.

'I hadn't realised that you and the little redhead were private detectives until the Duchess told us everything on that last evening at Duddingston. Lady detectives, well, well. Who'd have thought there were such things. It's a mad world, with men taking to the skies in machines made of wood and canvas, and women wanting the vote.'

Maud bristled at his comment, but if he'd seen her response, he gave no sign. He gestured for her to enter.

'You should have joined us for breakfast the following morning,' he went on, closing the door behind her. 'It would have been fascinating to learn the methods you employed to catch the Colonel.'

'Miss Cameron and I felt it more prudent to have breakfast in my room. We were of the opinion that after such an active house party, it would be less embarrassing all round.'

He laughed. 'Less embarrassing for whom? I doubt I would have been embarrassed.' His eye travelled over her in a most impudent manner.

Maud was shocked at his abrupt change of character. Where was the personable young man she'd meet at Duddingston House? Back on his home territory, this must be the real Douglas Laing.

She sent him a freezing look, which would have withered most decent men but didn't seem to make any difference to his perusal of her person.

'Mr Laing,' she said in an abrupt tone. It brought his attention back to her face. 'In my role as a detective, albeit a female one, I have been asked by Lord Miller to investigate the disappearance of his daughter, Miss Diana Miller, your fiancée.'

He narrowed his eyes as he puffed on his cigar, which made it difficult for Maud to identify what emotion lay there.

'I believe her father informed you he's asked me to act on his behalf in this matter.'

Mr Laing grunted and nodded, then gestured with his cigar for Maud to take a seat. He sat opposite.

'I hope you found my rooms without too much difficulty. Lawnmarket is convenient for court. When I have built up my reputation and of course my fortune, I shall look for a small country estate.'

Mingling with the aristocracy, a High Court judge for a father-in-law... 'It's clear to see you are an ambitious man, Mr Laing.'

Maud's gaze travelled round the room. Walls unadorned with pictures, serviceable oak furniture. A functional room; the room of a man with his mind on other things. She could see no photograph of his fiancée, but now she noticed on the desk a framed certificate of his qualification. He followed the direction of her gaze.

'I read law at the University of St Andrews. It also happens to be Lord Miller's alma mater.'

Of course. When Maud didn't immediately respond, he went on, 'I am a busy man, Miss McIntyre. You are fortunate to catch me at home this afternoon. I'm preparing for a High Court trial on Friday, as you see.' He indicated a pile of documents on the desk, the pink ribbon discarded by its side. 'One of those suffragette types.'

'I take it you do not approve of women's suffrage or the demands they are making?'

'No, I do not. Many of the women are from good families and should know better. They could stay at home and be quite comfortable whilst their fathers or husbands provide for them, but they choose to draw attention to themselves in a most unladylike way. And so, Miss McIntyre, I also do not approve of their methods.'

'Some of their tactics are extreme, I will allow you that, but their wish to be heard is reasonable, is it not?' She paused as he gave a short laugh. 'How is it that this case is being heard now? I thought the suffragette movement had agreed to be dormant out of respect for the coronation.' George V and his wife, Mary, had been crowned in June, but the truce was for the summer.

Mr Laing shrugged one shoulder. 'Which shows the suffragettes cannot be trusted.'

The look he sent Maud could only be described as challenging. She held his gaze and spoke in a measured tone.

'It seems the case you mention concerns only one woman. A woman who became a little overzealous, perhaps. Let us hope the Prime Minister keeps to his side of the bargain and at the end of the year addresses the suffragettes' demands. It would be refreshing to see a man, particularly a powerful man, willing to listen to the request of a weaker party, don't you think?'

He set down his cigar in the ashtray. 'I don't. The movement is causing disruption in society at a time when it is not needed. Surely the more intelligent amongst these women must see that with the possibility of a European war, the threat of civil war in Ireland and the rabble-rousers on the docks, we need domestic peace. There is dissent everywhere you turn these days.'

Society was changing, but in some respects that was no bad thing. 'After thirty years of peaceful campaigning by the suffragette movement, can you wonder there are now militant campaigners? It would be so simple to grant women the vote.'

'Women's suffrage is not my concern.' His nostrils flared white as he breathed in deeply. 'I'm sure Mr Asquith knows what he is doing. It is my job to prosecute those who break the law. However, you are not here to debate legal matters, for which you have no training.'

'On that score, you are of course correct, Mr Laing. Any help you can give me in my quest to find Miss Miller would be greatly appreciated.' It cost her nothing to lay it on a bit thick, especially if his information led her to find the young woman.

His feathers now a little less ruffled and his sense of superiority returned, he sat back in his armchair and steepled his fingers just below his chin. It was a pose Maud could imagine him employing when waiting his turn to speak in court.

'I'm not sure that I can help, I'm afraid. Diana is very much her own girl, you know. I'm sure her father is worrying unnecessarily and that she's staying with a friend. No doubt she'll soon return home.'

Was he talking about the woman he professed to *love*? Where was the anxiety, the urgency he should be feeling? Maud decided that Diana Miller had almost certainly run away.

'She was last seen on Saturday morning. It is now Wednesday afternoon. That means your fiancée has been missing for at least four days. Are you not just a little concerned, sir? Can you think of nothing that might have made her abscond a fortnight before your wedding? Because if you cannot, then I must start to look at this case as a possible kidnapping.'

He dropped his hands and held her gaze. For a moment, Maud read something very like hatred in his eyes. 'I would never attempt to restrict Diana's movements and I don't expect her to restrict mine.'

He smiled and that look vanished. 'Regardless of what may have prompted her to take herself away for a while, I'm sure she'll soon come to her senses.'

'Then perhaps she hasn't been kidnapped, but has run off to join the Women's Freedom League.' Maud wanted to snatch back the words as soon as they left her mouth and his expression confirmed they should have remained unsaid.

He picked up his cigar and got to his feet. 'If you will excuse me, Miss McIntyre, I have work to do.'

Unbelievable – the man showed no concern. Maud knew she had to test him on another matter which continued to worry her. 'One further question, if I may.'

He waited with bad grace.

'Who do you think is the Duddingston jewel thief and murderer?'

'What?' His voice was sharp as he stared at her. 'The case is solved.'

'Is it?' Maud held his gaze.

'Yes. Now you must go. I am a busy man.'

Maud allowed him to show her out of the building, and she thanked him for his help, while a voice in her head told her that neither he nor his story was to be trusted. After all, wasn't that what advocates did, construct stories?

She rounded the corner into Bank Street, leaned against the wall and shut her eyes. Despite the appearance he'd cultivated at Duddingston House, Mr Laing was certainly not a pleasant man. He was overbearing and a bully, and showed indifference to the disappearance of his fiancée and satisfaction at the thought of prosecuting a suffragette. A chill went down her back just thinking about his callousness.

'Are you all right, lass?'

Maud's eyes flew open. A middle-aged man stood in front of her, his brow wrinkled.

She managed a smile. 'Yes, thank you.'

'Well, if you're sure.' The man tipped his hat and went on his way.

The stranger had shown more concern for her than Douglas Laing had for his fiancée. Her throat was suddenly dry.

TWENTY

'How is your friend's mother?' Maud asked Daisy the following morning, as she spread a generous portion of marmalade on her toast. Doing *pliés* and the like always gave her an appetite.

'Much better, thanks. I think the poor wifie's lonely, more than anything else. She enjoyed my story about the agency, anyway – just the one where I grabbed the wrong wee dog,' she added, seeing the alarmed look on Maud's face. 'How did you get on with Mr Laing yesterday?'

'There's no love lost between him and the suffragette movement.'

'What did he say, then?'

'He's prosecuting a suffragette tomorrow. His view is that most of them are from respectable families and should stay at home to be looked after by their fathers or husbands.'

Daisy scowled. 'The man's a gowk.'

Maud couldn't disagree with that.

From outside came the distinctive beep of a Napier's hooter. 'The car – it's here.' Maud dropped her toast onto the plate and ran to the window.

Lifting the sash, she leaned out and looked down on

Archie's dark head – he never would wear a driving cap – and called out to him. 'Archie!' He looked up, grinned and waved back.

'Come on, Daisy,' Maud prompted her astonished friend, 'let's go down and admire our new temporary possession.'

Maud clattered down the stairs, Daisy close behind, and flung open the door to the street.

'Special delivery,' shouted Archie above the chug of the engine as he climbed out of the car. 'Napier Colonial Tourer. She's a beauty.'

She was indeed. Bright blue with a cream top and chestnut-brown upholstery. Archie polished the gleaming paintwork with the sleeve of his blazer. Maud smiled. She was already as in love with the motor car as he was.

'Where would you like her?' Archie asked.

'There are the old stables round the back, but first come indoors and have a cup of tea,' she urged.

He shook his head. 'No time, sis. Sorry. Need to get the train down to Southampton, where I'll board the ship for Alexandria.'

'Then let me drive you to the railway station.'

'Good idea. Then you can see how she handles – and I can see how you handle her.'

'I'll be fine. You know I grew up driving father's car around the estate.'

'Yes, but a Rover isn't the same as a Napier Tourer.'

Maud jumped into the driver's seat. 'Hop in the back, Daisy.'

With Archie in the passenger seat next to her, she put the Napier into gear and, a wide smile on her face, she moved smoothly off and drove the mile to the station.

. . .

The shiny Napier tucked up in the stables for the time being, Maud and Daisy sat facing each other across the office desk, the typewriter pushed firmly to one side, as they reviewed what they knew about the Miller case.

'I feel sure Miss Miller has not been abducted,' Maud said. 'No one lurked in hiding and caught her unawares. There was no fracas in the street. The newspapers would have got hold of the story if there had been.'

Daisy agreed. 'It's not as if she was snatched in the dead of night. She disappeared in broad daylight.'

'According to her father, when she set off from home on Saturday morning she was in especially good spirits, which he put down to her imminent wedding. She was to call at her friend's house and then the two of them would make their way to the dressmaker's. Miss Miller didn't arrive at the house of her friend, Miss Grant, and she didn't keep the appointment with Madame Escoffier. When I interviewed Miss Grant, she was subdued, as well she might be, worried about her missing friend, but she spoke as if she had learned her response to my questions.'

'It sounds like she's hiding something.'

'Madame Escoffier was of the opinion that her customer was not as excited about her forthcoming marriage as a young bride usually is. Not only that, Miss Miller was becoming more quiet as the date of the wedding approached.'

'So, she wasna looking forward to her wedding,' said Daisy, 'but she was excited about the fitting of her wedding dress?'

'Which makes me think that she might have been excited about something else,' Maud murmured.

'A different appointment entirely?'

'Yes.'

'And there's the matter of her likeness taken as a gift to her faither, even though there would be a wedding portrait within a few weeks.'

'Exactly, Daisy.'

'Then the photographer told us that she'd been accompanied to the portrait session by a dashing young fellow in a kilt.' Daisy looked at Maud. 'Are you thinking the same thing I am?'

'I feel certain I am.'

'That she's run off with her handsome lover. I canna say I blame her,' Daisy added. 'That Laing is a nasty piece of work.'

'Hmm, yes, Mr Laing,' Maud mused. 'He's something of a dark horse. Miss Miller's father approves of him, but that seems to be based on his skill in the courtroom. Laing didn't appear concerned about Diana's disappearance, saying she will return in her own good time and—'

'Michty me!' Daisy suddenly exclaimed. 'He is involved in the Duddingston case!'

Maud stared at her. 'What on earth makes you say that?'

'He cares an awfa lot about money and status, wants to buy an estate of his own – this is from what you've told me, mind.'

Maud nodded, still staring at her friend.

'He's engaged to the daughter of a High Court judge,' Daisy went on, 'although he doesna care for her. He's been hobnobbing with Duchesses and the like—'

'And with his prosecution work, he'll know the right people to sell jewellery on without asking questions! Michty me, indeed.' They smiled at each other.

Maud sobered. 'On the night the necklace was stolen and the Viscountess murdered, Mr Laing and Lord Urquhart were the first two I saw out of their rooms. Lord Urquhart's bedroom was closer to the Viscountess's and he was already doing up the belt of his dressing gown, which led me to think he could be the guilty person. But equally Mr Laing could have done the deed and dashed back to his doorway. His dressing gown not yet fastened could have been a ruse.'

'But how did he get the jewellery out of the room? And why did he later throw it out of the Colonel's window?'

'Oh, those questions again,' Maud said, irritation in her voice. 'I don't know the answers – yet – but I'm sure we will discover them in due course.'

The subject of the Colonel was an uncomfortable one. 'Don't look so bad, Daisy; the evidence at the time, such as it was, pointed to the Colonel and I was also persuaded.'

Daisy gave a wry smile. 'Now we must start all over again with the Duddingston investigation.'

'Not quite. The suffragette trial is tomorrow. I'll attend to see if I can find out anything about Mr Laing. If I can't, then we'll go back to see the Duchess.'

'Laing must think we are dafties.'

'It doesn't matter what he thinks, if we've now got there.'

Feeling pleased with this morning's progress, Maud gave some thought to the afternoon.

'What do you say to taking a stroll round Charlotte Square in the hope of spotting Mrs Ferguson, the MP's wife, and perhaps learning something useful? We have only five days left to retrieve the stolen letters.'

Maud had no clear idea why she felt they should observe her, but she had a hunch it was the right thing to do. She didn't know the number of the Fergusons' house, so while Daisy nipped out to buy apples from the costermonger, Maud consulted *Who's Who*.

'We'll pretend to admire the imposing statue of Prince Albert on his horse,' Maud said, when Daisy returned with their makeshift early luncheon, 'but we'll be observing the houses around the square.'

They were coming to the end of the Trades Fortnight and children in their smartest clothes were being promenaded along George Street by their parents, while from Princes Street Gardens came the sound of a jolly tune as the brass band struck up in the Ross Bandstand. Maud felt as if she too were on holiday. Last month, the temperature in Perth reached almost ninety degrees, and this month, it was edging towards one hundred in the shade at Greenwich. It felt close to that here.

She took off her straw boater and dabbed at her forehead with her handkerchief. Her pale-blue cotton blouse tucked into the blue and white striped skirt felt stifling and her long corset didn't help; sweat was beginning to trickle down her back.

'Shall we have an ice cream?' Maud found herself saying. 'I'm rather warm and those ices do look so inviting.'

Daisy followed Maud's gaze towards the children and young men and women eating ices in the sunshine, bought from a man with a cart.

'I wouldna say no to a Penny Lick,' she said.

'Sorry?'

'Those ices. They're known as Penny Licks.'

As they watched, the glass goblets were licked clean and handed back to the seller. He rinsed them ready for the next customer. Maud weighed up the objections to a young lady eating in the street and her concern about poorly washed containers, versus the tantalising pull of the cool ices.

'Yes,' she said quickly, before she could change her mind. 'Buy one for each of us, Daisy.' Drawing her purse from the little bag on her wrist, she gave her two copper coins.

Daisy hastened away and returned within minutes with two glasses filled with vanilla-flavoured ices already melting. Maud felt positively daring, standing there on the street, letting the cold, sweet mix slide down her throat.

Seeing her face, Daisy laughed. 'You should enjoy yourself more often, Maud.'

Perhaps she should; it was quite a good feeling.

With the goblets returned to the man, they walked on and turned into Charlotte Square. It was quiet here, away from the busy street, and they were able to stroll along looking like nothing more than two young ladies out for their afternoon constitutional.

'Och, some bonnie houses here,' Daisy remarked.

'It certainly is a prestigious address, and one I can imagine Sebastian Ferguson and his wife not wishing to relinquish.'

Robert Adam had designed the town houses on the sides of the square as continuous blocks to make each set of frontages look like a palace, and he'd succeeded. The houses were grand, built in pale stone, with large windows and steps up to each front door. In the middle of the square stood the private garden surrounded by railings.

'Let's first admire the statue of Prince Albert,' Maud suggested. 'Anyone peering out of their window would expect to see two ladies do that.'

They wandered along the wide public path running through the centre of the gardens and stood for a while looking up at the statue of Albert astride a horse. Then they turned their attention to the base of the plinth and the four figures to represent science, labour, army and navy, and nobility.

'That's enough of that,' said Daisy.

She urged Maud through the gardens, just in time. As they emerged onto the pavement, a young woman came tripping buoyantly down the steps of an end house. She wore a white dress with lace and tucks, and a pale-pink hat with a rose at the brim. To shield her fair complexion from the sun, she held up a white lace parasol. At the bottom of the steps, the young woman turned in the direction of George Street, giving Maud and Daisy barely a glance as she passed by.

Daisy let out a breath. 'Do you think that was Mrs F.? She's so beautiful and elegant.'

'There's only one way to find out. Come with me...'

The woman had disappeared from view. Maud marched up the steps to the house she'd come from and pulled the bell at the side. Almost immediately the front door opened.

'Can I help you, madam?' The elderly butler looked at Maud and then Daisy.

'Is Mrs Ferguson at home?' Maud's heart was hammering as she prayed the woman they'd seen was Stella Ferguson. If not, they'd be confronted by a stranger, and she would need to think quickly why they wanted to see her.

'I regret, madam, that you have just missed her.'

So she *was* the bewitching woman. 'No matter, we will call again another time.' Maud turned to leave, glancing at Daisy to follow.

'What name shall I say?' called the butler.

Maud continued down the steps, as if she'd not heard the man. They walked as fast as they dared without attracting attention, not looking back until they reached the anonymity of busy George Street.

Maud felt hotter than ever. Mrs Ferguson had to be kept under observation, but where had she gone?

'Maud,' hissed Daisy. 'Look to your left.'

They were outside Clarissa's Tea Rooms. Maud glanced through the window.

There was Lord Urquhart, pulling out a chair at a small table, for afternoon tea *tête-à-tête* with Mrs Stella Ferguson.

Maud took Daisy's arm and almost dragged the poor girl along the road, until they were past the tea shop.

'I think you saw what I did,' Daisy said, a little breathless, as they came to a halt.

'Yes.' Maud nodded grimly. 'Now we can be certain that the lady is Mrs Ferguson, but what is Lord Urquhart playing at? He told me the relationship was over and yet there he was... Words fail me.'

Daisy gave a shrug. 'We are being paid to recover the letters and that's all that matters.'

She was right, although Maud didn't feel as reasonable as did Daisy. She felt as if she were being made a fool of, but she wasn't sure in what way. 'I need to think what this means. First, though, let's find another tea shop and have a cup of tea ourselves.'

'I'm not sure there is another one close enough for us to be able to keep an eye on his lordship and Mrs F.'

It occurred to Maud that there was something more they could do than observe the woman. 'It's time we put on a disguise,' she said and saw Daisy's eyes light up. 'This evening we will enter Stella Ferguson's house and examine the contents of her bureau. I don't believe she is as innocent as she looks. Come on.' They resumed walking. 'I noticed this afternoon there's a drainpipe at the side of the Fergusons' house. I will shin up—'

'You canna do that, miss! It's too dangerous. You might fall.'

Maud hid a smile at Daisy's temporary return to the role of her maid. 'I've been climbing trees since I was a little girl.'

That was one of the great advantages of having three older brothers. They were away at school during term time, but when they were home for the holidays, Maud followed them around, joining in their games which often involved climbing.

'But rhone pipes are nae the same as trees,' said Daisy, dodging round a young woman pushing a perambulator. 'They're smoother, for one thing.'

'They are, but they also have brackets to hold them to the wall.'

Daisy's horrified expression made Maud laugh out loud.

'Don't worry,' Maud said, 'I'll not be doing it in skirts.'

Daisy frowned. 'There might not be an open window to slip through.'

'The night is warm, so there's bound to be one open. I'll climb in, find her secretaire, which hopefully is in her bedroom or dressing room, and with any luck retrieve the missing letters.'

Daisy didn't look as convinced as Maud had hoped. 'As long as you realise something could easily go wrong,' she said.

What would Raffles do? Not that their situations were comparable, because he was interested in his own gain and she... well, Maud was trying to do the *right* thing.

Who was she trying to persuade? Breaking into another person's house was against the law, no matter what the reason.

Daisy interrupted her thoughts. 'Is it housebreaking if the window is already open?'

'I seem to remember reading that only if the window is opened further in order to gain access is it housebreaking. Although' – Maud skirted round a small boy on the pavement intent on bowling his hoop between the two women – 'the same is true if the window is at a distance from the ground, requiring a ladder – or a drainpipe – to reach it.'

'What if the letters aren't there? After all, someone else might have taken them from Lord Urquhart's study.'

'Such as a complete stranger who broke in looking for valuables, but came across the correspondence and realised their potential value?'

'Aye.'

'Yet our culprit has apparently done nothing with the letters, so there seems little point in having taken them.'

'Perhaps he's waiting for the husband to return and then will deliver the packet to him. Why don't we wait until Mr F. comes home, watch the place and get to the thief before he presents the letters?'

'Because' – *Dr Watson*, Maud mentally added – 'we have no idea who the thief is. We can hardly accost every visitor to their house.'

Daisy sighed.

'Don't lose heart,' Maud said. 'There are three broad possibilities. If the thief paid one of Lord Urquhart's servants to take the letters, presumably for political reasons, then it would be almost impossible to find the package.'

Daisy nodded glumly.

'A second possibility is that another ex-lover of Stella Ferguson, angry that she chose to marry Sebastian Ferguson, took the
letters with a view to publicly shaming her.'

'I canna see that,' said Daisy. 'For a start, we don't know that
she had any other lovers apart from Lord Urquhart.'

'Anyway, that's a long shot. Lastly, then, is the theory I'm
working on at present. Stella Ferguson herself arranged for the
correspondence to be stolen, to cause Lord Urquhart concern
and thereby punish him for not responding to her post-marriage
plea to resume their relationship.'

They'd reached the door to the side of the stationer's shop.
Daisy pushed it open, and they mounted the stairs. At the top,
Maud unlocked the office door and they entered.

'If it is her paying him back,' Daisy said, as she dropped into
a chair, 'how did she know that he hadna already destroyed the
letters?'

That was a good question, and one Maud hadn't considered. 'She didn't *know,* of course,' she said slowly, 'but I'm
certain she's confident enough in her own attractions to be sure
he hasn't.'

Daisy didn't look convinced. 'Why do you think they were
having tea together this afternoon?'

'That I can't explain. What if he wanted to tell her the
letters were missing, to avoid embarrassment if she found this
out from another source?'

'Then doesna that mean that someone other than her took
them?'

'No, only that Lord Urquhart *thinks* someone else is
responsible.'

Daisy blew out a breath. 'This is getting complicated.'

'I never said the life of a private detective was going to be
easy.' She glanced at her wristwatch. 'It's three o'clock. Can you
type up a progress report for Lord Miller and the invoice for the
Duchess? I'm going out for a while.'

'We've only just got in.'

'I know, but I want to see a demonstration of a new machine called the vacuum cleaner.' Maud had spotted the notice in Jenners' window the previous day on their way to the photographer's studio. 'It sucks up dirt and dust off floors and all sorts of surfaces. Think how much time that will save Martha.'

'It's nae the beast of a machine that was seen on the streets in London a few years ago?'

They'd pored over a picture in the newspaper of a large horse-drawn vehicle painted with the words The British Vacuum Cleaner Company. There was a special glass chamber on the other side to show the amount of dust collected through a long hose fed through a window of the house. 'No, this is much smaller. It looks like a broomstick with a dust-collecting bag on the end.'

Daisy muttered something about the unfairness of having to sit in front of the typewriter while Maud prepared to swan off.

'What you're doing is essential work,' Maud reminded her. 'We can't function if we don't receive payments.'

'Then you type and I'll go out.'

'You know I can't type.'

'You could if you'd let me teach you.'

'And,' Maud added firmly, ignoring her last comment, 'you need to be here as another client might come into the office at any time in urgent need of our assistance.' She softened her tone. 'When you've done that, go home and rest for a while. Tonight, we'll put on our disguises and return to Charlotte Square.'

She huffed, but Maud could see she was mollified. Before Daisy could say anything else, Maud went out the door.

TWENTY-ONE

The vacuum cleaner demonstration at Jenners was edifying, but Maud wouldn't be able to afford one for a long time.

Pushing aside her disappointment, she sat sipping tea at a little table in a tea shop on Princes Street and mulled over what she and Daisy had discussed today. She drew her notebook from her bag and started to jot down a new set of notes.

First, the Miller case. She focused on why Miss Grant had repeated exactly what Maud believed the young woman had been told to say. Then Maud went over the interview with Madame Escoffier and how she hinted at Diana Miller's unhappiness with her forthcoming marriage. And Mr Laing said Diana was sure to return home shortly, having come to her senses...

That was a particularly unpleasant phrase that told Maud nothing.

Did all know more than they were saying? She sighed.

She looked up as Lord Urquhart dropped into the chair beside her. He smiled. 'Are you working on my case?'

She put down her cup. 'Not at present.'

'Then you should be.' He raised a hand to call over the waitress and ordered a second pot of tea with an assortment of fancy cakes.

'I don't need any cake, thank you,' Maud said firmly.

'The sugar will improve thinking,' he said, equally firmly. 'I'm assuming of course that the notebook in which you are writing is for the purpose of keeping in order your thinking on the case.'

Maud closed the notebook to stop him from peeking, which she was certain he was more than capable of doing. 'This is a different investigation.'

'Can I help? Two minds are better than one.'

'No, I already have a very able assistant in Miss Cameron. Besides, you haven't signed the Official Secrets Act.'

He grinned. 'Have you?'

He was right. The legislation wasn't due to receive royal assent for a few more days and even when it became law, a private detective wouldn't be required to sign it.

'It's a question of client confidentiality. Think of it in the same way you would view a doctor taking the Hippocratic oath.'

'But I can be very circumspect. After all, you didn't notice me come into the tea shop until I sat next to you.'

Maud pursed her lips. 'That's not quite the same thing and you know it.'

'Ah, here we are. Thank you so much.' The waitress set the cake stand and teapot on the table.

'I'll just get your china, sir.'

The girl returned with a tray bearing another cup and saucer, two plates with knives and napkins, and set them on the table.

'Please have a cake,' he said to Maud. 'The madeleines look delicious.'

She picked up a tiny, shell-shaped sponge cake and bit into it. Sweetness flooded her mouth. 'Mmm, it *is* delicious.'

'There! What did I say? You look happier already. Perhaps I can be equally as helpful in other matters.'

She fixed him with a gaze. 'Do you have no gainful employment of your own you should be attending to?'

'Sadly, no. Which is why, when I was passing and saw you sitting here, I immediately resolved to make myself useful to you.'

She took a sip of tea and stared at him over the rim. Then she would make use of him, Maud thought. It would be interesting to know what he thought of Mr Laing.

'How well do you know the other members of the house party at Duddingston?'

He frowned. 'I thought that case was resolved.'

'I'm asking you for another reason.'

'Well, I've known the Duchess and her two daughters for some time. Swinton is a member of my club, and I've met him and his wife at a few social gatherings. Do you want me to include the Drummonds in my answer?'

'No, that's not necessary.'

'Very well. Let's see. Miss Taft I tend to avoid if at all possible. I'm aware that she's a fairly well-known novelist.' He folded his arms and shook his head. 'Have you read any of her books? They really are the most awful bilge.'

Maud raised an eyebrow. 'I'm aware they are romantic novels aimed at women, if that's what you mean.'

'I'm as romantic as the next fellow—'

She snorted.

'But her work is maudlin,' he continued.

'It is light, attractive reading,' she corrected.

'Hmm.'

Would he never get to Douglas Laing?

'I'd met Colonel Morrison at other country house parties,' Lord Urquhart went on, unfolding his arms. 'He attended a number of them, from what I'd heard. Which is not surprising, as it turned out.'

Maud waited for the last name.

'The other fellow, Douglas Laing, I've spoken to only once or twice at other house parties. Why do you ask?' He poured a second cup of tea for her and one for himself.

'I just wondered,' she said.

'How delightfully exciting this is! *No case too big or too small* should be your agency's motto. Or perhaps *McIntyre for hire.*'

'Shh, keep your voice down.' She glanced around the tea shop. The other customers were too involved in conversations with their own companions to have overheard. 'You are being ridiculous.'

He gave a melodramatic sigh. 'I suppose I should go. If we are frequently seen together, it might give the wrong impression.' He got to his feet, pulled some coins from his trouser pocket and left them on the table. There was more than enough to cover the cost of their teas and the cake.

'Goodbye for now, Miss McIntyre.' He replaced his straw boater and strolled out of the tea shop.

Maud drank the rest of her tea, replaced the cup in the saucer and turned to unhook the strap of her leather bag from the back of her chair.

'Excuse me, madam.'

'Yes?' She turned back to see the waitress holding out a folded piece of paper.

'This was left for you.'

'For me?' Maud took it from her. 'From the gentleman who left a moment ago, the one I was taking tea with?' Why had he not simply come back and told her whatever it was he wished her to know?

'No, madam. It was delivered by a boy.'

A boy?

Maud opened the single sheet as the waitress returned to the counter and she read the six words written in simple print across the page.

Stop asking questions about Miss Miller.

A slither of ice crept up Maud's spine. This was a warning note; the first she'd ever received. Pushing the paper into her bag and gathering up her gloves, she hastened over to the counter.

'The boy who left the note for me just now,' Maud whispered to the waitress as she was about to pick up a tray of tea things for a customer. 'What did he look like?'

The young woman paused and frowned. 'He was an ordinary-looking boy.'

'What sort of age? Was he dark or fair? There must be something you can tell me.' She kept her voice low.

The waitress shook her head. 'Not really, madam. He was just a boy with brown hair. Excuse me, but I have a customer waiting.' She lifted the tray and moved away.

Maud dashed out into the street. There were too many pedestrians passing in both directions for her to see an ordinary-looking boy with brown hair. Should she go right or left? Maud turned right and hurried along the pavement, peering into each shop she passed. There was no one fitting that description. She turned back and did the same in the other direction. Nothing. The boy had gone.

Maud was sure he hadn't written the letter, but had simply been paid to deliver it. The author couldn't have known that she'd be in that tea shop at that time, as it had been a spur of the moment decision. It had to be someone who was following her; someone who knew she was investigating the case. But who would leave a note for her – a note warning her off the case – and why?

TWENTY-TWO

Maud walked back to the apartment, looking over her shoulder perhaps a little too frequently, but she managed to keep a grip on her nerves.

The writer of the note would not frighten her off. Would Sherlock Holmes panic and run screaming to Dr Watson? No. He would calmly work out the clues and act on them, bringing the case to a successful resolution.

So why did the note make her heart beat faster than usual and have her glancing behind as she walked? Because this wasn't fiction but *real life*. And she had no idea if the note-writer was a murderous maniac. It suddenly occurred to her that she didn't own a gun. And that since a person over the age of eighteen could purchase a licence by paying ten shillings at the counter of any Post Office, it was possible that her stealthy pursuer had a firearm.

Maud did have a hat pin, though, and that was a dangerous weapon, as long as her attacker came in close enough for her to make use of it. Straightening her shoulders, she strode on.

Eventually, the number of people about in the busy streets helped her to get things into perspective, and her rhythmic stride was strangely soothing. She reached Broughton Street almost before she knew it.

Daisy was sliding a shepherd's pie into the oven when Maud entered the kitchen. She closed the oven door and straightened. 'You have a note.'

Maud paused in the act of removing her hat pin. There was something about the way Daisy said it that made Maud think it wasn't just any old note.

'Is it a note warning me off the case?' she asked.

Daisy's eyes widened. 'How did you ken that?'

Maud dropped her hat onto the table. 'Because, in a tea shop a short time ago, I received one with the same message.' She produced the sheet of paper from her bag and passed it to Daisy. In return, Daisy handed Maud her note. The wording and handwriting was the same: *Stop asking questions about Miss Miller.*

'How was this one delivered?' Maud asked.

Daisy glanced at the note in her hand and dropped it onto the table. 'It came to the office, but I didna see anyone. When I went to lock up, I noticed it had been slipped under the door.'

'At least we can be grateful the author doesn't know this address.' Maud looked again at the note she held. 'Would you say the writing was a man or woman's hand?' Now she considered the matter, the print suggested it had been written by a woman.

'A wifie's hand, I think.' Daisy pointed to one of the letters. 'See how the i's have a wee circle above them, rather than a dot.'

'I agree that it looks like a female's writing. And with those rounded letters, probably one who has been taught by a governess. You'll notice, too, the wording. It's not particularly threatening.'

Daisy laughed. 'You mean a man might have added, *or else.*'

Maud smiled. 'That's exactly what I mean.' She put the note on the kitchen table, next to the other sheet of paper, and settled in the chair. 'So who might have written these notes? Miss Grant, Madame Escoffier, Diana herself?'

'They're the names we have, but it could be any female. Even assuming we're correct about the writer being a woman.' Daisy shrugged.

Maud took a breath. 'I know this will sound ridiculous, but could it be possible that Miss Miller's been kidnapped by a suffragette?'

Daisy frowned and took the chair opposite Maud. 'Why on earth do you say that?'

'Oh, it's just a silly thought, but because her fiancé Mr Laing is prosecuting in the suffragette case tomorrow. Have you got today's newspaper?' She took the copy of *The Scotsman* Daisy passed to her.

Scanning through the pages, Maud found the relevant piece. 'Here we are.' She paraphrased her reading as she went along. 'To be heard tomorrow in Court three by the Honourable Lord Miller.' She looked up at Daisy. 'Not only is Miss Miller's fiancé the prosecutor, but her father is the judge.'

Daisy stared at Maud. 'Isn't that a bit of a coincidence?'

'A particular judge and advocate-depute are bound to appear in the same case from time to time.' Maud returned to the newspaper. 'Catherine Brown, suffragette. Broke a shop window valued at four shillings and assaulted a police officer. It must be a serious assault to be heard in the High Court.' She threw down the newspaper. 'I'll go to court tomorrow, to see if there's anything useful I can learn about Miss Miller's father or fiancé.'

'Do you think Miss Miller has been kidnapped with a view to somehow having an effect on the case?'

'Not really,' Maud admitted. 'That theory doesn't work for three reasons. First, neither her father nor her fiancé has received any communication from a supposed kidnapper.'

'At least, nae that we know of.'

'True.' Maud nodded. 'But if her father knew the reason she had been taken, why would he ask us to look into her disappearance without passing on this vital information?'

'Hmm.'

'The second reason is that the case would not be dropped by the Crown without a very good reason. Thirdly, the guilt or otherwise of the accused is a matter for the jury, not the judge.'

'But if Catherine Brown has broken the law, they will have nae choice but to find her guilty,' said Daisy. 'Look at all the guilty verdicts on suffragettes in England.'

'Yes, but in Scotland only a majority is needed to decide one way or the other. Perhaps eight of the fifteen jurors will be sympathetic towards her case.'

She scowled. 'All the jurors will be men.'

'Even if women were allowed to sit on a jury, it might not help. Incredible as it seems, some women are against suffrage for their own sex,' Maud reminded her friend. 'They believe that women should stay at home to look after their husbands and children, and stay out of public life.'

Daisy pushed back her chair. 'Curse the Prime Minister for refusing to put the bill through Parliament.'

'You can curse him all you like, but it won't solve anything. And right now, we need to get this case solved.'

Maud went back to pondering Mr Laing. She didn't like the way his name kept cropping up and how he'd behaved during the interview. 'You know, Daisy, I'm tempted to make Mr Laing the number one suspect in Miss Miller's disappearance.'

'Even though he was at Duddingston on Saturday and we think the warning note was written by a woman?'

'Even though. He might have disguised his handwriting or he could have a female accomplice.'

'Who?'

'I don't know.'

'If he's as awful as you say he is, Diana Miller probably just ran away.'

'If only it were that simple, Daisy. A young woman like her couldn't manage on her own.'

'Perhaps Laing's had her kidnapped so that he can be the one to rescue her and be the hero, so that she'll be more keen to marry him.'

Maud shook her head. 'That sounds like a plot for a Miss Taft novel.'

'I can't believe,' said Daisy after a brief pause, 'that Laing has turned out to be such a wrong 'un.'

'A wrong 'un?' Maud laughed. 'Where did you pick up that expression?'

She grinned. 'When working as a lady's maid.'

'Surely not in my father's house?'

'No, in the Duchess's.'

They laughed. Joking was all very well, but it wasn't getting them anywhere. Maud took her notebook from her bag and began to doodle on a new page. 'We need to find Diana Miller.'

Daisy frowned. 'Do you think this case is too big for us?'

Maud continued to scribble. She wasn't ready to admit defeat. '*No case too big or too small* should be the agency's motto.'

Daisy smiled.

'It was a suggestion made by Lord Urquhart this afternoon over a cup of tea,' Maud admitted. She refused to consider his alternative idea: *McIntyre for hire*.

Daisy snorted.

'What do you mean by that snort?'

'Why does he keep turning up?'

'He saw me in passing and wanted to know how his case was progressing.'

'Tell him to get in the queue.'

Maud smiled. It was rather a pleasant image, a queue of clients for their agency.

After dinner, Maud cleared the dishes from the table and Daisy put them to soak, ready for Martha when she came in the morning. Maud asked Daisy to wake her at eleven o'clock, when they'd each had a short rest, and they parted for their respective bedrooms.

Maud lay down on her bed and closed her eyes, but she was both too excited and a little nervous to be able to sleep. She'd decided they would disguise themselves as clergymen. A man was necessary as Maud needed to wear trousers for the climb. A working man out late and not under the influence of alcohol would attract attention, but a member of the clergy would arouse no suspicion.

What if they were stopped by a police constable on their way there, questioned and their answers not believed? Or, even worse, stopped on their way back? A kirk minister found in possession of love letters between a peer of the realm and the wife of an MP... They'd have to make a dash for it.

What if she were caught climbing the drainpipe? There could be no reasonable explanation for anyone to indulge in such behaviour. Or she might be discovered creeping about in the Fergusons' house close to midnight. That would be the end of her investigative career. The thought of being sent to prison and the shame that would cause her poor father sent a chill down Maud's back.

As she lay there, looking at the dusky light on the ceiling from a chink in the curtains, she toyed with the notion that she should cancel the whole risky venture. It wasn't fair on Daisy. But Maud knew she had to go ahead, otherwise how could she call herself a detective?

Daisy knocked on her door a few minutes before eleven and entered.

'You know you don't have to come with me tonight if you don't want to, Daisy,' Maud said, as she climbed off the bed. 'What I intend to do is illegal and I shouldn't involve you in that part of the job.'

Daisy shook her head. 'That's a choice for me to make. This opportunity means a lot to me, to make something of my life. I'm with you, miss, whatever happens.'

Maud was touched by her loyalty. 'Thank you, Daisy. We must trust that all goes well.' She pulled open the wardrobe door and the two of them considered the store of assorted costumes and other accoutrements.

Daisy stepped forward and examined the shelves. 'I've never worn a proper disguise before. Which outfits are we to wear?'

'Male ones,' Maud said, her voice firm. 'Two women walking along the road at night would draw unwanted attention.'

Daisy tutted. 'I look forward to the day when that is no longer the case.'

'Amen to that.' Maud began to pull various items from the cupboard, piling them onto the bed. 'We won't need to bind our breasts as it will be dark enough and clergy attire is sufficiently loose and plain.'

'Clergymen!' Daisy exclaimed. 'I never thought I'd be dressed like one of them.'

She quickly undressed down to her chemise and drawers, drew on a white shirt and tucked it into a pair of black trousers. A round-necked black waistcoat came next. She pinned her hair into a bun and shrugged on a long black coat. Searching the top shelf of the cupboard, she found the collar she wanted and secured it round her neck.

Daisy had copied Maud with the second set of clothes and now she smiled. 'We look the part.'

'One further thing.' Maud pulled a pair of grey whiskers from the drawer containing moustaches, beards and wigs, dabbed a little theatrical glue on each of her cheekbones and pressed the side-whiskers into position.

'Almost there.' She drew a couple of lines on each side of her mouth to give the appearance of deep wrinkles. Daisy handed her one of the two black hats lying on the bed and Maud pulled it on, covering her hair.

Maud stood in front of the long looking glass and assumed a slightly stooped position. Daisy laughed at the spectacle she had created.

'What better disguise than a minister and an elder of the kirk on their way home after a Bible-reading class?' Maud picked up her copy of the Good Book.

'No one will think to stop us and ask what we're about at this time of night in these outfits,' said Daisy.

'Let's hope not. Come and sit down, and let me show you how to put your whiskers on.'

A short while later, two respectable clergymen were making their way to Charlotte Square.

It was a warm night and despite the late hour a number of people were out and about. Maud and Daisy adopted the digni-fied pace of a minister and his elder and attracted no attention. The Castle on its rocky peak at the end of Princes Street domi-nated the skyline and tonight as they drew close the ancient stone walls looked particularly grim and forbidding. No doubt because they were about to break the law. They reached the square and all was quiet. Maud breathed a sigh of relief. They had made it here with no questions asked.

The feeling of relief didn't last long. A police constable rounded the corner of the square, heading in their direction.

Maud heard Daisy draw in a sharp breath and suddenly her own heart was beating fast. They kept up their steady pace even though the officer was almost upon them. They had no choice but to walk past the Fergusons' house.

'A fine night, good sirs,' the officer said in a deep baritone voice as he touched his helmet in greeting.

Maud deepened her own voice. 'And a few more souls saved for the Lord this evening. A good night to you, constable.'

He nodded and passed on down South Charlotte Street.

Daisy whistled out a quiet breath. 'That was close.'

'Too close.' Maud found she was clutching her Bible tightly.

They slowed their pace and Maud heard the officer's footsteps fade away on the stones of the deserted pavement. She glanced around. The policeman had gone. The square was clear.

'I think it's safe to turn back,' she whispered.

They retraced their footsteps.

'Here's the house,' Maud said, keeping her voice low. 'Are you still ready to do this, Daisy?'

'Aye, definitely.'

They moved to stand close to the wall, keeping to the shadows outside the circle of light from the street lamp. Maud looked up. As she'd hoped, the first-floor window of the Ferguson house was open at the bottom to let in the night air. The gap looked just wide enough for her to slide her legs through the sash window and lever it up as she sat on the sill.

'We should have sufficient time before the constable returns on his round. Here.' Maud gave her Bible to Daisy, then she slipped off the long black coat and handed it to her. 'It'll be easier for me without that. Keep an eye open while I climb.'

'And here was I thinking I'd come to sing and dance.'

Maud turned her attention to the drainpipe, to determine the best places for a foothold.

'There's a buddleia growing by the pipe.' Daisy pointed up. 'That will help.'

Just below the window, the purple-flowered plant grew out of a crack in the masonry. Maud hoped it was well-anchored.

'Here goes.' She put her foot on the first bracket holding the drainpipe to the wall and tested it. It took her weight. She sent Daisy a brave smile and began her ascent. Clutching the cast-iron pipe and using her sturdy boots to help, Maud climbed the first four feet or so. It was a lot harder going than climbing a tree with its rough bark and branches.

A further bracket and then the first joint in the pipe gave her feet some purchase. Making her slow way up, she put her boot on the next bracket and lifted herself. The pipe creaked. Maud's mouth went dry, and she froze. One of the two nails holding the drainpipe bracket to the wall loosened and fell to the pavement with a soft ping. Below her, Maud heard Daisy give a soft groan.

Maud could smell the sour-milk scent of the buddleia. Too late to turn back now; she was almost there. She reached up and grasped the plant, and hauled herself up and turned to sit precariously on the windowsill.

Then she looked down. The ground, where Daisy stood gazing up at her, appeared to be fifty feet below, rather than the twenty feet it must be. It's a funny thing, but there's a big difference between resting on the leafy branches of a tree when you're a child and perching on a granite windowsill when you're an adult.

Maud swallowed the lump in her throat, turned her head and peered through the pane of glass. Although it was dark inside, it was clearly a bedroom. And there was a shape under the eiderdown.

She waited for a moment until she heard a soft snore from

the bed. Then she took hold of the bottom of the window, swung her legs round and slid them through the gap. She prayed the window wouldn't creak when she lifted it to ease herself into the room.

'Maud!' Daisy's low urgent voice reached her. 'Someone's coming.'

The blood drumming in her ears had covered the sound of low talking and laughing from the street below. The occupant of the bed stirred and turned in Maud's direction, the face shrouded in the darkness of the room. Her heart seemed to stop. After what seemed an age, the snoring began again and so did Maud's breathing.

Maud held tight to the window and turned her head to look down where Daisy had been standing in the shadows. She wasn't there. As her eyes frantically searched the street for her, Maud saw her step onto the pavement towards an oncoming couple. By the look of their smart clothes, they were returning from a night at the theatre. Daisy nodded to them as she passed and continued walking away from her. For a moment, Maud's blood froze and her brain whirled. Was Daisy abandoning her at the first sight of danger?

Maud waited as the chattering couple passed under where she perched, all the while her heart battering the inside of her ribcage. The couple walked down the street and went up the steps of a nearby house. They were inside and the door closed behind them in only a couple of minutes, but it seemed to last a lot longer.

It gave Maud plenty of time to ponder on the recklessness of what she'd been about to do and the possible repercussions. She pulled her legs back out of the room, eased herself off the windowsill and started to climb carefully back down the drainpipe. Her pulse had steadied a little when, to her relief, she spotted Daisy hurrying back.

'I'm so glad to see you,' Maud whispered, snatching up her coat from the shadows on the ground.

'I'd never let you down, Maud.' Daisy's voice was low as she stepped up behind her and guided her arms into the sleeves of the coat. 'But glory be – that was a narrow squeak. What do we do now?'

Had Miss Gladden ever beaten a hasty retreat? Maud couldn't think of a case where the fictional detective had done so, but she reminded herself theirs was only a temporary setback. She looked up at the open window and shuddered. 'Let's go home. Tomorrow we'll think of another approach.'

'We will. We're learning all the time, aren't we, Maud?' Daisy gave an optimistic but nervous smile.

'We are.' Maud spoke firmly as she straightened her coat and took back the Bible. 'And now we are once again two respectable members of the clergy – who are taking a different route back to Broughton Street to avoid the possibility of being seen by the same police constable and arousing his suspicions.'

As they set off along Queen Street towards home, another plan was already forming in Maud's mind.

TWENTY-THREE

After a fitful night of dreams in which a police constable blowing his whistle climbed the drainpipe after Maud and pulled her by her legs out of the window, her nerves were on edge. She told Daisy her idea over breakfast.

The new plan was perhaps a more difficult one, but certainly less dangerous to carry out. Maud would befriend Stella Ferguson and, in that way, obtain entry to her house.

'Isn't that a bit risky?' Daisy asked, stirring sugar into her tea.

'More risky than climbing through a window into her house in the middle of the night?'

She set the spoon in the saucer. 'Fair enough. But how do you propose to get to know her – go to her house and present your card? Perhaps we ought to have done that yesterday.'

Maud passed swiftly over that comment. 'I think the best course of action would be for me to wait in the tea shop where we saw her yesterday with... our client. It's near Charlotte Square, so it's very likely she'll walk past when she leaves her house. Then I'll follow Mrs Ferguson, contrive to bump into her in some way and take it from there.'

'You might have to sit at a table for a while.'

'I'll drink my tea very slowly. This morning, though, I'm going to the High Court.'

'I'll get put up the spare copies of my *Have You Seen This Dog?* posters.' Daisy sighed. 'Wee Max has been missing for over a week now, so I hope he's being well looked after. When I've done that, I'll go to the office in case anyone comes with news of him.'

Maud arrived in Parliament Square in good time for the case starting at ten o'clock. Passing the medieval St Giles' Cathedral, she glanced up at its imposing façade and smiled. A month had gone by since she'd joined the crowds in this very place to see the newly crowned monarchs on their coronation tour. Such a wonderful spectacle, with King George V and Queen Mary seated in their open carriage and the long procession of horse-mounted guards.

Coming back to the present and her sobering task, she walked on to the next building, Parliament House. When she entered the grand Hall, her gaze went up to the magnificent oak hammer-beam roof and the grotesque faces carved on the corbels, and she felt the same shiver of awe she'd experienced when seeing it for the first time. The huge stained-glass window, paintings and niches with statues, fireplaces and parquet floor – it was a place to admire and to make you feel justice would surely be done. She'd dressed with even more care than usual that morning, but still she found herself smoothing down her smart dove-grey embroidered jacket and matching skirt.

The trial was to begin shortly. She wanted to be in the public seating in the well of the court, as close as possible to Mr Laing, so she passed through the doorway under the Great Window and along the corridor to Court three. A buzz of anticipation hit her as she entered. Almost every seat in the gallery above was taken and there weren't many left in the public area where she now stood. Maud squeezed into a place in the second row.

The judge's bench was empty. Mr Laing was in wig and black gown, sitting on the left-hand side of the long table, and Maud watched him as he idly flicked through his documents. The counsel's seat opposite him was empty. Did Miss Brown mean to conduct her own defence?

Sunlight filtered through the panes of the high windows. It was almost ten o'clock and the room already felt airless. Time ticked slowly on and the hubbub grew. The seats reserved for the press were taken, as Maud had expected. Stories of suffragettes sold newspapers.

A door at the side opened and at once the courtroom hushed. Miss Brown was brought from the cells into court between two officers, her slight build further diminished by the larger men. She carried a sheaf of papers. Maud's fear was confirmed; Miss Brown was representing herself. Stepping into the dock she looked young, perhaps eighteen or so, and pale but composed in her green worsted hat and coat. Her glance went round the court and when it reached a group of women she recognised in the public gallery, she smiled at them. A small cheer went up from her supporters, which was quickly subdued by a court official.

A door opened on the other side of the court and the jury filed in. Evidently, they had been picked and sworn in the previous day, for they took their seats in an orderly fashion. Some of the men looked well-fed and affluent; others were working men judging by their patched jackets. A few of them stared at Miss Brown, while most averted their gaze. Not one of their faces told Maud where their sympathies might lie.

From the back of the room, the macebearer entered, followed by the judge.

'All rise!' the macer called.

As everyone got to their feet in a scuffling, ragged fashion, Maud could see it was indeed Lord Miller in the wig and red and white robe. He lowered himself into his splendid chair, the macer hung his mace on the wall behind it and the room dutifully resumed their seats.

The clerk of court pushed his spectacles back up on the bridge of his nose and read out the indictment from a sheet of paper. 'Catherine Brown of Leith Street, Edinburgh. You are charged with, on third of August 1911 in Hanover Street, Edinburgh, you did one, damage the property of Duncan Cook, tea merchant, by throwing a stone and breaking a window at the premises; two, assault Police Constable James Williamson while he acted in the execution of his duty, by a cut to his face as a result of flying glass from the broken window.' He looked up at her. 'How do you plead?'

'Guilty to the first charge. Not guilty to the second.' Miss Brown's voice was soft, but she spoke with confidence.

As the clerk noted her replies, Maud relaxed a little. Perhaps she would make a success of her defence.

Mr Laing got to his feet and addressed the judge. 'My Lord, as the accused has accepted her guilt on the first charge, I will call only one witness, Constable Williamson.'

A burly police officer entered the court, his helmet under his arm, stepped into the witness box, took the oath and, when prompted, began his account. 'I was patrolling Hanover Street when I saw the accused standing outside the premises of Duncan Cook. At first, I thought she was a customer about to go inside the shop. As I drew closer, she looked at me and suddenly produced a large stone from her jacket pocket and hurtled it at the window.' Constable Williamson's stern voice, amplified by the curved wooden canopy over the witness box, resonated around the court.

'She saw you, waited until you were close and then

produced the stone?' repeated Mr Laing, with every appearance of satisfaction.

'Yes,' said the constable. 'There was no doubt in my mind that she wished me to see her break the window and for me to be injured by her action.'

Glancing at Miss Brown, Maud saw her shake her head. There were further questions and answers, which she half listened to while watching Miss Brown's pale features and the horrid self-assured look on Douglas Laing's face. He resumed his seat, steepled his fingers as she had guessed he would, and Miss Brown rose to begin her cross-examination of the police officer.

'I was looking into the shop to ensure there was no one close to the window who might be harmed by my action.'

'That is not a question,' said Lord Miller, peering down from the bench.

'I'm sorry, My Lord.' A little flustered, she glanced down at the papers in her hand. This was not a good start.

'I apologised for the cut on your cheek caused by a piece of flying glass, did I not?' she asked Constable Williamson.

'Aye,' he said, jutting out his chin.

'Did you accept that apology?'

'No, I did not. It was not meant and therefore a blatant cover for hypocrisy.'

There was a collective intake of breath from the women in the public gallery, Maud included. This was followed by a burst of laughter from some of the men seated there.

In a shaken voice, Miss Brown said, 'I repeat that I am sorry for your injury, which I had not meant to happen.' She glanced up at the women, gathered her confidence again, and continued. 'The cut to your cheek was slight and you were able to carry out your normal duties after an examination at the Royal Infirmary?'

'Aye.'

It was not a serious assault, then, Maud thought. An injury, yes, and to a police officer, but an injury with no deep wound or causing permanent disfigurement. Why had the decision been made to send the case to the High Court, rather than the sheriff court? Was it to make an example of the suffragette?

Miss Brown was speaking again. 'You refused my apology. Do you consider yourself a Christian?'

'Confine yourself to your case,' said Lord Miller, his voice sharp.

'I should be able to ask any question.'

'Put a relevant question to the police officer.'

She had no further questions and she produced no witnesses. Maud's sense of foreboding grew.

Mr Laing stood, tugged his gown back over one shoulder, and summed up the evidence for the prosecution. Already the trial was almost over. Maud glanced across to Miss Brown's friends and they looked as concerned as Maud herself felt.

Miss Brown took a breath and began her speech in defence. 'I consider I have been brought up on a wrong charge. I should not have been charged with assaulting a police officer, which I never intended to do. I lacked the necessary' – she glanced at her papers – '*mens rea*. I was sorry when I found out what had happened because of course I had no quarrel with Constable Williamson.'

Lord Miller peered down at her from the bench. 'You are doing your case no good by persisting with this attitude. The definition of assault is an attack on the person of another, with evil intent to cause injury or fear of injury.'

'I have told you, My Lord. I had no intent, evil or otherwise, to cause injury.'

'An assault can be committed indirectly.'

She consulted her papers again. 'But an assault cannot be committed accidentally or recklessly or negligently.'

'You waited until the police officer came close, therefore you had an intent to cause injury.'

'I waited only to be sure he saw me break the window. After the incident, I stood there and waited for the constable to arrest me. I did not wish to evade the law. I have a right to explain my motive.'

'You have not. You have already gone on far too long.'

With desperation in her tone, she began again. 'Action by suffragettes is the only kind of argument which Mr Asquith appears to understand. You should realise the unfair way in which women are treated.'

'That is no reason why you should break a window and assault Constable Williamson.'

'The suffragette movement is doing these things with the highest motives. We are acting on behalf of women who cannot speak for themselves. We appeal to the men in Parliament to save us from the necessity of doing any more on behalf of the cause.' She sat down abruptly, her eyes lowered.

The jury was sent away to consider its verdict, and Lord Miller ordered a break for luncheon. Feeling uneasy for Miss Brown, Maud had no appetite. She left the court and wandered around inside the cathedral until her wristwatch showed it was almost two o'clock, when she hastened back.

Miss Brown was brought into court, Lord Miller returned and the room fell quiet. The jury filed back to their seats, the men's grim faces revealing the decision. When asked, the spokesman stood and gave their unanimous verdict. 'Guilty.'

Mr Laing looked down at his documents on the table to try to hide a smile.

'Stand up, please,' said Lord Miller, addressing Miss Brown.

Looking as though she might faint, she gave a small shake of her head.

'I find you guilty of breaking a window and assaulting a

police officer in the execution of his duty. I sentence you to twelve months' imprisonment.'

There was a loud gasp from the public gallery, followed by cries of 'Shame!'

'I protest, sir.' Miss Brown spoke bravely, but her voice was subdued.

As she left the dock to applause from the gallery, she turned and called in a stronger voice, 'No surrender!'

'No surrender!' shouted her friends.

That was it; the case was over. Maud didn't think she would easily forget Mr Laing's smug look of satisfaction at Miss Brown's fate.

Shakily, Maud made her way back to her office. Daisy looked up from flicking a duster around the room.

'Maud, you're as pale as porridge. What has happened?' She threw the cloth onto the desk and pulled out a chair for her. 'Sit down. Let me get you a drink of water.'

Maud waited as she filled a glass and returned. 'Thank you.' She took a sip. 'It's not what has happened to me, but to poor Catherine Brown. Twelve months in prison. From the start it was clear that she was out of her depth in conducting her own case. Then the jury...' She shook her head. 'We need women as well as men to be able to act as jurors. And the sentence passed by Lord Miller seems unnecessarily severe. It isn't right that men are always the ones who decide important matters.'

'She'll probably be sent to Calton Jail.' Daisy shuddered. 'Cold, silent and harsh, it's the worst prison in Scotland.'

'We must hope that she doesn't go on hunger strike like some prisoners. What I've read about suffragettes in England who are forcibly fed is shocking. The bones of their face projecting, eyes half-closed, voice a whisper, wrists swollen and stiff.'

Daisy snatched up the broom and began to sweep the floor with vehemence. 'It's naething short of barbaric.'

'I got the distinct impression that not only was Mr Laing pleased with the outcome of Miss Brown's case, but also Lord Miller.'

Daisy threw the sweeping brush against the wall and dropped into the chair opposite Maud. 'Does this take us any further with Miss Miller's case?'

'I think we should conclude that neither of these gentlemen approve of women's rights and that they could, given the opportunity, exert a will of iron over Miss Miller.'

Daisy thought for a moment. 'What you said about her being kidnapped doesna seem so foolish any more. I'm thinking she might have arranged her own disappearance and kidnapped herself.'

'Our minds are once again on the same track, Daisy.'

They sat quietly for a while. Eventually, Maud broke the silence.

'I have a really bad feeling about Laing, Daisy. I'm convinced he's involved in the Duddingston theft, the murder *and* Miss Miller's disappearance – but how?'

TWENTY-FOUR

Maud's brain was buzzing, and she was unable to settle to anything. She decided she would attempt to strike up the temporary friendship with Stella Ferguson. She'd prepared a suitable outfit after breakfast this morning and had asked Daisy to take it with her to the office.

'Have you learned anything about the missing dog?' Maud asked her now.

Daisy looked downhearted. 'Naething. I'm beginning to wonder if the wee creature is still with us.'

'Goodness, Daisy, don't say that. We have to stay positive with all our cases. Besides, think of poor Max. He needs us to find him.'

'Besides the poster, I dinna ken what else to do. I can hardly chap on every door where I hear barking.'

'Indeed, you can't. We must hope that someone will come forward soon with information.'

Daisy sighed. 'I'll make us a cup of tea.'

As she busied herself with filling the kettle and lighting the Primus stove, Maud locked the office door, opened her Gladstone and lifted out the costume.

The top item was a purple velvet hat with ostrich feathers, which she carefully smoothed and placed on the desk. Next Maud unpacked the lemon dress, shook it out and laid it over the back of her chair. It looked as good as it had on the hanger; you could never go wrong with silk. The furled parasol Daisy had carried in with her was now hooked on the back of the door.

By the time Daisy had brewed the tea, Maud was an elegant lady in a lemon silk dress with matching parasol.

'Very nice, Maud,' Daisy said approvingly.

'I would have liked to wear my large straw boater with yellow and purple flowers, but I doubt it would have taken kindly to being packed in a bag.' Stella Ferguson must see her as well-dressed as she, if Maud were to have any chance of striking up a friendship with the woman, no matter how brief it would be.

'If that costume doesn't persuade Mrs F., I don't know what will.' Daisy set their tea on the desk.

Maud sat carefully on the chair and lifted her cup and saucer. 'I need a name.' She held the china suspended in midair. 'Nothing too grand, else she might wonder why she hasn't heard of me. I must be up from the country. The Honourable Jean...'

'Ballater,' said Daisy.

I frowned. 'Ballater?'

'It's a village in the Highlands. I have a cousin who farms by there.'

'That will do nicely.' She finished her tea quickly and set down the cup and saucer. 'Wish me luck.'

Maud rose, unhooked the parasol, unlocked the door and sailed from the room.

As it happened, Maud didn't need to wait for Stella Ferguson to pass by the window so that she could follow her and contrive a meeting, because she opened the door of Clarissa's Tea Rooms and walked in.

Maud's pulse beat faster. A vision in pale-pink, Stella Ferguson halted just inside the threshold and gazed around the busy tea shop. Was she looking for someone in particular, a friend perhaps, or trying to find an empty table? There were no free tables, but there was a spare seat at Maud's. Maud sent the woman a brief but friendly smile and returned her attention to buttering the scone on her plate.

'Excuse me.' She heard a woman's voice and looked up. 'Is this seat taken?'

It was Stella Ferguson and Maud had to suppress a laugh. 'You're welcome to sit here,' she said with a smile and a gracious nod of the ostrich feathers in her hat.

'Thank you.' Mrs Ferguson raised an elegant hand to summon a waiter. He hurried forward to pull out the chair for her. 'This is very kind of you,' she said to Maud, as she lowered herself gracefully onto the seat before ordering a pot of tea. Her eye fell on Maud's scone. 'And a scone,' she added to the waiter.

When he had left, she turned to Maud. 'I really shouldn't, but yours looks so tempting I couldn't resist.'

Maud sent her a conspiratorial smile and said in a lowered voice, 'That's what corsets are for.'

She laughed, delighted at Maud's indecorous comment, and for a moment Maud felt sorry for what she was planning to do. Perhaps she really was as innocent as she looked. But that was what Maud had to find out.

Before she could speak again, Stella Ferguson said, 'It's very busy in here today, is it not?'

Was she naturally friendly or simply lonely? Either way, it worked to Maud's advantage. 'I'm afraid I don't know what it's usually like here, as this is my first visit. I'm up from the country for a few days. My father has some friends to see.' Maud smiled, then took a risk and rolled her eyes. 'When they get going, they are such bores, talking only about shooting and fishing. My father allowed me to come out by myself as long as I didn't speak to any strangers.'

She returned my smile. 'But I am a stranger.'

'Then let us introduce ourselves,' Maud broke off as the waiter brought the tea and scone. 'And then we won't be. I am the Honourable Miss Jean Ballater, but you may call me Jeanie.'

'And I am Mrs Ferguson, but please call me Stella.'

And just like that, the preliminaries were out of the way.

'I think you must come here quite often, since you mentioned how busy it is.' Maud cut her halved scone into four pieces and placed one morsel daintily in her mouth while she waited for her to reply. Stella wasn't going to invite her to Charlotte Street on the basis of one accidental meeting, but she might on a second such occasion.

'I like to come here once or twice a week,' Stella said.

'What a pleasant thing to do.'

She took a sip of her tea. 'My husband is always so busy that I find I have rather too much time to myself.'

Could Maud ask what he did for a living? No, that would sound too forward and anyway she knew the answer.

They chatted about this and that, Stella recommended the best shops for Maud to visit, and the time passed quickly. Maud could admit that on first acquaintance she liked the woman, which made her feel uncomfortable as she intended to betray this blossoming friendship. But if Stella didn't have the letters, Maud reminded herself, then she wouldn't be betraying her. And if she did have them, then she was playing some cruel game at the expense of Maud's client and so she need feel no self-reproach.

Eventually, Maud said, 'I must go now,' and gestured to the waiter for the bill. 'My father expects me back at the hotel shortly.'

'And I should return home. The dog must have a walk.'

Instantly, Maud was on the alert. 'You have a dog?' She tried not to sound too interested. 'How charming.'

She shrugged. 'Not really. He's always bothering me to go out and is becoming a bit of a bore.'

Was she now seeing the real Stella? 'How long have you had him?' Maud kept her voice casual.

'Not long. About a week, in fact.' Maud noticed that she didn't meet her eyes as she spoke. 'He'll improve as he gets used to me, no doubt.'

If it was Maximilian, would she know his name? It was possible Lord Urquhart had mentioned the dog next door to him. And if she did know, would she have given him a new name to allay suspicion?

'I'm sure it will all turn out well. I'm fond of dogs myself, especially small ones; they are such dears.' Maud gave her an encouraging smile. 'What breed is yours?'

Stella dabbed her mouth with her napkin and dropped it beside her plate. 'Rex is a Pekingese.' She reached for her purse as the waiter approached.

Rex! Maud would have laughed if her throat weren't suddenly so dry. Like Max, Rex was a grand name for such a small dog. Importantly, though, it sounded similar to Max, so Stella might have misheard any name mentioned by Lord Urquhart or she might have changed the name to something the animal would probably answer to.

Maud paid her bill and got to her feet. 'It's been very pleasant talking to you, Stella. I do hope we meet again.'

They most certainly would. One way or another, Daisy would retrieve the dog – if it were indeed Max – and with luck Maud would retrieve the letters.

Barely had Maud told Daisy the news than her friend rammed on her hat, said, 'I'm away to Charlotte Square,' and was out of the door.

While Maud waited for her to return, with or without Max-Rex, she reflected on her conversation with Stella Ferguson and jotted down anything she thought might be relevant, which wasn't much.

Stella had a new dog, it was the right breed, had a similar-sounding name to the stolen one – and she didn't like the poor animal. Then why did she have it? It could have been her husband's idea to buy a dog, but she hadn't said so. It looked very much as if it were Lady Argyll's Peke. Maud would know when Daisy returned and if it were Maximilian, what was the connection with Lord Urquhart's missing letters? There had to be a link.

Maud wandered over to the bookshelf to pass the time and saw a little book on palmistry she'd bought on a whim at a second-hand bookshop. A strange subject to be studying, perhaps, but she liked to keep her mind occupied and besides, all knowledge was potentially useful to a detective.

She was absorbed in the fascinating topic when the door burst open and Daisy almost flew into the room. She shut the door quickly with one hand, her chest heaving and her eyes wild. In her other arm, she clutched her jacket made into a bundle. Poking out of the top was a black furry face with large dark eyes.

Maud dropped the book and leaped to her feet, the chair scraping along the floor. 'Is it...?'

Daisy peeled back the jacket, and Maud saw a small dog with a biscuit-coloured body. He began to bark.

'You've found Maximilian!'

At the sound of his name, the dog stopped barking and looked with interest at Maud. She stepped closer, keeping a wary eye on his jaws.

'How did you manage that, Daisy?'

Still clutching him, Daisy dropped into a chair and puffed out a breath. 'It was easy enough to find him as I had Mrs F.'s address, and this time I avoided a stushie getting hold of him.'

Tentatively, she set the dog down on the floor. He shook himself and set off round the room, head down and sniffing, wagging his cropped tail as he went. Maud continued to keep a wary eye on him, only this time it wasn't on his jaws but a different part of his anatomy. To his credit, all four legs remained on the ground. She relaxed a little and looked at Daisy. Her heightened colour was fading back to normal.

'I went straight to Charlotte Square,' Daisy said, 'and by the time I got there, I had two possible plans. Chap on the door and demand the return of the dog, which probably wouldna have worked, or bide until someone came out to walk the dog and then snatch him.'

Maud didn't much like the sound of either, but Daisy was correct that there was no other way of getting hold of him. 'Which plan did you opt for?'

She smiled. 'The second one. It wasn't Mrs F. who came out with Max on the leash, but a housemaid. I'd grabbed him and was running before the lassie realised what had happened. I nipped into North Charlotte Street, then St Colme Street where I pulled off my jacket and wrapped him in it. Then I walked at a normal pace, carrying him like a babe in my arms. You didna mind at all, did you, Maxie?'

The dog paused in his exploration, shot her a humiliated glance and continued his second tour of the room.

'Well done, Daisy,' Maud said with real admiration. 'It appears he's been well looked-after by his temporary owners.' She peered at him. 'I wonder if it's his dinner time.'

'I'll take him back to Lady A's. I feel as if he and I have developed a bond, and I'm sure he wouldna mind me carrying him again.'

Maud saw the dog's ears twitch, but he clearly decided not to respond. 'Tell Lady A. – that is, Lady Argyll – that the account will be in the post.' She moved over to the Primus stove. 'I'll make us a cup of tea first. You deserve to have a sit-down before you go out again.'

As Maud busied herself picking up the book she'd dropped and replacing it on the shelf, putting on the kettle and preparing the teapot, she watched Daisy playing with the dog. He was rather sweet, and she could see why Daisy was already fond of him. When the tea was made, Maud gave him a saucer of the milky liquid and he lapped it up.

Her tea finished, Daisy addressed the dog. 'Up you come, young Max.' She scooped him into her jacket again and cradled him. 'He makes a bonny bairn. I bet he'll be asleep before I get him home.'

Asleep... That gave Maud an idea. 'Daisy, could you buy a sleeping draught from the pharmacy on your way back here?'

She shot Maud a look. 'For yourself?'

'Thankfully not.'

Maud opened the door for her, and with a quizzical look, Daisy disappeared out of the office.

One case definitely solved, Maud thought with pride. Turning back into the room, she saw she'd been pleased too soon. The little creature had left a puddle against the table leg. A cleaning charge would be added to Lady Argyll's bill.

As she mopped up – how could one small dog expel so much bodily fluid? – Maud tried to work out how and why Stella Ferguson had stolen the dog. She couldn't see her in all her finery climbing over the wall and into the other woman's garden to grab the Peke. Nor could she imagine what Stella had to gain by doing so. But the letters... she knew they existed because she had written them, and very likely she knew or could guess where Lord Urquhart would keep them.

The floor clean again, Maud hung the cloth under the basin

and turned her thoughts to the visit she was to make tomorrow, Saturday, to her father's house in the country. It would involve a day away from the missing letters investigation that she couldn't afford, but when she moved to Edinburgh, she'd promised him she would do her best to return for lunch once a week, and Maud was a woman who liked to keep her promises.

TWENTY-FIVE

Maud's father usually sent his chauffeur Carstairs to pick her up from Broughton Street, but now she had her brother's motor car and she was keen to take it for a run in the country. It was a pleasant drive to her father's house and the blue Tourer sped along in the sunshine. After a few miles of white clouds of dust sent up by the dry country roads, though, she was grateful for her veil and goggles.

The front door of the house stood open to the heat of the day as she drew up. Maud threw off the rug protecting her clothes and climbed out of the Napier. Carstairs came running round from the stables to admire the motor. Crichton, her father's ancient butler, stood at the top of the house steps ready to greet her.

'Good morning, Miss Maud,' he greeted her in his solemn, measured tone. He'd been known to intimidate unwelcome guests, but he was a dear and she was fond of him. Looking at him now, no one would believe when Maud was a small child, he'd go down on all fours and let her sit on his back as if he were a horse.

'Hello, Crichton.' Maud smiled at him. 'Another scorcher of

a day,' she remarked and eased the goggles down over her nose, to rest around her neck like a piece of unusual jewellery.

Maud caught the glimmer of a responding smile on his wrinkled, flushed face. He was proud of his butler's uniform, but the poor man must be sweltering in his dark suit of clothes. The sun beat down on the stone steps and bounced up again to hit them.

'Let's get out of this heat,' she said and entered the house, already stripping off her gloves. 'There's no need for you to announce me to my father.'

The young housemaid came forward and Maud handed the girl her gloves, hat and, once she had extricated herself from them, the motoring goggles.

'Thank you, Agnes,' she said at last, patting her hair. 'Am I tidy enough or should I clean up first? I feel I must look a terrible fright.'

'You look very well, miss.' Agnes gave her a shy smile and bobbed a curtsy. 'The master's on the north terrace.'

Maud made her way through the delicious coolness of the hall with its black and white tiled floor, and out onto the shaded terrace at the back of the house.

'Hello, Father.'

He removed the pipe he was smoking. She leaned over the wicker chair where he sat and kissed his warm cheek. He smiled and set his book on the table.

'Did you have a good journey?' He poured a second glass of lemonade and slid it towards her as she sat down opposite him. 'The Napier all right?'

Maud took a long draught of the warm but welcome lemonade. 'She goes like a dream. And both the motor car and I are still in one piece.' Her eye caught the title of the volume her father had been reading.

'*The Great Illusion?*' She raised an eyebrow. 'The author is of the opinion that a war in Europe is extremely unlikely because of the economic cost to all countries involved.'

'This fellow Angell' – her father tapped the book with a forefinger – 'puts forward that argument, but I'm not convinced.'

'I have to agree with you, Father. Anyone who can read a reputable newspaper can learn of Germany's aggression towards the French in Morocco.'

'I'm pleased to see you still keep up with world affairs despite having a busy working life.'

The twinkle in his eyes made her smile. 'Our government is quite rightly incensed, as perhaps I should be about that little quip.'

He laughed, then the smile slid from his face. 'As Lloyd George said, the situation is intolerable.' He was quiet for a moment. 'Some might say that Angell wrote his book with the aim of discouraging Germany from its bid to become a great naval power.'

Maud looked at her father. He was a kind man, a liberal by both political inclination and paternal nature. His understanding of her desire to earn her own living if possible, and certainly of her need to live a useful life, had encouraged her to start the detective agency. 'All I want is for you to be happy,' he'd said when she had told him of her intention. 'But if for any reason the business doesn't work out, Maud, I am here; and when I'm gone, your brothers will step in.'

Maud frowned as she thought of her father no longer in her life. He mistook the reason for her look of concern as she faced him across the table.

'But let us not dwell on the political situation on such a fine day,' he said.

She took another drink of lemonade and let her gaze wander down from the terrace and onto the lawn and flower beds basking in the sunshine. 'We could be mistaken for thinking we are in the Garden of Eden.'

'Although it is hot enough to believe we might be about to meet the devil.' He smiled. 'But should you not be wearing a hat, my dear? I wouldn't want you to suffer from sunstroke.'

'It's delightful to be free of a hat outdoors for a change.' She would have liked to unpin her hair too, but that might have scandalised her father. 'The breeze keeps my brain cool.'

He was immediately interested. 'How are you getting on with your cases?'

'You know very well I can't discuss them, so stop asking me!'

Sergeant McKay had taken the credit for the Duddingston case, and her name had not been in the newspapers, which suited Maud given her disquiet at the Colonel's arrest.

'There seems to be all sorts of crime reported these days. I wonder if the police need Sherlock Holmes to lend them a hand.' Her father had a twinkle in his eye again.

'Or Monsieur Dupin,' she said.

'Or Miss Maud McIntyre,' he added.

Maud couldn't deny the idea wasn't an exciting one, but...

'Can you imagine the police accepting help from a female private detective?' She laughed. 'They haven't even appointed a female police officer.'

Her father puffed on his pipe. 'There was Big Rachel of Partick some forty years ago.'

'Yes, but that's Glasgow for you. Big Rachel was six foot four inches tall, weighed seventeen stone and her approach was to throw rioters into the River Clyde.' Maud shook her head. 'You didn't send me to finishing school to behave like that, did you?'

'That is true. The year at Château Mont-Choisi was to teach you social graces, how to find a husband—'

Maud drew in her breath sharply. 'As if any short cut to happiness lay that way!'

He laughed and continued, 'And for a more academic education than your long-suffering governess could provide.'

'What do you mean by long-suffering?' She knew the answer even as she posed the question.

'Trying to prise you away from those detective novels.'

Maud knew he was teasing her, for he was supportive of female education as well as a fan himself of detective novels. He had allowed – encouraged, even – her reading of them as she grew older. Her governess hadn't approved, but she couldn't stop Maud because of her father's consent.

Women had been allowed to matriculate from a Scottish university for the last twenty years, but Maud's father sent her to finishing school because that was what her mother had wanted for Maud. But he chose a finishing school with a serious programme of education.

'Your time in Lausanne was well spent,' he said. 'It improved your languages considerably.'

Maud smiled as she remembered sitting by the shore of Lake Geneva, reading *The Murders in the Rue Morgue* in French. In the winter, she'd skied and in the summer, she had hiked in the mountains, away from the chatter of the other girls who talked of nothing but the men they would meet.

'Anyway,' Maud pointed out, returning to their original conversation, 'the police have not asked for my help in solving any crimes.'

'More fool them.'

The gong sounded.

'Luncheon,' she said, getting to her feet.

Daisy wasn't home when Maud returned to Broughton Street later in the afternoon.

She went into the sitting room, tossed her gloves and goggles onto the low table and dropped into a chair without removing her dusty travelling hat. On the journey back, as she had pondered upon the Miller and the Urquhart investigations, she wondered if there could be a connection between them. The two gentlemen knew each other, but not well, Lord Urquhart had told her in the teashop. And there was nothing to connect Miss Miller with Lord Urquhart. Maud shook her head; she was looking for links that didn't exist. Yet hadn't Leonardo da Vinci said *all things are connected*?

Whoever had said it, time was running out to solve the cases. Miss Miller went missing a week ago, and Sebastian Ferguson was due home in three days' time.

The door opened. 'Hello, Maud,' Daisy said, as she came in. 'Did you have a braw day?'

'Yes, thanks. And you?'

'Nae bad. I closed the office at midday as we agreed. That Lord Urquhart came in this morning.'

Maud tutted. 'The sooner we get his case solved, the better. That will stop him plaguing us.'

Daisy took off her hat and sat down. 'He was carrying a bunch of pinks fairly drooping in the heat. "You shouldn't have," I told him, and he said the place needed cheering up and did we have a vase? Their scent of cloves was really bonnie, but I told him, "This is a detective's office, not a lady's boudoir."'

Maud laughed. 'Good for you, Daisy.'

She grinned. 'I washed the empty milk bottle at the basin in the indoor sanitation, took it back into the office and said, "It just so happens that we do have a suitable receptacle."

'Then he made himself at home while I put the flooers in the water and he asked how we were getting on with his investigation. "Yours is not our only case, you know," I said and rearranged the notes on the desk to look busy.'

'Did he mention having tea with Mrs Ferguson at Clarissa's Tea Rooms two days ago?'

'I asked him,' she said. 'He looked embarrassed.'

'As well he might, given he employed us to retrieve letters resulting from a relationship he professed no longer existed.'

'And he said he was impressed that we knew, and we were rather good investigators.'

'Of course we are. So what was his explanation?'

'He wanted to let Mrs F. know about the missing letters, so that if she were approached by a blackmailer, she would tell him immediately.'

Fair enough, although Maud couldn't imagine what he thought he'd do about it. 'What did you tell him about our progress?'

'I said you'd tried to get into the Fergusons' house through an open window, and he fairly jumped out of his seat.'

Maud didn't know whether to smile or frown at Daisy's revealing this.

Daisy went on: '"Good heavens," Lord Urquhart said, "I think I have hired a female Raffles!"'

The smile won.

'I told him we thought the letters might have... found their way back to Mrs Ferguson.'

'Well put, Daisy.'

'When he asked if they had, I said we didna know because we were disturbed, and you had to climb back down the drain-pipe awfa quickly.'

'What did he say to that?'

'He laughed and said, "That must have been a sight to behold." So, I couldn't resist adding, "Especially as Miss McIntyre was dressed as a minister of the kirk at the time."'

Maud laughed again. 'Oh, Daisy, you make a wonderful assistant and friend.'

'And then he said in an amused voice, "A woman minister? That is as unlikely as a police officer in petticoats."'

The smile disappeared from Maud's face, and she pulled out her hat pin with such force that Daisy looked at it with alarm. Maud wrenched off her hat and thrust the pin back in. 'I hope you told his lordship in no uncertain terms we have a new plan and that he can leave the matter safely in our hands.'

'Let me take that before you do yourself a mischief.' Daisy removed the hat from Maud's hands. She collected her gloves and goggles from the table, and with her own hat took them out into the hall.

'Now,' she said, returning to the sitting room. 'What is this new plan?'

'Did you buy the sleeping draught I asked for?'

'Aye.' She rummaged in her bag, produced a small envelope and held it out to Maud.

'Thank you.' Maud took it, slipped it into her skirt pocket and glanced at the mantel clock. 'I've done nothing useful today and it's not yet four, so I'll return to the tea shop and hopefully will bump into Stella Ferguson. I need her to invite me into her house, where I intend to snoop around to see if she has the letters. For that, I will need the powder.'

After a quick wash to get rid of the dust from the drive, Maud dressed in her blue suit consisting of a little bolero, skirt with panels and a wide belt, and hooked the short chain of her beaded purse onto her wrist. There was just time to effect a ladylike stroll to George Street.

She picked up her parasol.

There was no sign of Maud's quarry in Clarissa's, so rather than enter and wait she walked a little further on in the direction of Charlotte Square. The sky had begun to look heavy. A summer shower threatened and all she had to protect herself and her wide-brimmed hat was a rather silly parasol. An umbrella would have been a better choice.

Maud was on the verge of returning to the tea shop and taking her chances with Stella appearing, when the realisation hit her. Getting wet in the rain would be the perfect excuse for taking shelter in her house.

Striding into Charlotte Square, she welcomed the first splashes of rain – until they turned from a few damp droplets to a heavy downpour. Should she put up the parasol and save her hat or keep her parasol furled and ruin the hat? Before Maud had made the decision, the front door of Stella's house opened, and she appeared on the threshold.

'Miss Ballater!' She waved at her. 'Come in from the rain, do!'

Maud didn't have to pretend to be grateful. Her hat was about to collapse about her ears and her clothes felt decidedly damp. Picking up her skirts, she ran up the steps and into the hall.

'Thank you,' Maud gasped, with only a slightly exaggerated shiver. 'The rain was so sudden and unexpected.'

'It was lucky that I was looking out the window, considering whether to venture out or not, when I saw you. I couldn't possibly let you get any more soaked. Come into the drawing room where there's a fire. You'll be warm in no time.'

A hovering butler took Maud's parasol and hat. Stella told him to bring tea and gestured for Maud to follow her along the passage.

The drawing room was large and elegant, with a tall mirror over the high mantel, overstuffed sofas and potted plants dotted about. In the corner of the room stood the item of furniture Maud wanted to see. Her secretaire bureau, a little key nestling in the lock. Her heart gave a thump. The letters could be in there.

She dragged her gaze away and focused instead on the hearth. Although the day was still warm despite the sudden shower, the grand room would have felt chilly without the flames burning in the grate.

'I always think a fire is so comforting. Sit near it and dry off your dress.' Stella indicated the two wing-backed chairs arranged opposite one another near the hearth.

'Thank you. I should have kept a better watch on the weather.' Maud took a seat and Stella did the same.

'Not the best day for a walk, I think,' she said, looking enquiringly at Maud.

Had she seen through Maud's pretence? 'It was pleasant enough when I set out.'

She nodded. 'And you were intending to walk to Charlotte Square?'

Maud arranged her damp skirts to avoid meeting Stella's eye, and in doing so surreptitiously slipped her hand into the pocket. Thank goodness; the envelope remained dry. 'I was going to take tea in Clarissa's Tea Rooms' – that much was true – 'but found myself walking on, enjoying the exercise.' Would she believe that?

'Well, I am pleased to see you, Jeanie, for I find myself feeling rather lonely. My husband is away from home.'

'Then it is fortunate I came along when I did.' Maud looked pointedly around the room. 'Where is your charming little dog? He must be company for you.'

She shrugged. 'He has disappeared.'

'Oh, that is a pity. But I think you said that you'd had him for only a few days. I'm curious, how did you come by him?'

If she thought the question intrusive, she gave no sign. 'I heard him barking in the gardens in the square. Somehow the silly thing had got in – presumably when a neighbour unlocked the gates to enter – and then he couldn't escape through the railings. I sent the footman to investigate the noise and he came back with Rex.'

Plausible, but Maud wasn't convinced. 'Perhaps he's found his way back to his original owner,' she said. 'I'm sure I saw a poster in a shop window somewhere; a plea for the return of a missing dog.'

'I can't say I ever read notices in shop windows. Ah, here is our tea.'

The butler entered the room and Maud watched in silence as he placed the laden tray on a low table beside Stella. When he left, she continued, 'I wonder the posters weren't mentioned by your servants. They must have seen them.'

Stella gave her a sharp look. 'If the servants had read the notices, they obviously had no reason to think it was the same animal. Or if they did, then they could see how fond I was of the creature and said nothing.'

Fond of the creature? She didn't sound it, and Maud distinctly remembered Stella telling her the dog was becoming a bit of a bore.

'Milk and sugar?' Stella asked, lifting the pot and pouring tea into Maud's cup.

'Just milk, thank you.'

She placed the teapot back on the tray and took up the milk jug.

'Only a little.' Maud leaned forward to take the cup and saucer from her. As she did so, the envelope containing the sleeping draught shifted in her skirt pocket, as if eager to be of use.

They drank their tea and chatted of inconsequential things – places Stella had visited, people she knew – and Maud was relieved there was no overlap between their two circles. To Stella, Maud was simply an acceptable female with whom to pass the afternoon.

A maid came in to add more coals to the fire and went out again. Their conversation continued. Maud was beginning to wonder if she would ever get an opportunity to slip the powder into Stella's cup.

'More tea?' Stella asked.

Instantly, Maud saw the way to do it. The bell to summon a

servant was set to the side of the mantelpiece. Stella would have
to rise and turn her back to her to press it.

'That would be delightful,' said Maud.

As if Maud were directing her movements, Stella rose,
turned, took the few steps to the mantel and pressed the bell.

In a flash, Maud pulled the envelope from her pocket and
tipped the contents into the remainder of the tea in Stella's cup.
Within seconds, the powder had dissolved in the pale-brown
liquid.

She was pushing the paper back into her pocket when
Stella turned back towards her. Fumbling, Maud drew out her
handkerchief and blew her nose.

'Oh dear,' Stella said. 'I hope you have not caught a chill
from the rain.'

Maud smiled and returned the handkerchief to her pocket,
making sure the crumpled envelope was securely inside. 'I'm
sure I have not. The fire and the tea are having a beneficial
effect.'

The maid reappeared. Stella gave her instructions to the
girl, who bobbed a pretty little curtsy and went out again.

'You mentioned your husband was away from home,' Maud
said. 'Will he return soon?'

'In a day or two. When he has dealt with constituency
business.'

'Constituency business?' Maud's hand flew to her chest in
what she hoped was realistic astonishment. 'You don't mean he
is Mr Sebastian Ferguson, the Member of Parliament?'

Stella nodded wearily. 'Yes. And he is devoted to his work.'

Was this the reason for her dissatisfaction with her
marriage? A husband paying little attention to his young bride
must be vexing for her, but there were worse things to have to
put up with in marriage, Maud was sure.

'How splendid that he is doing such good works.' Maud had

no idea if he was or not, as she had not read anything of the sort in the newspapers.

'Is he?' Stella sounded bored.

'The world of politics must be thrilling,' Maud continued, determined to continue on this theme, 'although I suppose there must be a lot of malice and such like.'

She shrugged. 'None we have experienced.'

The maid brought a fresh pot and set it on the low table. Stella poured Maud a second cup of tea. Maud held her breath and willed Stella to top up her own cup. It would help to dilute the taste of the powder. She did. Maud let out her breath, but her heart continued to thud. The other woman still had to drink the tea.

Stella picked up her cup and began a litany of complaints about life married to a politician, sipping her tea between each assertion. With each sip her concentration appeared to loosen. Maud doubted she'd reveal such tedious and repetitive thoughts to a stranger. The powder must be working.

Finally, Stella put down her cup and saucer and rested her head against the back of the chair. 'The fire is so delightfully warm, I fear that if I stay seated for much longer, I shall be in danger of falling asleep.'

Maud murmured something about the heat of the flames being most welcome, as Stella's eyes fluttered closed. Her speech became a murmur and with longer gaps between each sentence. Her breathing slowed. At last, she was snoring.

Rising quietly from her chair, Maud hastened across the room to the bureau. Turning the little key in its lock, she carefully let down the lid. Slots for writing paper, envelopes, bills, receipts. She rifled through them. Definitely no packet of correspondence. She opened a small drawer on the right-hand side and stared. A bundle of letters, tied with a red ribbon.

Maud snatched them up and checked the name and address

on the top envelope. *Lord Hamish Urquhart, 72 Frederick Street, Edinburgh.* Got them!

Quickly, she slid the drawer shut and went to close the lid of the bureau. It slipped in her nervous hands and dropped back down with a bang.

Her heart seemed to stop.

TWENTY-SIX

Maud turned her head sharply to look at the woman in the chair by the fire. Stella shifted in her drugged sleep and settled again.

This time she took greater care as she locked the bureau and returned to her chair to pick up her bag. Stella lay back with her mouth open and continued to snore. Maud kept an eye on her as she opened the clasp on her bag and slipped the letters inside. Then she crept out of the room.

Maud stood in the hall, breathing fast and praying no servants would appear. None did. They must be occupied with their duties elsewhere. Treading silently, she stepped across the hall, took up her hat and parasol, and let herself out of the front door.

'I'd like to treat you to luncheon today, Daisy,' Maud said the following morning, 'to celebrate our successful beginning in business.'

Daisy smiled. 'That's awfa nice of you, Maud.'

After yesterday's little adventure, she'd hurried back with the correspondence, keen to lock the bundle in the drawer of the bureau in their sitting room. Unlike Mrs Ferguson, she had not made the mistake of leaving the key in the lock.

Now they both stared at the bureau.

'When do we give them back to his lordship?' Daisy said.

'After luncheon, I think. It won't do him any harm to wait a little longer.'

'I wonder what the letters say,' Daisy said after a pause.

'You will have to continue to wonder, I'm afraid.'

She sighed. 'Aye.'

Maud unlocked the drawer, removed the package and placed it in the blue leather purse she used for kirk, before hooking the strap securely around her wrist. Her Sunday costume was completed with a matching midnight-blue hat and parasol.

Maud and Daisy went to the morning service at St Giles' as usual. Maud resisted the impulse to pray for divine inspiration in her work as it didn't seem the right thing to do. But something about the Colonel languishing in jail didn't sit right with her and she couldn't get it out of her mind.

After the service they made their way along the street to a small restaurant she was keen to try.

'What about here?' Maud peered into the window. 'I'm famished.'

A voice behind them said, 'Then allow me to take you both to luncheon.'

Maud turned to see Lord Urquhart. Of course, in a city with a population of something over three hundred thousand, who else could they expect to see?

'Do say yes, ladies. You'll save me from having to eat another dreary meal alone.'

Maud doubted that. 'Are you following me?' She was cross and didn't hesitate to show it.

He looked offended. 'No, I've just come from the High Kirk. I spotted you in the congregation, but there were too many people to be able to speak to you.' Now he looked a little shame-faced. 'I seem to have confessed to following you, after all. The truth is, I have some information which I think might be important. Regarding a mutual acquaintance.'

Whom did he mean? Daisy nudged Maud and nodded towards her bag.

'And I have something for you,' Maud said.

He raised an eyebrow. 'Is it what I think it is?'

'Yes.'

'Then let us not exchange information in the street. Please, let me buy you ladies a meal.'

'It's perhaps a little early.' Annoyingly, her stomach rumbled at that moment.

His eyes opened wide. 'You are hungry, therefore it is exactly the right time. Think of it as a business appointment,' he said, as Maud continued to hesitate.

'Come on, Maud,' said Daisy. 'Lord Urquhart is paying.'

He gave a good-natured laugh.

His offer to pay was very tempting, and she and Daisy did have to return the letters. This would save a further meeting with him.

'Something light?' he went on. 'What about a few oysters, a plate of soup, a little meat?'

'Not oysters. There is no letter R in the month,' Maud said.

'Isn't that just an old wives' tale?'

'Old wives are often right,' Daisy pointed out.

'Then we won't have the oysters.'

Even the thought of the food he mentioned made Maud's mouth water. He turned the handle of the door to the restaurant and opened it. Delicious aromas wafted out onto the pavement. Maud had to swallow to stop from dribbling.

'We accept. Thank you.' She marched in.

There were half a dozen or so small tables with white linen cloths. No doubt due to the early hour, there was only one other diner, an elderly man eating alone. One wall had framed pictures of famous city sights. The Eiffel Tower in Paris, the Colosseum in Rome, the canals of Amsterdam.

'International cuisine?' she asked in a low voice, as they followed the waiter to a table.

Lord Urquhart shook his head. 'But very palatable.'

'Thank you, sir,' said the waiter, straight-faced, as he turned to pull out a chair for Maud. 'We do our best.'

Lord Urquhart suppressed a smile, as he held the other chair for Daisy and asked the man to bring three glasses of wine.

When the waiter had gone, Daisy picked up the menu. 'It a' looks tempting.'

Maud placed her leather purse on the table. Lord Urquhart glanced at it but was too polite to do more.

When the waiter returned with their wine, Maud was still perusing the menu. She looked up. 'I can't decide what to have.'

'Shall I order for all of us?' Lord Urquhart asked.

Annoying as it was to let him do that, they were there on business and the sooner it was completed, the better, so Maud nodded.

'Suits me,' said Daisy.

'Windsor soup and mutton cutlets.' He handed their menus to the waiter.

'Which mutual acquaintance were you referring to outside the restaurant?' Maud asked as soon as the waiter had gone.

'Let us eat something first. Business should not be conducted on an empty stomach.'

'Very well.'

Conversation between the three of them was on neutral topics and by the time Maud had supped the delicious soup and drunk the wine, she was feeling more kindly towards Lord Urquhart. After all, he was a client.

'Now to Mr Laing,' he was saying.

Maud shot Daisy a look and sat up taller, suddenly alert.

'At my club, by some accounts, most actually, the view is he is a bit of a bounder.'

Lord Urquhart paused as the waiter placed their second course on the table. The aroma wafting up from the mutton was heavenly.

'What exactly do you mean?' Maud asked, as the waiter retreated to the kitchen.

He flushed. 'A womaniser.'

'Isna that just the talk of the steamie?' Daisy said.

'My club is hardly a steamie. But no, it's not mere gossip. I had thought it was, which is why I didn't repeat it.' He cut off a piece of his cutlet.

'And now you have proof?'

'A feature of the Saturday-to-Monday, I believe, and the reason why some people attend country house parties is... certain activities. At Duddingston House, I saw Cynthia enter Laing's bedroom during Sunday's post-luncheon siesta. It appeared she was expected – and was welcome.'

So much for the Duchess's matrimonial plan for her elder daughter.

'I'm sorry to say that Cynthia is not alone in her affection for the cad,' he went on.

'He's got more than one other woman?' said Daisy.

Lord Urquhart nodded. 'Usually, his taste runs to females less affluent than Cynthia. Apparently, he pays them off when they find themselves in what I believe is known as "an interesting condition."'

'The devil take him.' Maud cut furiously into her cutlet. To get a woman with child and then cast her aside was one of the lowest things a man could do in her book. She lifted a piece of the mutton on her fork and chewed it. Had Miss Miller discovered her fiancé's behaviour?

She swallowed the meat. 'Why did you not tell me this three days ago when I asked you about him?'

'I'm afraid there's more.'

Her pulse rate was increasing by the minute. 'Yes?'

'The... um... package you said you have for me...'

'Yes,' she almost shouted. *Get on with it!*

He lowered his voice. 'In one of the letters, the lady refers to a liaison she had with Mr Laing.'

'Why on earth did she write that?' Daisy said, looking up from her plate.

He shrugged. 'To show me she was desirable to others, perhaps? I cannot really say, but I do know that the foolish young woman had a lot to lose if the content of those letters was revealed.'

Maud let out a slow breath. 'Why did you not tell me this before?'

'I really am very sorry. The truth is I was embarrassed. The subject is something no gentleman should speak of to a lady.'

And yet what he had told Maud about Laing put a different complexion on the Miller case. She needed to talk to Daisy in private as soon as possible. But first there was one other question she had for Lord Urquhart. Maud finished her meal, put down the knife and fork, and dabbed her mouth with the napkin.

'What made you decide to tell me now?'

'Having thought about it, I realised the information might be crucial. And I could see that you are serious about carving out a career as an investigator.'

Yes, Maud was. She smiled. 'Thank you for the information, Lord Urquhart.' She glanced around the restaurant. The elderly man had gone, the waiter hadn't yet returned to clear their plates and they were alone.

She reached into her bag on the table, extracted the ribbon-tied package and slid it over the tablecloth.

'These are for you.'

TWENTY-SEVEN

'You've done it!'

Lord Urquhart stared at the little parcel for a moment before pulling off the ribbon and dropping it onto the table. From the top envelope, he took out a couple of sheets of paper, which Maud could see were covered in a large scrawl in violet ink, and ran his gaze over them.

'Yes, these are her letters.' He raised his eyes to Maud's. 'Did you really find them at Stella's?'

Maud felt sorry for him, with that wounded look on his face. She brushed the thought aside. 'I'm afraid they were in her house. She had them in her bureau.'

'I don't understand how the letters got there.' He shook his head. 'Nor how you managed to get hold of them.'

Maud held his gaze.

'Quite right, Miss McIntyre. You should not reveal your methods to anyone but the police. I think perhaps the constabulary could take a few tips from you and Miss Cameron.'

Maud wondered if Stella Ferguson had yet discovered the letters were missing and if she had realised it was the not-so-Honourable Jean Ballater who had whisked them away. Maud would have liked a confession from the woman, but it wasn't essential. She'd done as her client instructed and retrieved the package. That didn't stop her imagining Mrs Ferguson easing round the slightly open door from the back lane into Lord Urquhart's garden, skirting the lawn and keeping close to the wall, climbing – in divided skirts – through the window and into his study, stealing the package and out again. She must have been less quiet during her exit, perhaps with relief that she'd secured the letters, or Maximilian had only just been let out by his owner, as then the barking began. Maud could picture the dog attempting to hurl itself at the low stone wall between the two of them. Either Stella panicked, or she had always wanted a Peke – who knows? – but she must have leaned over the wall, snatched up Max and shot out of the garden. Maud had to admire her, in a way.

Lord Urquhart dropped the letters onto the restaurant's swan-white tablecloth and slumped back in his seat. 'Then Stella took them, or arranged for someone to take them for her. Not a thief coming across them by chance when breaking into my house.' He ran a hand across his forehead. 'But why would she do such a thing? What did she hope to gain?'

Maud was pretty sure she knew: to cause Lord Urquhart worry about the disappearance of the letters, and of his and her possible humiliation. It was either in revenge for his not responding to her post-marriage plea to resume their affair, or an attempt to bring him closer to her again. But what she said was, 'Perhaps it's a case of hell hath no fury like—'

'I'm aware of Congreve's quote, thank you,' he said. He looked at the letters lying on the table. 'I can't think why I began the affair in the first place.'

He gathered up the letters.

'You should burn them,' Daisy said.

'I will.' He pushed the bundle into the pocket of his jacket. 'I can't thank you enough for what you've done.'

Maud inclined her head. 'You can thank me by paying your bill in good time.'

'Send it to Frederick Street in the morning and I will see to it immediately.'

'And perhaps...' She left the remark hanging. It wasn't her place to comment on his behaviour.

'Yes?'

Oh, why not say it? Maud finished the sentence. 'You won't be so careless in future.'

'I promise.' He stood. 'Would you two ladies excuse me if I leave now?'

'Of course.' Maud was eager to discuss with Daisy what they'd just learned.

'Would you both like coffee?' he said.

'Yes, please.' Daisy smiled.

Maud nodded. 'Thank you.'

'I'll settle with the waiter at the desk,' he said.

Maud and Daisy thanked him for luncheon and soon afterwards they were alone at the table with their cups of coffee.

'Well,' Daisy said, lifting her cup and taking a sip.

'Exactly. Lord Urquhart's information changes the Miller investigation considerably.'

Daisy nodded and set down her cup. 'I think Laing's betrothed discovered his tricks. All those poor women, not to mention Mrs F. and Lady C.'

'We suspected the warning note was written by a woman. But what if Cynthia has kidnapped Diana? That would free Laing to marry her, instead.'

'Then what would Cynthia do with Diana? Murder her?' As soon as Daisy had spoken, she stared horrified at Maud.

'I can't see that,' Maud reassured her. 'The question is: does Laing have a sufficient motive to get Diana out of the picture?'

'I think Lady C. is just another bit of fun to him.'

'You're right. He must know the Duchess would never

accept him as a son-in-law, no matter how rising he may be. Whatever the reason for Diana Miller's disappearance, we need to find her, which is what her father asked us to do.'

Daisy took another sip of coffee. 'What if we could discover where she was hiding and encourage her to face up to her father and fiancé? Then she and her new sweetheart could marry and live happily ever after.'

Maud smiled. 'That sounds like the perfect outcome.'

Daisy finished her coffee in a few gulps. 'Do you mind if I dash home to the apartment?' she said. 'Only I've got a letter to write to my cousin.'

'Off you go.' Maud picked up her cup. 'I'll saunter back after I've finished this delicious coffee.'

Maud set off along Princes Street, her furled parasol tucked under one arm, swinging her other arm in a jaunty fashion. Another case solved.

The road was as busy as ever and it was with some relief that she turned into South St David Street. There were fewer people here, and it was pleasant to feel she could breathe more easily. She began to skirt round St Andrew Square.

Suddenly, hard metal pressed into her back. Maud opened her mouth to cry out, but the gun jabbed harder into her ribs. Her heart hammered.

'Keep quiet, you interfering *witch*, and step into the shop doorway.' The man's voice hissed in her ear, his breath hot against her skin.

Maud's hands shook, but she wrenched the parasol from under her arm and rammed the tip down as hard as she could on his ankle.

He swore, released his grip and she ran, clutching her parasol in one hand and her skirts in the other. The blood pounded in her head, the image of being found dead in a doorway spurring her on.

She reached the corner of the square and realised she could hear no footsteps running after her. Slowing down, she glanced back over her shoulder and couldn't see her attacker. Maud came to a halt, her breathing ragged.

She steadied her breath to calm herself and walked onto York Place. Thankfully, it was busy again here. What should she do now?

There was no point in looking for a constable. The man had slipped away, and she had nothing to prove that she had been attacked. Besides, she hadn't actually seen him, so she couldn't even give a description.

It was a man; Maud knew that from his voice. What was it he had said? *You interfering witch.* Not the same as the warning in the letters: *Stop asking questions about Miss Miller.* Similar, but not the same. And there was the conviction both she and Daisy had that the notes were written by a woman.

As Maud turned into Broughton Street, she tightened her hold on her trusty parasol and walked on.

'Heavens,' Daisy said, putting down her pen as Maud walked into the sitting room. 'You look frayed round the edges.'

Maud's knees felt weak, and she sank onto the sofa, giving Daisy an account of the attack.

'And you didna see his face at all?' Daisy said, when Maud had finished.

She knew she should have turned to look at the man before running away, and it didn't help that Daisy thought so too. Now all she knew for certain was that someone was prepared to do physical harm to warn them off the case.

'Any distinguishing features?' Daisy asked.

'Such as, given I didn't actually see him?'

'A missing finger, perhaps?' She looked hopeful.

'I can't say I noticed. But he could be missing some skin where I rammed the end of my parasol into his ankle.'

'That's not awfa helpful,' Daisy pointed out. 'You hear about investigators being attacked,' she went on, 'but this is the second time. First in the rose garden at Duddingston and now here.'

Maud felt like telling her this sort of thing was a feature of Sherlock Holmes's life, but that would have made her sound a little disturbed.

Daisy made them both a cup of tea and they discussed this new incident.

'A missing lassie soon to marry, an anti-suffragette faither and fiancé, a lover, a female note-writer and a male attacker. It doesna add up to much, does it?' Daisy said.

'On the face of it, no. But we mustn't forget Diana's friend. I'm sure Miss Grant knows more than she's saying. Another visit to that young woman is due.'

'Shall I come with you this time? To try a different approach.'

'Intimidation, you mean?'

'If it works, why not?'

Why not, indeed? Although Maud preferred to think of it as gentle persuasion. She didn't want to frighten Miss Grant, but the presence of the two of them might be enough to persuade her to tell whatever she knew. And if they were in disguise...

'Shall we go in some sort of disguise?' Daisy added, her face brightening.

Opening the wardrobe door, Maud considered its contents.

'Gypsies, I think. Fortune-tellers. Miss Grant has met me, so I need to change my features. Eye colour can't be altered, but a new nose makes a marked difference.' Maud handed Daisy two tubs. 'We'll create new noses for ourselves with the paste and blend them into our faces with the greasepaint.'

Maud showed her how to mould the putty into whatever shape she wished. 'You start on that, while I sort out the gypsy costumes.'

Daisy took the pots to the dressing table and began to work on her face in front of the mirror. From the wardrobe Maud pulled out brightly coloured blouses and skirts, belts made from strips of fabric, a plain shawl, dark wigs, a headscarf and strings of beads, and arranged them on her bed. She would be the old woman, as it wasn't fair to ask Daisy to put a small stone in one of her boots to produce a painful hobble.

Maud slipped out of her jacket and skirt, unhooked the front of her long-line corset and gave a small sigh of relief when she was down to her chemise and drawers. Next, she drew on one of the long, loose skirts and a blouse with billowing sleeves tight at the wrist. A belt round her waist, beads hanging at her neck, and she was almost ready. While Daisy dressed in her disguise – the brighter-coloured clothes left for her on the bed – Maud pressed a lump of paste onto her nose and made it broader. Next, she blended the new nose into her skin using the dark greasepaint Daisy had been applying and smoothed some over her own hands.

Maud stood, pulled a dark wig over her fair hair and threw a shawl over her head.

Miss Grant had met her only five days ago, so she also needed to disguise her voice, as voices were often even more recognisable than faces. In the street earlier as she'd turned for home, she'd spotted fresh dates for sale on a barrow and had stopped and bought half a dozen. 'And a little basket of blaeberries,' Maud had added to the man. Now, rather than eat all the fruits, they would put some of them to use.

Firstly, Maud rubbed the juice of the blaeberries on her

teeth, gave a stained-toothed grin and bid Daisy do the same. Daisy gave a delighted laugh and snatched up the little punnet of berries.

'Your gypsy is much younger than mine, so you won't need as many,' Maud cautioned.

In less than twenty minutes, they were transformed. Over her red hair, Daisy wore a dark wig and a bright headscarf tied at the back of her neck.

'We'll do very well,' Maud said. 'Remember that people see what they expect to see. Miss Grant will expect gypsy fortune-tellers and that's what she will see.'

Daisy watched in surprise as Maud took a date from the brown paper bag, removed the pit with her fingers and pressed the sticky fruit against the roof of her mouth.

'Simple, but effective,' Maud told her in her newly thick-ened voice. She dropped the pit into the waste-paper bin and licked her fingers clean, pulled a spotted handkerchief from the drawer and wrapped the fig in it. 'I won't put it in until we get to Hope Street, to ensure it stays in place.'

From a shelf in the wardrobe, Maud took the tray containing a small collection of cheap tin items. 'And, finally, the lucky charms. You will try to sell one to Miss Grant, and I will offer to read her palm.' She slipped the string over Daisy's head, and Daisy held the tray in front of her. Maud stood back to examine her appearance. 'You really do look the part.'

'I feel it.' Daisy looked down at the jumble of trinkets and moved them with a brown-stained finger. 'A four-leafed clover, horseshoe, heart, ladybird, wishbone...'

'With all these charms,' Maud said, 'we should be in luck.'

TWENTY-EIGHT

The afternoon was wearing on by the time they reached Miss Grant's house. The street was quiet, and Maud took the small stone she'd earlier placed in her pocket, bent and slid it inside her boot.

'It won't go into position,' she muttered.

'Shoogle your foot,' Daisy advised.

Maud shook her foot as best she could inside the boot and the stone slipped under her heel. Putting her weight on it, she grimaced. It might have been a tiny obstacle, but it made itself known.

'We must go to the side door,' Maud reminded Daisy. 'Follow me.'

She slumped to give herself a stoop and hobbled down the steps at the side of the front door. Through the window of the semi-basement, she could see the cook and maid in the kitchen, preparing dishes for the evening meal. As Maud's and Daisy's shadows crossed the glass, both servants looked up.

'This is so exciting,' Daisy whispered. 'And we don't have to worry that Miss Grant is going to attack us.'

'Young ladies of her class don't go in for that sort of behaviour.'

'Some might,' she said, her tone as sassy as her costume.

Maud sent her a warning look and discreetly used her hand-kerchief to press the date securely to her palate, while Daisy knocked on the door.

'I'm hoping Miss Grant will be too delighted by your lucky charms to look at me,' Maud said, as she pushed the large spotted cloth back into her pocket. 'And then I will offer to tell her future. Few females can resist that.'

'I'm sure you're right, but first we have to get past the servants.'

The door opened and a maid stood there, the same one Maud had seen when she came to question Miss Grant. The girl's attitude was very different now. She looked them up and down, and scowled. 'Aye?'

'Are the ladies of the hoose at hame?' Maud wanted only the daughter, but it would look strange if she asked just for her.

'Bide here.' She shut the door in their faces.

'Wee crabbit quine,' Daisy murmured.

The cook was still at the sink but staring towards the window. 'Stay in character,' Maud warned Daisy.

They waited in silence, until eventually the door was wrenched open again by the maid. 'You're in luck. The mistress is out but her daughter will see you.'

This was even greater luck than the girl realised. She stood back for them to enter. They followed into the kitchen. The cook stepped forward, blocking their way any further. Fisted hands on her wide hips, she glared at them.

'Now you twa listen and listen well,' she said. 'See that you behave yourselves while you're in this hoose. Make sure that you mind your manners with the young mistress. And don't you be touching anything or sitting on the furniture.'

Neither of them said anything but nodded their understanding and followed the maid through the kitchen and up the back stairs. She stopped at an open door on the ground floor.

'The two gypsy women to see you, miss.'

Giving them a glare, she spun on her heels. They stood in the doorway of the sitting room. It was arranged to be admired rather than to relax in. The furniture was over-large, the numerous paintings showed no flair. A gilt-framed wedding photograph on the mantelpiece depicted a young couple Maud presumed to be Angela Grant's parents. He stood tall, thin and severe; she, seated and clasping a large bouquet, also stared unsmiling at the camera. Maud found the atmosphere dispiriting and quite unlike the exuberance of the garden, which Miss Grant had told her was her domain.

Angela Grant rose from her chair by the low fire burning in the grate. Despite its warmth, she looked pale. Like a woman with something troubling her conscience.

She gave a weak smile. 'This is an unexpected treat. Please, come in.'

'Much obliged to you, miss.' Maud stepped into the room. 'As you see, we have some lovely wee fairlies, only a few pennies each.' She beckoned Daisy to come forward. 'Lucky charms for a lucky lady.'

'I'm not sure that I am lucky.' Her voice was rueful. 'But let me see what you have.' She selected the little four-leafed clover. 'To find one of these growing is a particularly good omen, I believe?'

'Aye, miss,' said Daisy. 'It's a Celtic charm. The four leaves represent faith, hope, love and success.'

Miss Grant sighed, slowly replaced the clover and picked up the horseshoe.

'Now that, miss,' said Daisy, 'is another favourite amongst ladies.'

'Why is that?'

'Well, some say it's because the curved shape is like the

moon, which means the moon goddess will protect you from evil and give you good fortune.'

'And what do others say?' She smiled.

'They say,' said Daisy, clearly getting into her role, 'that evil spirits are afraid of horseshoes because they are made of iron and can't be destroyed by flames.'

As Angela Grant turned it in her hands, the horseshoe slipped. 'Oh.' She caught it quickly and looked in dismay at her palm. Maud's gaze followed. The charm was upside down. Miss Grant's voice trembled. 'That is bad luck.'

'Nae at all, miss. The right side up is said to keep the luck in, but with the tips down it pours good fortune out to others.'

Maud sent Daisy a quick glance. She was indeed getting into her role and was making an excellent job of it.

Miss Grant returned the horseshoe to the tray. 'The lady-bird is pretty.' She touched it lightly with her fingertips. After selecting each item in turn and considering it, she finally settled on one charm.

'I'll have this.' In her left hand, she held the four-leafed clover towards Daisy.

Maud caught at the soft white hand and held it in her brown-stained one. 'You have an interesting palm, lady. Let me read it for you.'

She tried to pull her hand away, but Maud held on to it. 'Which is your favoured hand?'

She hesitated. 'My right.'

Maud nodded. 'It is the other hand – with you this left one – that shows you what will be.' She prayed she could remember what she'd read in the little book on palmistry.

Miss Grant glanced at Daisy, who nodded encouragingly, and her hand relaxed a little in Maud's. She transferred the trinket into her other hand and closed her fingers around it.

'That's better. Now I can see your lines more clearly. Look.'

With her forefinger, Maud traced a line across the top of her palm. 'This is the hairt line. And this one below is the heid line.'

'What does the heart line tell you?' Angela Grant asked, her voice low.

'Aye, that is what all the young ladies want to know. See how the line begins below your middle finger? You fall in love easily. This includes making friendships,' Maud added, watching her face. 'Friendships with those you really care about.'

Miss Grant's interest quickened, her gaze still focused on her palm.

'And see,' Maud went on, 'how the line curves? This means you freely express your emotions.' All this was true according to the book, which was fortunate.

Her hand jerked in Maud's and she glanced up, searching Maud's face. Maud held her breath, but no recognition showed in the young lady's eyes. 'And my head line? What does that tell you?'

Maud drew Miss Grant's gaze back down to her palm. 'It is a deep, long line, which means your thinking is clear.'

The other woman gave a small nod in agreement. Maud needed something to persuade her to reveal whatever was on her conscience. 'But wait. You see here a small cross in the heid line?'

She peered more closely. 'I think so.'

'Oh, my poor lady. This tells me you are going through emotional turmoil, unsure about the right thing to do...'

Miss Grant gasped and pulled her hand away. 'How did you know?' She stared at Maud.

Maud pulled the shawl more firmly over her head and shrugged. 'I know nothing, my lady. It is your palm that is telling me so. Everything that happens to us is written in the hand, but only the person themselves can interpret what the hand shows. I hope your dear mama can help you through the storm to come.'

'Oh, miss,' put in Daisy softly, 'I hope so too. The palm is never wrong.'

Angela Grant gave a small sob and collapsed white-faced into her chair. 'It is true, everything you say. Usually, I am a sensible woman, but I have a dear friend and it pains me not to express my deep concerns about her, even to my mama, but I am sworn to secrecy.'

She passed a hand across her forehead. 'My friend has... has run away with a man, and they are living together as husband and wife.'

Maud waited with bated breath. It was as she expected. Was she about to tell them where Diana Miller was hiding?

'She made me promise not to disclose where they are,' Miss Grant continued, 'yet her father is desperately concerned about her.'

No mention of the fiancé's concern, Maud noticed.

'It is no wonder you are so worried. If not your mama, then there must be someone you can tell where she is biding, to unburden yourself and aid your friend.' Maud pressed her fingers to her temples. 'I sense the presence of a tall young lady with fair hair. She wants to help.'

Daisy shot Maud a look that said don't overdo it, and she dropped her hands.

Miss Grant, her eyes blurred with tears, shook her head. 'That might ease one part of my conscience, that which is concerned for my friend's father, but not the other part. I have promised her.' A tear rolled down her cheek.

'What do we do now?' Daisy mouthed over Miss Grant's bent head.

They couldn't do what Maud usually recommended in such situations – offer to make a nice cup of tea. She nodded towards the fireplace to indicate to Daisy that she attend to the dying flames. The warmth of a properly burning fire can give some comfort.

As Daisy raked the coals with the poker and Maud tried to think of their next step, Miss Grant slowly opened her hand. Where she had gripped it so tightly, the four-leafed clover had made a small red cut in her palm. She dropped the charm into her lap and wordlessly held out her palm.

Again, Maud took her hand.

'The line that begins near the thumb and travels down in an arc is the life line.' Hers was short and shallow, which meant she was manipulated by others. As that included her, Maud skipped over that part of the reading. 'The spot of blood in the middle of the line indicates an injury...'

'Why did you tell her that?' said Daisy, as she walked and Maud hobbled alongside her onto the street.

Maud chewed the date and swallowed it. 'Because it's true.' Her voice had resumed its normal dulcet tones. 'A circle in the life line shows injury.'

'Aye, well, that circle of blood *was* the injury.'

'For that matter, why did you tell her those stories about the horseshoe?' They rounded the corner and Maud bent to unlace her boot.

'Because they're true.'

She managed to look up at Daisy and raise an eyebrow as she leaned against a house wall and pulled off her boot.

'That is,' went on Daisy, 'they're stories my mither told me.'

Maud tipped her boot upside down. The stone fell out and skittered across the pavement. She glared at it; the pain and damage inflicted by the thing was out of proportion to its size. Quickly, she pulled her boot back on, snatched up the stone and dropped it into her pocket. She might need it again one day, but her foot hoped it wouldn't be soon.

As soon as she'd climbed up the first flight of stairs and was through the door into the sitting room, Maud sank onto the sofa, wrenched off her boots and dropped them to the floor. The sole and heel of her foot were stinging. She massaged her foot, but that made it feel worse. She leaned back with a sigh.

Daisy removed her headscarf and wig, and scratched her head. 'This false hair makes your scalp hot.' She glanced at Maud's feet. 'I'll get you a bowl of warm water.'

'Thanks, Daisy.' Gingerly, Maud peeled off her stocking.

She heard Daisy clattering about with the kettle, first at the sink and then on the stove, before she came back into the room.

'The water won't be long.' She took the armchair opposite me. 'What do you think of this evening's adventure? Was it worthwhile?'

'It was definitely worthwhile. Angela Grant might not have told us where Diana and her new beau are currently ensconced, but she knows. All we have to do is watch and wait. I think Miss Grant's conscience is plaguing her sufficiently that it's very likely she will pay her friend a visit.'

'To persuade Miss Miller to leave the love-nest and set her faither's mind at rest?'

Maud nodded. 'This means another disguise will be in order.'

Daisy touched her putty nose. 'I hope this clart comes off our faces easily.' Maud smiled at her, and Daisy grimaced. 'And the staining off our teeth.'

'A little alcohol on a cloth will remove the putty,' she reassured her. 'And then soap and water on our faces and bicarbonate of soda to clean our teeth. Now, as to tomorrow, I wonder which disguise would be the most appropriate to observe Miss Grant's house.'

'A flower girl,' suggested Daisy. 'If you do that, I will collect my photograph from Ovinius Davis and then look after the office.'

'You don't want to watch the house?'

'Nae, I'd best get the photograph.' She grinned. 'I dinna like to keep dear Ernest waiting.'

A whistling came from the kitchen. 'That's the kettle,' she said, getting up from the armchair.

'Don't worry about my foot,' Maud called after her. 'Can you use the water to make us both a cup of tea? There's some cake in the tin on the shelf. I'll take my tea and cake and have a soak in the bath. Then I'm off to bed, as it will be an early start tomorrow.'

Maud slept well, rose early feeling refreshed and, ignoring her tender foot, set out immediately after breakfast to buy a few bunches of whatever was in bloom. Then she would set herself up on the corner of Hope Street, where she could keep an eye on any comings and goings. If Miss Grant was going to make contact with her friend, she'd do so at the first opportunity she had without arousing suspicion. Maud guessed that would be this morning.

She found a flower girl not far from the apartment and, after taking careful note of how she dressed, Maud looked into the basket on her arm. She was tempted by the dahlias in their riot of yellows, oranges, whites and reds, but they might attract too much attention from Miss Grant. She wanted to be unobtrusive enough to follow her.

'Going to a funeral, miss?' the flower girl asked, giving her an odd look when Maud asked for half her stock of daisies. Their yellow wasn't too ostentatious but would provide cover for her surveillance.

Maud gave her a tight smile and hurried away, feeling conspicuous behind her floral arrangement. Once she reached the sanctuary of her apartment, she changed into the nearest costume she owned to the one worn by the girl. Brown hat with feathers and brown jacket, apron tied round her waist and pretty scarf knotted roughly at her throat. She selected a pair of cheap but delicate-looking long earrings and screwed them on. At the bottom of the wardrobe sat a wicker basket with a handle, which was perfect for her purposes. Filling it with the daisies, she sallied forth.

Maud walked with purpose, not making eye contact with anyone in case they should try to stop her to buy a bunch or two. It wouldn't do to arrive at Hope Street with no flowers left to sell. When she reached her destination, positioning herself with a clear view of the Millers' front door, she plucked a bloom from the basket and held it out to passers-by.

'Bonnie yellow daisies for your sweethearts,' Maud called. 'Buy a single flooer or a wee posie.'

Maud had sold a few posies by the time the door opened. Just as she hoped, Miss Grant stepped out. She looked around nervously but didn't give Maud's flower girl a second glance. Straightening her shoulders, she stepped out along the street. As soon as she'd gone a reasonable distance, Maud followed, Miss Grant's black and white striped blouse with white collar distinctive enough to spot amongst the throng on the street.

Angela Grant turned left onto Princes Street, dodged a tram as she crossed the road and weaved her way through the pedestrians on the opposite pavement. Passing the gardens, she headed south, still moving at a smart pace, across Waverley Bridge and towards Old Town. Maud hurried along behind her, keeping her distance but always with her eye trained on the blouse.

The surroundings were becoming increasingly down-at-heel. No longer did Maud see the occasional little boy in a sailor suit or small girl wearing a pretty dress with lace on the collar, walking by the side of a nanny. Here the children were dirty and barefoot, playing with a rope around a lamp post or sitting on a kerb rolling clay marbles in the gutter. Maud's heart went out to these bairns, and she thought of their parents, who might well be amongst those striking in an attempt to bring an end to their poor pay and dreadful working conditions.

Her quarry turned into a close off the High Street.

Maud stopped in the shade of a dingy building at the corner and peered round, just in time to see Angela Grant enter a low doorway about halfway down the alley. Hastening forward, she reached the shabby door and pushed gently.

It swung open.

TWENTY-NINE

The passage, painted in brown and mustard colours, was gloomy after the bright sun, but Maud could make out the staircase ahead and two doors on the ground floor. Had Angela Grant gone into one of those?

She shut the street door quietly and tiptoed in, as her eyes became accustomed to the semi-darkness of the tenement. Above her, she could hear female voices. They must be no further up than the first floor. Leaving the flower basket in the hall, Maud put one foot on the concrete steps and heard an upstairs door close. She sped up the stairs and came to a halt on the first landing. A meagre light penetrated through the dirty glass cupola on the roof, but it gave no clue as to which of the four doors here Angela Grant had entered.

Then she heard raised voices, including a man's, from behind one of them and Maud crept forward to put her ear to the door. The voices were too muffled to make out what they were saying. Was Angela telling Diana Miller about Maud's enquiries, and perhaps the visit of the gypsies, and trying to persuade Diana and her lover to come clean to Lord Miller and the obnoxious Douglas Laing? If so, it didn't seem to be going well.

The voices were growing louder, and they were coming closer to the door. Maud flew down the stairs, snatched up her basket of flowers and let herself out of the tenement. As soon as she was back in the High Street, she took up an inconspicuous position and waited, her heart thudding.

Before long, Miss Grant entered the street again, walking slowly this time and looking pensive. The poor girl really was suffering with her conscience.

Maud continued to wait, hoping that Diana would come after her friend, and she wasn't disappointed. Minutes later, a young woman rushed out of the close. Her handsome features, the dark hair piled on top of her head in the pompadour style and her large dark eyes as Maud had seen in her photograph, confirmed it was Diana Miller. To her credit, her hair was as neat as in the likeness, despite her present somewhat straitened circumstances.

'Angela!' Diana called to her friend's retreating back.

Angela Grant spun round, and Diana ran down the street towards her. They embraced and there was a low conversation before Diana retraced her steps. Miss Grant shook her head slightly and resumed walking away.

Maud was satisfied Diana was staying in those lodgings with her man. She returned to the tenement, mounted the stairs to the first floor and knocked on the door.

It flew open. 'Angela!' began Diana's pleased exclamation. It died in her throat as she saw it wasn't her friend. 'I'm sorry, I thought you were someone else.'

That was reasonable, as Maud quite often was someone else.

Diana's gaze fell on the flowers in Maud's basket. 'No, thank you. I already have flowers.'

As she moved to close the door, Maud caught a glimpse of a

table and on it a little vase filled with the jewel-blue flowers of love-in-a-mist. This might be a man's lodgings, but Diana was clearly making it into a home.

Maud put a foot out to stop the door. 'Miss Diana Miller?'

The young woman frowned and opened it wider. 'Yes?'

'My name is Maud McIntyre and I'm a private detective. Your father has engaged me to—'

'No!' She tried again to shut the door.

'What is it, dearest?' came the man's voice. He came into the hall and stared at Maud as she stood in the doorway. Very tall and rather dashing-looking, he fitted the description given by the photographer. Today he wore a cream waistcoat over a white shirt and dark trousers, rather than a kilt, but he looked none the worse for it.

He looked enquiringly at Diana. 'What is going on?'

'This woman,' whispered Diana, 'is a private detective and has been sent here by my father.'

'You can tell him—' The man took a step towards Maud, looking considerably more menacing than a minute ago.

Diana put a restraining hand on his arm. Maud's knees wobbled as the memory of being assaulted in the street yesterday afternoon leaped back into her mind.

'Was it you who attacked me in St Andrew Square?' she asked.

He took a step back. 'Of course not. I would never do such a thing.' He looked so stricken that she was sure he was telling the truth. Besides, someone as tall as this fellow, even seizing her from behind, would have been obvious.

Diana's hand had flown to her mouth. 'Someone attacked you?'

'I dealt with it,' Maud said. 'But I do have another question, this one for you, Miss Miller. Did you send me two letters warning me off the case?'

She dropped her hand. 'Yes,' she whispered, 'I did. I paid a boy to deliver them. I wanted only to stop the investigation. I was afraid you would find me – and you did.'

So, she and Daisy were right about a woman writing the letters, Maud thought, although she hadn't really suspected Diana herself. But if her sweetheart hadn't been the one to attack her, then who had? And more importantly, why didn't this person want her to find Diana?

'But how did you know where I was?' Diana's question brought Maud back from her musing.

'We private detectives have our methods.'

The man, Diana's true love, caught her in his arms as she threatened to swoon against him. 'She followed Angela Grant here, I imagine. You should sit, my love.' He led Diana away and through the open door into the sitting room Maud saw him help her into an armchair. Maud stepped into the flat, quietly closed the front door behind her and moved into the sitting room. The man now sat on the arm of Diana's chair, his hand tenderly smoothing back a stray lock of hair from her face. Against one wall stood a sofa on which was placed a pillow and a neatly folded blanket. A door stood ajar to another room which contained a bed.

'Following a witness is part of our methods,' Maud went on, 'and I assure you it's not quite as easy as it might look.' She went over to Diana Miller and crouched down in front of her. Maud took one of her hands in both of hers. She gazed at Maud, a look of defeat on her pale face.

'Now I have found you,' Maud said, 'I am obliged to inform your father.'

'But—'

Maud squeezed her hand and released it. 'You are of age, so I don't need to tell him where you are,' she continued. 'But I will let him know you are safe and well. You are safe and well, I take it?'

'Oh, yes.'

'And happy?' Maud had to be sure.

'Blissfully.' She smiled up at the man, and he took her hand and kissed it.

Maud blinked a tear from her eye and nodded. 'Then my report will advise him of that and little more.'

'Thank you,' Diana said.

'I love Diana and she loves me,' said the man. 'We wish to marry as soon as possible, but Diana desires that her father bless our union and that seems unlikely. At least, not until I am able to support her. I'm trying to make my way in the world as a journalist.' He gave a rueful smile. 'My name, by the way, is Jack Buchanan.'

'It's really the Honourable John Buchanan,' put in Diana, gazing up at him, 'as he's the younger son of a Baron.'

Then all hope might not be lost. It wasn't as though he were the younger son of a night-soil man. 'Perhaps your father will come round, Miss Miller.'

'Perhaps, but there's also my fiancé.'

'Is he very much in love with you?' Maud thought she knew the answer.

'No, he's not, and I don't believe he ever has been.'

Maud was right. It gave her no pleasure for that to be so, but, on the other hand, she no longer felt bad about keeping Diana's whereabouts a secret.

'Don't let his charm fool you. Douglas Laing despises women' – there was an unexpected strength filling Diana's voice – 'and suffragettes in particular.'

'So I've noticed,' Maud said dryly.

'The more he belittled suffragettes, the less affection I felt for him. And then Jack came along. He helps with addressing envelopes for the movement and I do the same. I'm paid two pounds a week.' She smiled. 'I know it isn't much, but it gives me real pleasure to be of use to society and to earn some money.'

Maud knew exactly what she meant. 'What are you going to do about Mr Laing?'

Diana sighed. 'I don't know. My father approves of him, which makes it difficult.' She looked hopefully at Maud. 'Perhaps, if you wouldn't mind, you could put in your report how much I loathe Douglas Laing?'

Lord Miller was in court during the day, so Maud would delay her visit to him until the evening. Daisy would be wondering how she'd got on with following Angela Grant. First though, Maud needed to return to Broughton Street and change out of her flower-seller's costume. She also hadn't had time to do her fifteen minutes of ballet warm-up exercises this morning and now she felt an ambitious cambré would be just the thing.

Once again dressed as Maud McIntyre, private detective, she walked with a spring in her step to the office. Between the two of them, she and Daisy had returned Maximilian to his rightful owner, retrieved Lord Urquhart's potentially ruinous letters and found Miss Miller alive and well. But there was still the unsatisfactory resolution of the Duddingston theft and murder.

Maud turned the handle of the agency's door and walked in. Daisy looked up from the typewriter, an eager look on her face.

'Did Miss Grant lead you to Diana Miller?'

'She did.' Maud removed her hat and jacket and hung them on the peg behind the door. 'As we surmised, Diana is living happily with her handsome beau, otherwise known as the Honourable John Buchanan.'

Daisy smiled. 'I do like a happy ending.'

'Let's hope it is. I still have to inform her father, which I'll do this evening.'

Maud looked about the room. It needed a tidy-up and she'd

start with the pinks from Lord Urquhart, their frilly-edged petals now brown. She plucked the wilted blooms from the milk bottle and dropped them into the waste-paper bin. She'd rinsed the makeshift vase and was putting it beside the door to remind herself to return it, when her eye lit on Mr Davis's photograph of Daisy, propped up on the bookshelf. He'd captured her seated primly in the chair by the hearth, but Maud could see the glint in her eye.

'A good likeness,' Maud said to her, nodding at the picture.

She grinned. 'It's nae bad.' She pulled the sheet of paper from the Underwood. 'Lord Urquhart's invoice,' she said, as she folded it into an envelope.

'The agency is doing well, Daisy, but...'

'There's still the Duddingston case?'

Daisy knew Maud as well as Maud knew herself. 'Yes.' Maud sighed. 'I can't deny I'm disappointed that my instincts were wrong about Laing, that he wasn't involved in Diana's disappearance.'

'But you can see why she wanted to escape such an awfa man.'

Maud nodded. 'I'm convinced he must be involved in the murder and theft at Duddingston, but I just can't work out how.'

At once an idea came to Maud and she glanced at her wrist-watch. 'I need to leave now to speak to Lord Miller. Could you telephone the Duchess and tell her we've solved the crime? Ask Her Grace to summon everyone back to her drawing room for three o'clock tomorrow afternoon, when the real villain will be identified.'

'To get Laing to show his hand, as it were?' Daisy smiled. 'Aye, it could work.'

'I expected you to bring Diana home.'

Lord Miller wasn't too happy when Maud arrived at his house that evening to give him a verbal report and return his daughter's portrait.

He took the photograph with a frown. 'I've had a busy day in court...'

Sending more suffragettes to prison, no doubt, was her response to his abrupt manner. Maud kept it to herself, though. It wouldn't do to offend a client, particularly not a powerful man like Lord Miller.

'... and now you come to me with this news and say you are not willing to complete our agreement. A man would not go back on his word.' He dropped into a chair and rubbed his face with his hands.

'I beg your pardon, Lord Miller, but you will recall that was not our agreement. You engaged me to find your daughter and that is what I have done.'

He looked up and sent Maud a sharp look. For a moment, he didn't speak. Then he said, 'You are indeed correct, Miss McIntyre.' He gave a wry smile. 'Your quick mind is worthy of the legal profession. I cannot believe I did not specify exactly what I wished you to do.'

The poor man seemed to have aged since she had last visited his house. 'You were understandably upset,' she said in a gentle voice.

'Even so...' He shook his head.

She found herself saying, 'Shall I ring for a whisky?'

He nodded. 'If you would be so kind.'

Before long Maud was sitting in the armchair opposite him, he staring at his whisky and she politely sipping hers as she waited for him to speak.

Eventually, he said, 'It's not been easy.'

'What hasn't?' Maud put down her glass.

'Managing a daughter without her mother to guide her. I've always wanted to do the right thing for Diana, but...' He broke off and took a gulp of his drink. 'You've come to tell me she doesn't want to see me again.'

'That isn't the case. She wants to see you, but only if you're prepared to acknowledge the man she loves.'

'I don't know that I can.'

'You could try.'

After a while, he got to his feet, crossed to a table in the corner of the room and pulled open a drawer. 'Are they, my daughter and this man, residing in the same set of rooms?' he asked, his back still towards Maud. 'Has the blackguard...? It doesn't matter. It will soon be known that she ran away with him. Her reputation will be as naught. Laing will never have her now.'

And she did not want Laing. 'Diana and the young man are very much in love, My Lord.' Maud remembered the sofa made into a temporary bed and the separate bedroom. 'I do not think he is the kind of man who would take advantage of the situation.'

Lord Miller paused and then took a cheque book from the drawer. 'I must pay you.'

'My assistant will send you the account.'

'Very well.' He turned back towards Maud. 'The maid will show you out.'

'Before I go, My Lord, do you wish me to convey a message to Diana?'

'I wish nothing more from you. Good day, Miss McIntyre.'

The maid arrived to show her to the door. Maud had very much hoped this whole affair would have a satisfactory conclusion, but she was afraid it didn't look promising.

It was a little after eight o'clock and the sun low on the horizon when Maud stood on the step and breathed deeply as the maid closed the door behind her. The city air smelled of fumes from motor cars. For a moment, she wished she were back in the country, breathing in the fresh, sweet air.

Maud walked down the path towards the anxious young couple walking up it. The three of them stopped and smiled tentatively at each other.

'Tread carefully,' Maud told them.

'That bad?' he said.

'I cannot be certain how he will receive either of you.'

'Then we had better get it over with,' she said. And with that the handsome couple resumed their stroll towards the door, arm in arm.

'Good luck,' Maud called after them. Diana Miller and Jack Buchanan were going to need it.

Maud and Daisy had barely arrived in the office the following morning when the telephone rang.

Daisy answered. Her eyebrows rose and she said, 'I will pass you over, miss.'

Across the desk, she handed Maud the instrument.

'Who is it?' Maud mouthed.

Daisy shook her head and whispered, 'I'm nae sure, but whoever it is, she's in a rare state and asked for you.'

Maud cleared her throat and spoke into the mouthpiece. 'Good morning. Maud McIntyre speaking.'

'Oh, thank goodness I have got you.' It sounded like a young woman, and she was clearly agitated. 'You must come straightaway to Duddingston House. Something awful has happened.'

'Of course.' Maud got to her feet. 'But what is it?'

'Please hurry!' The telephone line went dead.

Maud replaced the receiver and turned to Daisy, who was staring at her. 'Something's up at the Duchess of Duddingston's place. She wants us to go immediately.'

'Did the girl say what's happened?'

'No. We were cut off before she told me. Either she was too flustered or—'

'Someone deliberately broke the connection,' Daisy finished the sentence.

They stared at each other.

'We have to go at once,' Maud said.

'Your brother's car.' Daisy was putting on her hat.

Maud stuffed a fresh notebook and pencil into her bag as Daisy's boots were already clattering down the stairs. Maud locked the office and dashed down after her, her long coat flying. The door to the street banged shut behind them.

'What could have happened at Duddingston to require our immediate presence?' Maud was breathless as they hurried along the pavement. A crime, of course, but of what sort? It was unlikely to be a theft, as that wouldn't need them there urgently. Another death? A chill went through her.

'We should have telephoned the Duchess to ask for more details,' Daisy puffed.

She was right, but it was too late now. Maud had even forgotten to put on her gloves. Quickly, she pulled them from her bag and drew them on, although it was something a lady should never do in the street.

They quickened their pace and at last reached Broughton Street. They ran round to the stables.

'Get in, Daisy, while I start the engine.' Maud had started her father's motor car on occasions, but now Archie's voice was clear in her head as she followed his instructions. *Hand brake on, gear in neutral.* Yes, that was how she'd left the Napier after she'd taken her brother to the railway station. *Take starting handle from boot, go round to front and slide handle in to line up with crank shaft...* In her haste, she couldn't get it to line up. Taking a deep breath, she tried again and this time the handle went into smoothly. *Turn on ignition.*

'Turn on the ignition, Daisy,' Maud called to her.

'Just a minute. I need to find it first.'

'The key is already in; turn that.'

A brief pause and she called back, 'That's done.'

Grab handle, keeping thumb out of way to avoid breaking thumb. Good advice. *One complete turn – slowly – of the handle. On second rotation press down hard...*

The engine sprang into life. Thank goodness.

Maud jumped into the driver's seat, slammed the door shut, tied a scarf over her hat to keep it in place and they were off.

The city roads were so much busier than those she was used to in the country. Maud navigated round an open-sided milk cart being drawn by a big black horse, the bottles rattling in their crates.

'We forgot to put out the milk bottle,' said Daisy.

Maud nipped in front of a motor car, pressing the horn as she went.

Daisy glanced at her. 'It's quite something, isn't it, this speed lark?'

'The girl did say it was urgent.'

They said nothing more until they were through the city and out into the open country heading south. Maud pressed the accelerator harder, and they gained speed. She had the sudden, rather worrying realisation that they were rushing towards an unknown incident. But this was the sort of thing that must happen to police detectives all the time...

'Whatever it is,' said Daisy, voicing Maud's thoughts, 'the Duchess wouldna ask us to come if it weren't important.'

'Except that it wasn't the Duchess herself. It must have been one of the maids.'

'Do you ken which one?'

Maud shook her head. 'She didn't identify herself.'

'Hmm.'

That 'hmm' didn't sound good. 'You think we might be heading into a trap?' Maud was annoyed that she hadn't asked herself that same question and telephoned Duddingston House to confirm the Duchess's phone call. 'It's possible.'

'Why would the girl, whoever she may be, want to trick us in this way?'

Maud frowned. 'We're private detectives. We must have enemies.'

'We've only been doing the job for a few weeks. Could we have made enemies in such a short time?'

Maud considered the question. Very likely.

The blast of a horn pierced the air, and a green motor car passed them at speed.

'What the—?' Maud caught her breath. 'The passenger's got a gun!'

'What?'

'Get down!'

THIRTY

Maud's heart skittered, she heard a burst of gunfire and the windscreen cracked. Daisy screamed as the Napier skidded on the road. Maud regained control and righted it again. Beads of sweat prickled her forehead, her palms were damp. She took her eyes off the road for a second to check on Daisy.

'Are you all right?'

'Yes.' She took her hands from her head and looked at Maud. 'We're both still alive.'

'The shot missed us.' Maud's voice was grim. 'Looks like the driver was travelling too fast for his passenger to take an accurate aim.'

The bullet hole was high on the windscreen. The green Austin had raced on. Maud pressed her foot on the pedal.

'What are you doing?' Daisy cried.

'I'm not letting them get away with it.' Maud didn't know which was the faster motor, but she was determined.

'We dinna have a gun!'

They flew round a bend. Daisy put out a hand and braced herself against the dashboard.

'Where have they gone?' Maud muttered.

The road ahead was empty. She slowed as they approached a crossroads bounded with high hedgerows. They peered from right to left. No sign of any motor car. She sped up again and they dashed across the junction.

There was a screech of tyres from behind them.

Daisy turned in her seat and looked back. 'It's shot out from the side junction.'

The Austin loomed up alongside them. Maud's heart threatened to jump out of her mouth.

It kept abreast of them for a few yards. The passenger in the front seat, his hat low down on his face, pointed his revolver at Maud and signalled her to stop.

'Get ready to hold tight very soon,' Maud shouted to Daisy above the noise of the car engines.

Maud's stomach twisted into even tighter knots as she slowed down. The green motor did the same. When they both had almost stopped, the passenger door of the Austin opened and the man prepared to get out.

'Here we go.' Maud threw the Napier into low gear, accelerated, changed up quickly and sprinted away at top speed.

'You've done it.' Daisy let out a breath.

'Not just yet,' Maud said, glancing back over her shoulder and seeing two blinding headlights fast approaching. This was not how she'd planned to die.

The other driver started to overtake them but misjudged the curve. Their motor swerved violently, came off the road and struck a tree with a terrific bang.

'Lord have mercy.' Daisy's voice was a whisper.

Maud brought the Napier to a stop, opened her door and made to step out.

'Wait!' Daisy grabbed her arm. 'It may be a trap!'

'I don't think so.' Maud climbed out and Daisy followed. 'Look at them.'

Only a few yards ahead, the front of the Austin was crumpled like a squeeze-box. Both the occupants lay slumped forward, unmoving, in their seats.

She walked towards the car, Daisy close behind. Maud's legs were shaking. Where was the gun? She had a vision of the man lifting it and firing at them, his last remaining action on this earth.

Maud looked through the twisted open window. The passenger's face was cut and bloody, his eyes closed; the hat no longer on his head, the revolver fallen from his grasp. She stared at the young man. A complete stranger. Why would he try to kill her, to kill them?

'Is he... dead?' whispered Daisy.

Maud's throat was dry. She swallowed, reached in through the car window and felt for a pulse in the man's neck.

'Not yet. It's weak, but there is a pulse.'

'And the driver?'

She moved round to the other side and Daisy came with her. She repeated the motion and shook her head. 'Too late for him. It looks like his neck was broken on impact with the tree.'

Daisy shuddered.

'We should call for an ambulance for the other man,' Maud said. 'I seem to remember there's an inn a couple of miles further along the road. One of us can telephone from there.'

'I'll stay with him,' said Daisy, 'in case he comes round. To be injured and alone – I wouldna wish that on anyone.'

'What he tried to do to us was awful.' Maud saw the look on her face and sighed. 'Let's see if we can get him out of the car. It will be quicker to take him to the infirmary ourselves than wait for an ambulance.'

She put her hand on the door and tried to open it. 'It's jammed.' She ran back to her car and opened the bonnet.

'Hurry,' Daisy shouted.

Maud took out a spanner and ran back to where Daisy stood. She'd slipped her hand in through the window of the

Austin and was holding the man's hand, but she moved out of the way as Maud worked the spanner into the gap beside the door.

'This should work,' Maud said. 'Stand well back.'

Daisy stepped away from the car, and Maud put both hands onto the spanner and used it to lever the door open. The man's eyelids fluttered and their eyes met.

A spasm of pain crossed his face. 'It was supposed to be an easy job...'

'Why did you try to kill us?'

'Paid to do it.' His voice faded and he was again losing consciousness. Under the bloody mess on his face, he was as white as a sheet.

'Who? Who paid you?' Maud said, her tone soft but urgent. She bent to hear him.

'Laing,' he muttered.

Laing! Maud glanced at Daisy. Her look told Maud she had heard.

'Stay awake!' Maud knew only a little about first aid, but she was aware that an unconscious man is in danger of choking. 'You must stay awake!'

'We have to get him to hospital,' she said. Daisy reached into the car, removed the gun from the floor and tipped into her hand the unspent bullets from the chamber. She passed them to Maud, and Maud slid the bullets and gun into her coat pocket before leaning into the car again and slipping an arm around him.

'Help me take his weight, Daisy.'

He gave a groan that chilled Maud's blood.

Daisy put her hand on Maud's arm. 'Moving him might make his injuries worse. You go for help. I'll stay here with him.'

Maud hesitated. 'I don't like to leave you here.'

'He can't harm anyone now.'

'Can you hear me?' Maud said to him. 'I'm going to telephone the hospital for an ambulance.' She turned to Daisy. 'And I'll inform the police.'

A deathly rattle sounded from the man's throat. As Maud watched his shallow, laboured breathing, time seemed to slow. He fell silent. She felt again for a pulse in his neck. There was nothing. She looked at Daisy. 'He's gone.'

Daisy spoke slowly. 'It was Laing who wanted us dead.'

Maud nodded. Her suspicions about him had been confirmed, but they needed more – and now both witnesses were dead.

'Best report this, Maud.' Daisy returned to the Napier and sat on the running board. 'I'll wait here.'

Daisy was still seated there when Maud returned.

'I've telephoned for an ambulance and the police. They should be here shortly.' Maud sat next to her, and they waited in silence. Her legs were still trembling from the shock of being shot at, and at seeing the man's cut and bloodied face.

They got to their feet when a heavily built policeman came pedalling along the road. He reached them, braked and dismounted.

'Police Constable George Peacock,' he said. His eyes went from Maud to Daisy, to the other car. He addressed Maud and touched his helmet. 'What's happened here, miss?'

She nodded towards the Austin. 'They tried to kill us.'

The constable leaned his bike against the stone wall at the side of the road. He pulled out his notebook and pencil and took a step towards the wrecked motor.

'They're both dead,' she added.

The clip-clop and rumble of a fast-approaching horse-drawn wagon signalled the arrival of the ambulance. The driver and his companion reined in the horse and came to a halt. They jumped down from their seats at the front of the wagon, ran to the crushed car and spoke in low voices to the police officer. Maud watched as the constable made a few notes in his pocket-book and the ambulance men assessed the situation. The two men were pronounced dead, then were each eased onto a stretcher and slid into the back of the covered wagon. Maud and Daisy gave their statements, and Maud handed the gun and bullets to Constable Peacock. The ambulance driver turned the horse and the wagon moved away, and the police officer mounted his bicycle. It was over.

'I think I'm going to boke,' said Daisy, her hand to her mouth.

'You are not,' Maud said firmly. 'Come and sit away from the motor car, and breathe deeply through your mouth. That will settle your stomach.'

She led her over to a tree stump at the side of the road, facing away from the wrecked Austin. Apart from Daisy's slow panting, they sat in silence.

'Did you telephone the Duchess?' Daisy said after a while.

'She told me that she'd not asked anyone in her household to contact us and there was no emergency.' Maud had failed the basic rule of detection: double-check everything. 'We've asked the Duchess to gather everyone together this afternoon to reveal the true thief and murderer. How could I have been so foolish as to risk both our lives like that?'

'I didna try to stop you,' Daisy said. 'And someone made that telephone call.'

'Laing probably put up one of the maids, telling her it was a practical joke.'

Maud remembered what Lord Urquhart had told her of the Duchess's daughter creeping into Laing's bedroom that after-noon at Duddingston House. Would Cynthia have been so foolish as to make that telephone call?

'And those men?' Daisy said.

'Poor wretches who were persuaded to do it for money, I

imagine. My bright-blue Napier is certainly distinctive, so they had no fear of shooting at the wrong car.'

'Laing must have been the man who attacked you at Duddingston and in St Andrew Square.'

A thought struck Maud. 'The red rose Laing put into my hat band at Duddingston station, saying it was to remind me of the rose garden...'

'Aye?'

'I'd thought he meant it as a pleasant memory, but now I see he wanted only to remind me of the dangers of interference. Well, at least we have proof now that he's a villain.'

'But our witnesses are dead.' Daisy finished the sentence.

'Laing doesn't need to know that. Are you feeling better?' She nodded.

'Then let's get to Duddingston House.'

The Duchess had sent telegrams to all who had been at the house party as Maud had requested and now everyone was gathered in the drawing room. The Duchess sat stiffly on the edge of an overstuffed chair. Lord Urquhart lounged on the sofa next to Miss Taft. The Earl and the Countess looked uncomfortable in separate chairs, leading Maud to wonder if she had discovered his infidelity. Lady Violet sat alone on another sofa.

Not quite everyone was here. There was no sign of the Viscount, Lady Cynthia or – importantly – Laing.

Daisy took a seat near the door, while Maud stood in the middle of the room.

'Thank you for coming this afternoon,' she began. 'Forgive me, Your Grace, but I notice that we are not all here.'

'I'm afraid the Viscount is too unwell to attend,' the Duchess said, her tone soft.

Maud inclined her head. That was understandable and his presence wasn't needed.

The Duchess glanced at the ornate ormolu clock on the mantel. It showed less than a minute before three. 'I'm sure my daughter will be here on time. As to Mr Laing...'

The clock struck the hour, its chimes loud in the quiet room. On the third stroke, the door opened and Maud turned to see Lady Cynthia. She was not alone. Mr Laing's gaze fell on Maud and his face went white.

'Lady Cynthia,' Maud said.

Cynthia entered and made herself comfortable. Laing hesitated on the threshold.

'And Mr Laing. Do join us,' Maud said encouragingly.

He stepped into the room, his eyes never leaving hers, and took an armchair. It irked her to be the one to look away first, but time was passing.

'I've called you here today to explain the case,' Maud began, her gaze moving from one face to another around the room. 'I'm sure you are all curious to know how the culprit managed to steal the necklace, commit murder and apparently get away with it.'

There was some murmuring in the room.

'I thought it was resolved,' said Miss Taft.

'So did the police, but Miss Cameron, my assistant' – Maud nodded towards Daisy, to reaffirm that she was not her lady's maid – 'and I have discovered new evidence.'

The murmuring grew louder.

'If I could ask for your attention.' Maud cleared her throat. 'This whole sorry business began with the theft of jewellery from country houses and was sadly followed by the murder of the Viscountess. A short while ago, the crime spree came to an end with the attempted murder of myself and Miss Cameron.'

'My dear,' exclaimed the Duchess.

There were other astonished voices, so Maud clapped her hands for attention and raised her voice. 'It is what happened at Duddingston which concerns us here.'

Everyone grew quiet and she continued. 'When the thief entered the Viscountess's bedroom that night, she woke, saw the thief taking her precious diamond necklace and was smothered by the panicked thief. Her scream drew us all onto the corridor, including the thief who, because he was in his night attire, managed to hide himself in plain sight. All persons present, and later their rooms, were searched and no necklace found. The sergeant conducted the same investigation below-stairs with the same result.

'The following afternoon the stolen necklace was thrown from the window of the Colonel's room. He denied he had done this, but the evidence seemed to point to him.'

'Do get a move on, Miss McIntyre,' said Miss Taft. 'I have a dinner engagement in the city this evening.'

'I'm coming now to the denouement,' Maud said, fixing her with a stern look. 'First onto the corridor that night were Lord Urquhart and Mr Laing. My suspicion initially fell on Lord Urquhart because his room was closer to the Viscountess's and he was tying the belt of his dressing gown, which suggested he had been out longer than Mr Laing whose garment was not yet tied. But that was a mistake on my part. The thief and murderer was someone in financial difficulty.'

Maud gazed round the room. More than one face looked anxious.

'Afraid that he – it is a man I am about to name – was about to be caught, he'd acted to draw attention from himself and cast suspicion on another.' Maud thought of their conversation when Laing had made the disparaging remark about the murdered Viscountess's age. 'The Colonel was chosen because the villain sees elderly people as dispensable.'

'Good Lord,' said the Duchess.

Maud nodded. 'Knowing we were to gather here today where he would be named, the miscreant paid two men to shoot my assistant and me on our drive here. One of those men is dead; the other, who has confessed all, is with the police.' That was almost the truth.

Laing's face was white.

'As to my reasoning, that is based on the following. Firstly,' Maud said, as the thought came to her, 'he was quick to pass the hand mirror when I asked for one to check if the Viscountess was breathing, which meant he was familiar with her room.'

'Anyone could guess that a mirror would be kept on a dressing table,' said Miss Taft.

True. Maud passed over that.

'Secondly, he has a number of criminal contacts who can dispose of the stolen items on his behalf. Thirdly, the culprit needed money to pay for expensive gifts for you, Lady Cynthia.' Maud was guessing here, but it seemed a reasonable assumption. 'He's been stealing valuable jewellery since the beginning of your affair.'

The Duchess drew in a sharp breath.

'Mr Laing also has a fiancée to provide with perhaps less expensive presents.'

The Duchess would have drawn in another breath if it were possible. Instead, she let out her breath in a seething sound through her teeth.

'Fiancée?' Cynthia stared at him, tears starting at the corner of her eyes. 'Douglas?'

Stony-faced, he said nothing.

'How did he manage to smuggle the necklace out of the Viscountess's bedroom?' Violet asked, her forehead creased with a deep frown.

'Do you want to answer that or shall I?' Maud turned to meet that hard glare he kept fixed on her. She hoped he would take the opportunity to show how clever he was, as she had no idea how he'd accomplished the feat.

Laing shrugged and relaxed back into his armchair. He crossed one leg over the other and let it swing for a while. 'Oh, why not? You know the answer, anyway. I made a pouch to fit inside the front of my pyjama trousers.'

Violet wasn't the only one to wrinkle her nose.

'Which you continued to wear to hide the jewellery,' Maud went on confidently, 'until you threw the necklace from the Colonel's window.'

'I didn't kill her,' he said, his voice sullen.

'Then who did?'

'Her husband.'

'I think not. The man is devastated. No, Mr Laing, *you* killed her. Your need for a scapegoat is understandable. Murder means hanging; a lawyer would know that better than most.'

Laing glared round the room. 'Can you not see she is trying to incriminate me, an innocent person? It was the Viscount, I tell you.'

'You also tried to put the blame on the Colonel, Mr Laing. But then I suppose in your opinion the Colonel is old and expendable, like the Viscountess and her husband.'

'The Colonel is a boring old fool.'

'I don't think you meant to kill her, but she woke and saw you in her room. She screamed and, not knowing what else to do, you covered her face with the pillow but pressed down too hard. She was old, frail and could not resist the attack. When you lifted the pillow, you could see it was too late and ran from her room. In the corridor you blended in with everyone else, looking as if you too had risen from your bed on hearing the scream.'

For once in his life, he could find no eloquent courtroom words to turn the tide of opinion in his favour.

'You're responsible for the death of an innocent person,' the Countess said in wonder. 'Was stealing the jewellery worth that?'

He shrugged. 'Cynthia has expensive tastes.'

'It became clear to me,' Maud continued, 'when I was investigating the disappearance of his fiancée, that Mr Laing would once have been content with marriage, no matter how loveless, to the daughter of a High Court judge.'

Cynthia looked as if she was about to swoon, so Maud hurried on. 'When I found he was indifferent to the disappearance of his fiancée, my doubts about his good character were alerted. I realised that if she came back to him, he would have to go through with the wedding. A breach of promise case against an advocate-depute would not sit well with his reputation. If, however, she chose another, as she did, fortunately for her—'

'Hear, hear,' said Daisy.

'Laing would be free to marry another. Namely Lady Cynthia, the elder child of the Duchess of Duddingston and her heir.'

The Duchess's hand went to her throat.

'He tried to murder Miss Cameron and myself,' Maud said, 'as he rightly believed we had found him out. He wanted nothing to ruin his chances with Lady Cynthia.'

'I would never have allowed my daughter to marry Mr Laing,' the Duchess retorted.

'Nae matter how promising?' Daisy muttered.

The Duchess sent her a sharp glance.

'Listen to yourself, acting like you're a real detective,' Laing said with a sneer to Maud.

She shot him a fierce look. 'I *am* a real detective. Just not one in the police service.'

He looked as if he were about to leap from his seat – and he did.

'I should have killed you before it got this far, Maud McIntyre,' he snarled. 'You know what they say about if you want a job done.'

He pulled a gun from his pocket and pointed it at her. 'None of this would have happened if you'd kept your nose out of it.'

Maud stepped back as he readied to fire. A flash of something gold and Daisy was lifting the brass candlestick from its place atop the long table. Looking like Boudicca must once have done when leading a revolt against Roman rule, she brought the heavy base of her weapon down smartly on Laing's head. He let out a gasping sound and crumpled to the floor, the revolver skittering across the carpet as he fell.

'Well done, Daisy!' Maud said, darting forward to secure the gun.

'It seemed like the best thing to do.'

'Absolutely. Now, before he wakes...'

Lord Urquhart had already snatched from the side of the window the cord that looped up the heavy curtains.

'Allow me.' He knelt, rolled Laing over onto his front and tied his hands behind his back. 'That should suffice until the police officer gets here.'

The Duchess had a dazed air about her, and Maud found it necessary to ring for the butler herself.

'It is curious,' said Violet, looking down at her sister's erstwhile lover, 'how you think you know someone and yet remain unaware of one side of their character. Who would have thought Mr Laing harboured such murderous inclinations, Miss McIntyre?'

'The murder of the Viscountess was done in the panic of the moment, but his attempt to murder Miss Cameron and me was in cold blood.'

The butler appeared at the door and, casting a startled glance at the bound man lying prostrate on the rug, forgot all his training. 'Gordon Bennett!'

'Thomson,' Maud instructed, 'the Duchess would be obliged if you could telephone Sergeant McKay immediately and ask him to arrest Mr Laing as soon as the gentleman wakes.'

'If he wakes,' said Cynthia, shooting a glance at Daisy.

The butler hastened from the room.

'I can't believe so much crime could happen under my roof,' said the Duchess. 'I must thank you, Miss McIntyre, and Miss Cameron, for all your detective work.'

Maud and Daisy beamed.

On the floor, Laing stirred.

'He wasna out long.' Daisy sounded disappointed.

They stood by Maud's car at the front of Duddingston House and watched Douglas Laing be taken into custody by Sergeant McKay. They had made their goodbyes to those left in the party and Maud felt relieved to be away, no matter how complimentary the others were of their efforts. The seriousness of the day's events suddenly overwhelmed her. She turned to Daisy, who looked a bit out of sorts herself, and hugged her, surprising them both. A tear trickled down Maud's face.

'We came through, Daisy,' Maud said, as she stepped away.

'Then dinna greit,' Daisy said with a laugh, the colour beginning to return to her face. In that moment, Maud knew Daisy was made of stronger stuff than her, no matter the confident face Maud managed to show to the world.

Maud sniffed and managed a watery smile as the sudden desire to go home, to her real home, washed over her. Everything she needed was already there, so she could go immediately. 'I'd like to stay with my father for a few days, Daisy. Do you mind?'

'Of course not.' She smiled. 'He'll be pleased to see you, but pinch those cheeks before you get there as you're looking awfa pale and no wonder. Och, and don't tell him about Laing pointing that gun at you, not if you want to keep doing this job for a living.'

'I'll do as you say and deflect the worst of his questions.'

'Nae by too much, Maud. This case is bound to end up in the newspapers sooner or later.'

'What would I do without you, Daisy Cameron?'

Daisy raised her eyebrows but smiled with pleasure.

'All the case files are marked closed,' Maud said. 'I'll have to get the Napier's windscreen repaired...' She put her hand on its door handle. 'Oh, but how will you get back to Edinburgh?' What had she been thinking? 'I'll take you to the city.'

'I'm happy to offer Miss Cameron a lift,' said Lord Urquhart, coming down the steps. 'I'm going the same way. A temporary repair for the hole in your windscreen,' he added, brandishing a cork.

Maud smiled – who could not like a resourceful man? She and Daisy stood quietly, watching as he plugged the bullet hole.

'I wanted to say,' he remarked, returning to where they stood, 'how much I admire your spirit, Miss McIntyre. Not many women would remain calm after facing a man with a gun.'

'Thank you,' Maud said, 'but Miss Cameron was the hero of the hour. She felled the villain.'

'Indeed.' He addressed Daisy. 'You're a plucky young lady.'

'Aye, that's what folk tell me,' she said to him, before turning to Maud. 'Now off you go,' she told her friend. 'Have a nice wee holiday and give my regards to your faither.'

Maud nodded, opened the car door and slid onto the seat. Before she could close the door, Daisy grabbed the handle. With a gleam in her eye, she bent down to be out of Lord Urquhart's earshot.

'Excellent, Holmes,' she said with a smile.

'Elementary,' Maud replied with a grin of her own.

A LETTER FROM LYDIA

Thank you so much for reading *The Scottish Ladies' Detective Agency*. It was great fun writing it, and I hope you found it fun to read.

If you enjoyed the story and would like to keep up-to-date with my latest releases, please sign up at the following link. Your email address will never be shared and you can unsubscribe at any time.

www.bookouture.com/lydia-travers

One of the pleasurable aspects of writing comes from learning the reaction from readers. This is the first cosy crime novel I have written – my earlier publications are romances under the name Linda Tyler – and so this is a new and exciting adventure for me. Did you root for Maud and Daisy all the way? Did you fall in love with the Scottish landscape? If you liked *The Scottish Ladies' Detective Agency*, and I really hope you did, I would be very grateful if you could leave a short review. I'd love to hear what you think and reviews also help other readers to discover one of my books for the first time.

Thank you for reading Maud's story.

Love

Lydia x

KEEP IN TOUCH WITH LYDIA

www.bookouture.com/lydia-travers

 facebook.com/LindaTylerAuthorScotland

twitter.com/LindaTyler100

 instagram.com/lindatylerauthorScotland

ACKNOWLEDGEMENTS

Thank you to the team at Bookouture, including my editor, Jess Whitlum-Cooper. I am indebted to Karen Glen, Building Manager at the Supreme Courts in Edinburgh, for allowing me to view the High Court, and to Michael Hendry for his advice on the Edwardian photographic studio. (I know he will forgive me for the one aspect I chose to ignore). Special thanks go to my friend Joan Cameron for her enthusiastic support of Maud's exploits from the beginning; and in particular huge thanks to my writing buddy Julie Perkins for our brainstorming sessions and her insightful readings that allowed this book to grow. I couldn't have written it without her.

Other influences on my writing have been *The Perfect Summer: Dancing into Shadow in 1911* by Juliet Nicolson; *The Adventures of Maud West, Lady Detective* by Susannah Stapleton; an account in the *Aberdeen Free Press* of the 1912 trial in Aberdeen of Emily Wilding Davison for breach of the peace (Emily Davison died the following year after being struck by King George V's horse during the Epsom Derby); the work of comic genius P.G. Wodehouse; and of course the various detective stories beloved by Maud.

Some liberties have been taken with the jurisdiction of the Scottish criminal justice system in 1911. Any mistakes are my own.

Made in the USA
Monee, IL
21 July 2024